OMEGA FALLEN

EVELYN FLOOD

Omega Fallen

Evelyn Flood

First published by Evelyn Flood in 2023

ASIN: B0BHLBZNB4
ISBN: 9798396108615
Imprint: Independently published
Copyright 2023 by Evelyn Flood

Cover and formatting by Diana TC, TriumphBookCovers.com

TRIGGER WARNING

The previous books in this series have contained some pretty heavy duty TWs. In comparison, this book is very light on triggers, but it does contain some references to sexual/physical assault. There are no on-page descriptions, and the FMC has not experienced the same level of trauma as Harper and Ava. Omega Fallen is very much about Gabrielle's discovery of what it means to be an omega, with all of the delicious nesting and bonding experiences that come with it.

There are some references to homelessness, claustrophobia and addiction.

Evelyn x

About this book

This book is an **omegaverse**. That means that the characters have some of the characteristics often seen in wolves, but they **do not shift.**

In loving dedication

For my mum.
This one's for you, ma.
No going past this page, though. x

PROLOGUE

My breathing echoes harshly around me.

Occasionally, I'll hear a snatch of voices overhead, a laugh from a guard.

But there's no light coming from the hatch above me. No light coming from anywhere.

I'm consumed by pitch black darkness. I can't see my hands, my feet. I know they're still there, because my hands arc burning, my nails ripped to jagged shreds where I've tried to rip myself free of the cage I'm trapped in.

Crying. Screaming. Begging.

They know how to break us.

All I did was pass Molly some of my shitty food ration, spooning a bit of rice onto her plate.

But punishment is harsh and swift here.

I don't know how long ago that was. I've lost any sense of time down here.

The scent of my own urine soaks into the filthy space around me, adding to the scent of fear and desperation. It's clear from the smell that I'm not the only person who's been down here.

How many other omegas have ripped their nails against these walls?

I didn't even know this existed until Enzo, one of the particularly creative guards, dragged me out, opening the hatch with a grin and pushing me in.

There's not enough space to sit down. All I can do is lean against the wall, my legs and back screaming.

When my thirst becomes overwhelming, I try calling out. Apologizing, asking for just a little bit of water to soothe the desert in my mouth.

But nobody comes.

What if they're not coming? What if I'm trapped?

My breaths quicken, the panic clawing at my throat. My broken nails rip at the dirt-packed walls until some of it starts to crumble in, and I stop.

I don't want to die here. So I wait.

Nobody comes for a long time.

And when they do, I'm not human anymore. I'm not Gabrielle.

I'm a terror-soaked, filthy thing, half-blind in the bright sunlight beaming into the hole. Faces lean over me, talking rapidly, arms reaching down to lift me out.

They help me get my feet underneath me, shaky but upright. The voices sound shocked, upset, kind. Offering food, pressing water into my hands that I gulp down in big swallows that hurt my chest.

They are not the people who put me in here.

They promise me I'm safe now.

But I learned long ago not to trust promises.

So I run, ignoring the panicked calls from behind me.

I stagger, nearly fall, but I keep going.

Because the gates are open.

The gates are *never* open.

And once I'm through, I don't look back.

FIVE YEARS LATER

CHAPTER ONE
GABRIELLE

I stare blankly at the scrappy little piece of paper taped to the flaking wood of my apartment door. The red text stands out like a beacon.

Eviction notice.

Muttering furiously and ripping the paper down, I twirl at the giveaway rustle as my sleazy landlord tries to quietly close his door. I'm across the hall in a split second. "Joe, wait!"

He grunts. "Nothin' left to say to you. You need to be out by tomorrow."

"But I'll get the money, Joe. You know I will."

I try to keep my voice even, but the squeak at the end of my words fills the dusty hallway with the scent of desperation. He gives me a mildly pitying look before his eyes slide downwards. "Business is business." He shrugs. "Got another tenant moving in tomorrow, so you need to get out, omega."

Repulsed, I tug the edge of my top up, and Joe's eyes flick away.

Asshole.

"Joe," I try, giving it one last chance. "Please, be reasonable. Where am I going to go?"

"Not my problem."

His hand slides down the back of his trousers to scratch his ass. I try not to recoil in disgust as his fingers come back up to rub at his chin. "Why don'cha try that place… y'know, the *center*. They'll help you out. You're one of 'em, ain't you?"

The way his lip curls tells me exactly what he thinks of my designation.

My hand clenches around the eviction notice. "That's not an option."

"And that ain't my problem, omega."

My head jerks back as the door slams, missing my nose by a bare whistle.

I blink, desperately trying to come up with a plan in my head.

I can't lose this place. I won't get another.

This is the shittiest of the shitholes, and if I can't even stay here…

Panic grips my chest as I shove the paper as far as I can down into my apron pocket, crumpling it up in my hand as I head slowly back across the musty-smelling hall. The bare lightbulb casts more shadows than light, making my fingers fumble as I slide the key into the old lock with shaking fingers.

Keeping my shoes on, I dodge the broken nails splitting out of the bare hall floorboards like a pro as I head into my tiny kitchen. With my luck, they'd give me gangrene, or some other equally disgusting infection.

Peeling black and white linoleum lines the floor, the various rips and dents matched only by the dilapidated cupboards. My shoulder bangs into the door hanging off one particularly battered unit, and I swallow back a yelp.

Rubbing at the bruised skin, I open up the refrigerator and stare bleakly at the scant contents. My stomach rumbles as I gingerly sniff the milk I bought a few days ago.

Yep, that's definitely gone.

Tossing it into the trash, I push my hunger down and shut the door, falling into a chair at the table and yanking my wages from the diner out of my apron.

The coins and a few paltry notes spill over the chipped wood. My heart sinks. I don't need to count it to know it's not very much at all.

Not enough to pay my outstanding rent.

And definitely not enough to tide me over until I can get another job.

The back of my eyes burn as I tip my head up to the ceiling, taking a deep breath.

No falling apart now, Gabby. It's just another tiny hurdle. Nothing you haven't done before.

But... I'm so *tired*.

And losing my job and my apartment in one day... I'm entitled to be a little upset.

Blowing out a breath, I take a minute before getting up, ducking into my tiny little living space.

There's not much here, even after two years. The carpet squishes slightly under my feet, courtesy of a few too many leaks from the apartment above. Joe's not the best at maintenance. Or repairs. Or anything, really.

I'll be better off out of here.

The thought feels hollow as I sink into the brown faded armchair that's been patched up one too many times, staring blankly out the window at the street below.

People walk past with purpose, everyone heading somewhere. I watch as one couple strolls along, the beta male saying something that makes the female throw her head back in laughter as their linked hands swing between them.

A lump appears in my throat. I can't remember the last time someone touched me like that.

Maybe never.

God. What I wouldn't give to feel a human touch that

doesn't want to grab me, hurt me or fuck me. Most of the ones I've known wanted all three, and they didn't care in which order.

My throat aches as I heat up a tiny can of soup for dinner, shoving the meager cash I have left back into my apron. Pouring half into a bowl, I cover the rest for later.

I'm a master at making food last as long as possible.

The pathetic portion disappears too quickly. Taking my empty bowl to the sink, I run my fingers over the cheap plastic, sucking up every bit of juice I can find.

After the quickest shower in history, I sit on my futon, clutching the towel around me and shivering as I try to think of a plan. Any plan.

I need cash. Funds for Joe, if he'll take them. If not, then I'll need more, for a deposit, hopefully somewhere furnished.

I need a new job. One where the boss doesn't see me as his own personal fuck-toy.

Decision made, I jump up and throw on my tidiest outfit before sliding on my sneakers. Glancing in the mirror, I ignore the bags under my eyes and tidy my wet hair as best I can, pulling the dark strands back into a braid.

The door slams behind me.

CHAPTER TWO
GABRIELLE

My feet are killing me.

I've dropped into every single diner, bar and possible job opportunity on this side of town.

And the response has been the same every single time.

"No vacancies."

The older, matronly beta who curled her lip at me. The younger, pretty beta with the mean eyes and the tossed hair. The exhausted looking bartender with a 'help wanted' sign who told me in no uncertain terms to fuck off out of his bar, bleary-eyed men jeering as I backed out rapidly.

Nobody wants to hire an omega.

It's asking for trouble.

It's a target on your back for pro-Creed hate groups. They're still out there, spewing their poison about omegas being the spawn of evil, only good for lying on our backs and popping out babies.

Shattered, I slump down onto a small set of white stone steps halfway up the street. The wind whistles sharply, slicing against my cheek as I huddle in, blowing on my hands for warmth and jamming them under my armpits.

Staring unseeingly into the street, I start to shake.

I'm out of ideas. Out of options.

A door creaks open behind me, warmth and music and laughter spilling out across my back. Closing my eyes, I take a deep breath, breathing in the delicious smell of well-cooked food and *happiness*.

Someone sniffs loudly.

"I'm amazed they let *that* hang around here," a woman drawls loudly. "I thought Hudson had more taste."

A male grunt of agreement makes my shoulders stiffen, and I huddle against the railing as they pass me, wincing as a heel catches me in the side. Not so accidentally, I'm sure.

The woman turns back to look down her nose at me with a huff before they move off down the street. Behind me, the door closes, leaving me with nothing but cold and bitterness.

Swivelling, I take in the glossy sign, the ivy trailing down the side of the glorious white building.

Il Piacere, the sign proudly announces in swirling gold font.

Swallowing hard, I scramble up.

I haven't got a hope in hell. I know that. But I just want a single minute to take it in. To feel warm, and hear music, and forget about my own fucked up world.

Even the bronze handle feels heated beneath my fingers.

As I pull the door open and slide inside, a few conversations die down as people turn to take in the newcomer. Lips curl, hands appearing over mouths as women whisper to each other, their eyes sliding down my worn blouse and faded trousers.

Gripping my elbows, I take another step, looking around at the ornate décor gilding the walls.

Flickering sconces send warm light across each table, tall cream candles and brightly-colored flowers creating a lovely, soft sweet scent in the air. Dark green ivy trails around pillars dotted through the room, decorated with white flowers alongside intricately painted walls.

A pianist plays quietly in the background.

My eyes must be wide as hell.

I could live here, quite happily.

My reverie is abruptly shattered by a hand tapping my elbow.

"Can I help you?" someone asks sharply.

I swing around, mouth open to present my prepared spiel, but I blink.

This isn't a beta.

This is an *alpha*.

A tall, lightly muscular, tawny-skinned alpha with honeyed eyes and dark bronzed hair, artfully mussed. He towers over me, narrowed eyes widening slightly as he takes me in.

His hand clenches around my arm, and I flinch. Picking up on my unease, he pulls it back immediately, offering me an apologetic half smile. "What can we do for you?" he asks.

Creamy toasted marshmallow and charred wood scent wraps around me, just as warm and inviting as the surroundings around us. Not him, though. He's staring at me like someone just walked me in on the bottom of their shoe.

Straightening, I hold out my hand for him to shake. He doesn't take it. Awkwardly, I let it hang there for a few seconds before pulling back.

"I… ah… I was looking for a job?"

My carefully prepared job hunting pitch goes down the drain as nerves take over. I wasn't expecting an alpha.

I don't *like* alphas.

And apparently, the feeling's mutual.

He shakes his head abruptly. "We don't, sorry."

Even though I expected it, it still hurts to turn around and face the door. I just need one more minute to breathe it all in. God knows I'll never be coming here again.

A throat clears behind me. "Wait."

I pause, hope expanding my chest as I turn to look back at him.

"I can help you." The possibility shatters in an instant as his eyes glance down, taking in my crappy old sneakers covered in all sorts of shit, thanks to my shifts at the diner.

Drawing myself upright, I take a step back, wrapping my arms around me protectively. The alpha's eyes widen. "I didn't mean—"

But I don't stay around to hear it. Embarrassment flushes my cheeks as I head for the door.

"Wait!"

Breaking into a run, I shove the door open and pound down the steps. My feet beat out a loud pattern on the concrete as I sprint around the corner before pausing for breath, resting against the wall.

I don't want to hear whatever offer the alpha with the pretty eyes was going to make.

Because from someone like him? In that place? I might actually be tempted to give the last little piece of myself up.

And that's the one thing I swore I'd never do.

CHAPTER THREE
NATE

My hand closes on empty air as the door swings shut behind the omega, leaving the faintest scent of butterscotch lingering in the air.

Someone clears their throat in front of me. There are customers waiting to be served, but my eyes are fixed unwaveringly on the door.

"It's Nate Reyne," someone whispers.

I've never shied away from who I am, but just once, I wish I was anonymous. My foot steps forward, instinct driving me to hunt the omega down, to find out why she's too thin and why the fuck her sneakers have a hole in the top.

My focus snaps when a hand claps on my shoulder.

"Nate? We've got customers," Hudson says, his tone chiding. He takes a step around me, opening his arms wide. "Welcome to Il Piacere," he announces warmly. "Here, let me take your coats."

He eyeballs me as he walks past, leading the disgruntled group to their table before reappearing.

"What's the matter with you?" he asks, poking my arm.

"I… nothing." She's gone, that delectable scent already fading from the air, as if she'd never been here at all.

Taking one last breath, I turn and follow Hudson back into the main restaurant, moving between tables, chatting and signing autographs until my feet ache and my mind feels clearer.

But I can't get the omega out of my head.

Petite, barely reaching to my shoulders, skinny as all hell with bags under her wide blue eyes. Dark hair hinting at thickness yanked back into a sloppy braid.

And fear in her gaze.

I swallow, shame creeping over me as the last customer leaves and Hudson flips the sign. I didn't mean to make her feel uncomfortable. I just wanted to *help*.

"Thanks," Hudson says with a sigh as he grabs a couple of wine glasses, pouring us a glass of red before collapsing into a chair. "They love it when you're here."

"No problem," I mutter.

Hud glances at me, his hawkish face lowering into a frown. "Everything alright?"

I nod, then shake my head, rubbing at my eyes. "Sorry. It's just… this girl came in earlier looking for a job. She looked like she needed it, but we're full, right?"

Hudson cocks his head. "We're not, actually. Zoe handed her notice in today, effective immediately. Going traveling."

Well, shit. Now I really feel like I fucked up.

His gaze turns curious. "You liked her? Beta?"

I swallow. "Omega."

He straightens. "Really?"

I nod, and he raises his eyebrows. "Not from the Center?"

"I don't think so. She didn't look the type."

Center omegas are notoriously well cared for, ferociously protected by Ava Grey and her pack, backed up by a number of volunteers. Every pack application for a match is carefully considered, a long and lengthy process before you get anywhere near an omega. And it's *always* their choice.

We've been working through their system for eight months. And I'd choose that every single time over the horror of the heat nests the fucking Omega Creed used to push.

"This one was alone," I say quietly. "And I just let her leave."

Hudson takes a sip of wine, his hazel eyes considering. "What else could you do? Maybe she'll come back. Don't beat yourself up over it."

We're interrupted by a rustle at the door. Axel lets himself in, a duffle bag swung over his shoulder and blonde hair yanked back into his typical messy knot as he locks it behind him.

"Where's your coat?" I ask. It's freezing outside, and he shrugs. "It's not that bad."

Axel runs a gym down the street. Between the three of us and Cade, we all have our own thriving careers. It's probably the only thing we have, truth be told. After a while, it all starts to feel a bit empty.

What's the point of success when you're lying alone at night?

My fingers begin to tap on the table.

"Nate met an omega," Hudson says sneakily, rolling his eyes at Ax. "*Not* a Center one."

Axel doesn't bat an eyelid, crossing his arms as he leans against a marble pillar.

"What was she like?" he asks in his gruff tone.

Shrugging, I take a swig of my wine. "Memorable. Doesn't matter now, though. I spooked her and she ran."

Axel frowns. "Is she okay?"

Meeting his eyes, I let him see my own worry. "I don't know."

CHAPTER FOUR
GABRIELLE

I'm lying on my crappy, spring-happy futon, staring at the cracks on my ceiling in the murky dawn light and wondering exactly when that damp patch is going to collapse through. At least I won't be here to get crushed by several pounds of falling plaster.

After a few hours of tossing and turning, I gave up on the idea of any sleep, spending the last few hours desperately trying to think of a way out of my current predicament.

And I've got...nothing. Zip. Nada. Zilch.

Annoyingly, my mind also keeps drifting back to a pair of certain honey-colored eyes.

Frowning, I stagger out of bed, pushing the useless thoughts away in favor of more practical considerations. Today, I get kicked out. And I have nowhere to go. A headache forms between my eyes, not helped by the sudden banging at the door.

Fuck. It's not even 7am yet. Joe must be keen for me to get out if he's dragged his ass out of bed this early. I don't think I've ever seen him before noon.

I pull the door open and slide out, pulling it closed behind me. Joe squints at me, his vest a funky mixture of dubious-looking stains and dirt as it strains over his beer belly.

Filthy nails scratch at his stomach. "Time to go, omega."

"Come on, Joe. Just hold off. Give me the day, at least," I plead. "I've got cash on me. I can pay."

He eyeballs me. "All of it?" he asks suspiciously.

I bite my lip. "Some of it."

Joe shakes his head. "Ain't enough. All or you're out."

"*Please*." I beg around the lump in my throat. "I have *nowhere* to go. I'll be out on the street."

"You ain't no child," he sneers. "You can earn yer keep on your back just like the others. Dunno why you're slumming it here anyway."

He scoffs, looking me up and down. "Now quit arguing, and pack your shit."

He stands there, arms crossed, as I move back inside and bolt the door behind me.

Turning, my back slides down the door, my legs collapsing as I fall on my ass. The tears come thick and fast, my hand clasped over my mouth to try and hold in the noise.

What the hell do I do now?

When I finally manage to pull myself together and Joe's banged on the door twice, it takes me all of three minutes to shove my clothes and some toiletries into a ratty old black duffle bag. I don't have much, which is probably a blessing right now. I wouldn't be able to take it with me anyway.

My sneaker lace catches on a nail and I glance down. This place was a shithole, but at least it had a lock on the door and warm water.

Joe is leaning against the wall outside when I leave, and he gives me a once-over that has my skin crawling.

"Keys," he grunts, looking away as he holds out his meaty hand.

I drop my only key into his palm with a little more force

than needed. "I'd say it's been fun, Joe, but it really hasn't. Enjoy explaining the smell of damp carpet to your next tenant. Hope they like gangrene."

He rolls his eyes and heads back into his apartment, slamming the door behind him with an air of finality.

Trudging down the stairs, I emerge out onto the street, sucking in a breath at the cold air of the bright winter morning. At least the sun is shining.

This could be good. Maybe it'll be a fresh start. I just need to look for a job.

CHAPTER FIVE
GABRIELLE

"Three dollars."

I blink at the librarian. She stares back at me owlishly, pushing thick-rimmed tortoiseshell glasses up her nose as her eyes scan me warily.

"For the day?" I ask weakly. She shakes her head, and my heart sinks.

"Per hour." She jabs her finger at a sign on the wall setting out the extortionate costs.

I definitely can't afford to stay here all day. I have a total of eighteen dollars and twelve cents in my pocket. I'll need food.

If I can get myself a shift somewhere this evening that pays cash and bust my ass for tips, I might be able to grab a cheap motel for the night.

I count out three dollars carefully, and the librarian holds her hand well below mine so we don't touch as the coins change hands. She points towards the bank of computers, retreating into the back room before I can ask for help.

It's been years since I used a computer. I barely remember how, but all I need to do is find the search, type in what I need, and write down the results. Easy peasy. It'll narrow down the list of places from an endless amount to ones with actual vacancies, and I can focus on them.

A few minutes later, I wave down the reluctant librarian after some significant arm waving and pitiful looks. She fingers her pearls, keeping a distance between us as she gingerly peers in towards the screen. "Yes?"

"Excuse me," I say with a smile, "I can't seem to get onto the search?"

She rolls her eyes. "You need to log in," she says pointedly.

My smile starts to feel a little wooden. "And how would I do that?"

"With an e-mail address and password."

She talks incredibly slowly like I'm a child, but I still blink. "I… don't have one of those."

She shrugs. "Sorry. You'll need one to use the computer."

My eyes move between her and the computer, the stupid screen blinking at me as it asks for information I don't have. "So… I can't use it?"

"It doesn't seem that way." She snaps off the end of her sentence.

"Can I have my money back then, please?"

She coughs. "No refunds. It says on the wall."

"But I didn't get to use it!"

"You switched it on," she says haughtily. "Not our fault you weren't able to access what you wanted. You've been using it for ten minutes, and we don't give partial refunds."

Breathe, Gabby. Just breathe.

"I… okay," I say in defeat. "Thanks."

For nothing.

So much for finding a job here. On foot it is.

After sliding past the librarian with my teeth bared in

some semblance of a smile, I find myself back outside on the street. This neighborhood has dozens of bars, shops, and restaurants.

Surely, someone will hire me.

CHAPTER SIX
CADE

My hands tap on my leg as I read through the contract, flipping pages over as my eyes skim the legalese, checking for errors or any last-minute changes the other firm might have slipped in, trying to pull a fast one.

My attention isn't fully where it needs to be, my eyes flicking between the complex confidentiality agreement and the folder on my desk.

My secretary, Sarah, fidgets in place as she waits opposite my desk for a response.

"What do you think?" I ask her suddenly, and she splutters.

"I don't know, sir," she says, and I cock my eyebrow.

"You just graduated, yes? Top of your class?"

Her eyes widen. "I… yes, but…,"

I slide the contract back over to her.

"I have some thoughts, but I'd like you to take a look at it too. I don't believe in wasting talent."

She brightens in front of my eyes. "I will," she promises. "I'll have it back to you today."

Smiling, I wave her out. "Thanks, Sarah."

When she's gone, my smile slips as I glance again at the black leather folder.

The symbol for the Omega Center is embossed in elaborate gold foil across the top, signifying the organization that's taken over the care of omegas since the Omega Creed collapsed five years ago.

Bracing myself, I crack it open, ignoring the spiel on the front page. My hands move straight to the back, to the little pockets storing a variety of cards.

Scent matching.

It's a new initiative, designed to help alphas and omegas make a strong connection from the beginning and avoid the awkwardness that comes from trying to casually sniff at someone you're meeting for the very first time.

I'm not entirely sure what I think about the whole thing, but curiosity gets the better of me.

My fingers slide a small, baby pink card from the folder, and I bring it to my nose, taking a deep inhale and choking on the sickly sweet stench.

The card drops to the table as I recoil. *The fuck is that?*

Gingerly, I pick it back up, flipping it over to reveal the scent of omega number one.

Coconut oil.

I grimace. I fucking *hate* coconuts.

Maybe there's something in this thing after all.

Sighing, I slide the card back into the folder, closing it up and resisting the urge to carry on flicking through. This is something we need to do together.

Taking a few gulps of air to remove the pungent scent of coconuts from my nose, I spend a few hours working through various contracts and checking in on my cases, before holding a lunchtime meeting with a prospective new client.

I'm interviewing them just as much as they're interviewing me. It's something I'm adamant about as CEO of the largest legal firm in the city.

Cade Reyne won't work with liars, cheats or assholes.

People used to roll their eyes at me. But my company grew, and grew some more, until we hit our first million and kept climbing.

As I pack up towards the end of the day, Sarah happily talking through her thoughts on the new Cromax contract, my hand lands on the folder again. For once, I'm leaving early, eager to get home and share the scent cards sent over by the Center with the pack.

An omega.

It'll be a huge change for us all. We're a close pack, but it's safe to say we're all mated to our work. I rarely leave the office before dark and Hudson is twice as bad as me with his obsession over his damn restaurant. If we didn't live above the place we'd never see him.

Then there's Axel, constantly working into the night at the gym, and don't even get me started on Nate and his world.

Sarah finishes her explanation and rocks back on her heels, twisting her fingers together.

She's good. Better than I thought she would be, even.

Nodding, I grab my briefcase.

"You're right. Make the changes and send it back to them. Add your name to the review list."

Her cheeks flush as she straightens. "Really?"

I wave her back to her desk. "I hired you for a reason, Sarah. I want someone who assists, not someone to take notes and fetch me coffee. I can get my own damn coffee."

I also don't have the heart to tell her that her coffee tastes like shit. She thanks me over and over again, full of bouncy excitement as she heads back, fingers flying over the keyboard.

My head is far away as I stand in front of the elevator

doors, watching the buttons light up before heading down through floor after floor. Colleagues get on and off, making small talk and asking about work. I'm absent, at best, and I shoot one of my associates an apologetic grimace as I exit.

"Sorry, Mullins. Focusing on a case. Give me a call tomorrow."

When I walk through the lobby, Jordan jumps up from his desk, casually turning over his phone. We both pretend not to hear the raucous noise of the hockey game he's watching in the background.

"Do you need the car, Mr. Reyne?"

Glancing outside, I shake my head. "I'll walk."

It's a beautiful day. Cold as hell but a blue sky and winter sunshine. It's not too far to get home, and I can get Axel from the gym on the way.

Making my way along the sidewalk, I dig my wallet out of my pocket to pay for a fresh, hot coffee from the stand on the corner.

I look down for a scant moment, and that's all it takes for someone to collide with me with a humph, sending my wallet scattering to the floor. The female bounces off me, landing heavily with an audible thump and a gasp.

"Shit – are you okay?"

I reach out a hand as she scrambles up and away from me. She's tiny, barely reaching up to my shoulders as she brushes down her thin jacket.

She must be freezing.

Taking in her threadbare outfit, I scowl. "You need a thicker jacket."

The beta blinks up at me, and I'm hit with a wave of warm, creamy butterscotch.

Fuck. My mouth actually waters, and I take a step forward, inhaling deeply.

"Omega?"

The word is pulled from my chest, deep with a vibration

just on the edge of a growl. The omega pales as she backs away, her hands outstretched. It's enough to shake me back into my senses, and I take my own step back, raising my hands.

"Steady," I soothe. "I'm sorry. Are you alright?"

What the hell is she doing? There's no bitemark, so she's unmated. And she smells fucking divine, like my favorite dessert. Any asshole alpha would think he'd won the lottery if he bumped into her.

"Fine. Sorry."

She pushes past me before I can open my mouth, although I'm not sure if it's to apologize again or to scold her for being so damn irresponsible. Taken aback, I watch her as she pelts up the street. She turns, and our eyes lock for a moment, hers widening as they flick downwards to something in her hands.

I follow her gaze, my hand dropping to my empty pocket.

"Hey!" I shout. "That's my wallet!"

The omega shrinks back before she darts away around the corner. With a curse, I give chase. I don't give a fuck about the money, but there's things in that wallet I actually need.

Skidding around the corner, I nearly trip over the discarded wallet. There's no sign of the omega. Picking it up with a sigh, I rifle through, surprised to find it full.

She didn't take the money. No... I count. Ten dollars.

Her face filters through. Thin and underfed. A thin jacket. And clearly desperate. Something in my chest clenches, and I look around for any sign of her. But the alley is empty, a dozen little paths coming off it that lead who knows where.

I consider hunting her down, but she could be anywhere by now. Frowning, I take a single step back towards the main road, ignoring the tugging in my chest that tells me to follow her.

Besides, what would I say? Demand a measly ten bucks back?

She clearly needs it more than I do.

With a final look back, I head back in the direction I came.

CHAPTER SEVEN
GABRIELLE

I slam my hands over my mouth, trying to hold back my heavy breathing as the alpha stares down the alley, his steel blue eyes skating across my hiding spot behind a dumpster.

The ten dollars in my hand is a burning brand of shame, and I swallow back the lump in my throat.

I've never stolen anything. Ever.

But I've only got fifteen dollars left. It's been another fucking useless day of getting turned away from the shittiest of places like I'm the worst thing to ever grace their doorstep.

The alpha looks back in my direction, and I shrink back against the dirty wall, holding my breath. Jaw setting, he runs a hand through his thick black hair before he finally disappears around the corner.

I crumple the money in my fist, not daring to move unless he comes back. When minutes tick by, I slide out from my hiding spot. The clear blue skies are fading away, the creep of early evening heading in as the sky darkens to dusky purple.

I need to find somewhere safe to sleep tonight. That has to be a priority.

I'll start again tomorrow.

I visit three different budget hotels, but I'm either turned away or don't have the funds to pay for a night. My stolen money itches in my pocket.

At the last place, the beta concierge leans in with a slight look of pity.

"There's a camp," he whispers. "Underneath the bridge. Lots of homeless."

I blink back tears of exhaustion. I don't need that. Besides, I can only imagine how a place like that would welcome an unmated omega.

I'll have better luck tomorrow.

I trudge up and down streets in one final last-ditch attempt to find something until it's well and truly dark and my legs are screaming with the need to sit down.

Ducking into an alleyway that looks a little cleaner than some of the others, my eyes fix on a doorway, a red security light blinking overhead. There's enough space to curl up, it's hidden from the main road and the building lights are off.

Glancing behind me, I make my way over to it, checking for any signs of life. When there's nothing, I throw down my duffle and sit on it, hugging my elbows for warmth.

It's just for tonight.

My eyes blink, but I fight the urge to sleep. I don't want any surprises in the night.

This is just one night, I promise silently. *I'll have a bed tomorrow.*

But it's starting to feel more and more unlikely.

CHAPTER EIGHT
AXEL

Hudson places a steaming plate of pasta in front of me, and I side-eye him as he passes similarly heaped plates to Cade and Nate.

He raises his hands defensively. "Nothing new! Just carbonara."

I've been his guinea pig before, with varying successes. He's a genius in the kitchen, but his experiments don't always turn out perfectly. There's silence around the large table as the four of us dig in. It's been ages since we all had chance to have dinner together in our apartment, and I've been craving some real food. Hudson would lose his shit if he knew how much trail mix I eat when he's not around.

Safe to say that I am *not* the chef in this pack.

"So," Cade begins as we push away empty plates. He gets up and grabs a folder from the side, holding it up. Everyone perks up at the symbol for the Omega Center.

Everyone except Nate. When I glance over, he's frowning down at the scant remains of his pasta.

Hudson gestures. "Let's have a look, then. Scent matching?"

Cade nods, flipping the folder and pulling out a pink

card. He hands it to Hudson using the tips of his fingers, and Hud laughs.

"Coconut," he announces with a wrinkled nose. "Not my favorite."

"You hate coconut," Nate mutters to Cade as he folds his arms.

"I do, but we all need to have a say." He opens another card and takes a deep sniff, his face neutral as he passes the card to Nate.

Nate begrudgingly takes the card, barely sniffing before he passes it onto me. I breathe it in gingerly. A sharp, almost acrid orange scent assaults my nostrils, and I wince.

Nate straightens. "Too much."

Every card is the same. Ylang-ylang, mint chocolate chip, fresh bread… none of them feel right. Cade sighs, slipping the last cherry-scented card back into its pouch.

"We're not out of options," he reminds us. "This is just the first batch."

Nate pouts. "I know what I want."

Across from me, Hudson rolls his eyes. "You're obsessed."

"With what?" Cade asks as he lifts his wine to his mouth.

"Butterscotch." It's almost a groan, Nate's toasty scent spiking as he leans back in his chair with a dreamy grin. Cade chokes on his drink. I lean in to pound his back as he waves me off.

"What did you say?" he croaks.

Nate leans forward with a glint in his eyes. "*Butterscotch*."

"Like the omega?" I ask, and Cade swivels to me.

"What omega?" His words have an unusual snap to them.

Hudson looks between us. "Nate met an omega yesterday. She came in looking for work but she ran off."

Cade blows out a breath. "Tiny, dark hair, petrified?"

Everyone turns to face him, and Nate half jumps out of his seat. "You know her?"

"She stole ten dollars from my wallet," he grumbles.

Nate's brow drops down into a frown as Cade explains. "She needs help," he mutters. "And she must be somewhere close."

Cade grabs his arm when he makes to jump up from the table.

"Hold it." He shakes the folder. "What about this? You can't just go haring off after some random omega, Nate. Jesus. Have some self-control."

Nate folds his arms stubbornly. "None of those scents even come close to hers," he points out. "Do they?"

He smirks as Cade doesn't answer. "Knew it. This omega… I feel like there's something about her. We need to at least look for her, make sure she's safe."

"Wait," Hudson says reasonably. "She might have a pack already."

Cade purses his lips. "I didn't see a bitemark," he admits.

Nate looks fit to burst. "Besides, no decent pack would treat their omega like that," he snaps.

"Then she might not want a pack at all," I say quietly. Nate turns to me, a wounded look in his eyes.

"We need to tread carefully," I add. "See if we can find her but keep it on the low-down. We don't want to scare her if she thinks a pack is after her. There has to be a reason she's not linked to the Center."

Cade points at me. "*Thank you* for being reasonable."

Nate rolls his eyes before looking to Hudson. "You agree?"

Hud hesitates. "I don't like the idea of someone out there needing help," he says carefully. "But I don't want to commit to anything. Not without even meeting her."

Cade straightens. "Okay. So we need to find her first and make sure she's safe. I'll put someone on it tomorrow."

Nate opens his mouth, and Cade gives him *the look*.

"In the meantime, I'll let the Center know we're not interested in these." Cade taps his finger on the folder.

Rubbing my neck, I pull the wine towards me, pouring another glass. Hudson stays seated as Cade and Nate leave the room, Nate offering up suggestions that make Cade's shoulders tense.

"Well," Hudson mutters. "This should be interesting."

"We might not even find her." I study my glass, considering. "Even if we do, she might not want us – or vice versa."

Hud sighs. "Nate's already set on her."

It's a good sign. Most alphas in a pack tend to have similar tastes. But not always. Shrugging, I down the last of my wine, and Hudson scowls at me.

"Heathen. That was a vintage."

"All tastes the same to me," I shoot back. I'll admit though that Hudson's taste for the finer things is starting to rub off on me.

Stretching, I groan as the knots in my back pop. "I'm heading in. See you tomorrow."

Heading down the hall to our rooms, I duck into mine, pausing to shuck off my clothes before stepping into the en suite shower.

Hot water cascades down my back as I tip my head up and reach for the soap, washing off the grime from a day down at the gym.

My thoughts jump to the discussion at dinner. We've all been keen to bring an omega into the pack. Someone to balance us out, center us – and to have kids one day.

I've never truly thought about what it's like from their side.

There was a massive public outcry a few years back when it was found that the Omega Compound was abusing omegas in their care. Until then, no one really paid much attention to the Omega Creed, a list of rules restricting omega movements and keeping them tied to the government.

Frowning, I rest my hands against the wall. Maybe we're jumping ahead. Maybe this omega had a bad experience.

Something pulls at my chest.

We'll need to tread carefully. And reel Nate in. He can be overwhelming at the best of times and he's used to getting what he wants.

This has to be about what *she* wants.

And that might not be us, whatever Nate wants to think.

CHAPTER NINE
GABRIELLE

I jerk awake, my eyes flying open as a horn blares. Blearily, I peer around. My little makeshift sleeping area is untouched. My hands feel numb, and I tuck them under my arms to try and warm up a little, yanking up my top to breathe against the material and try to warm my face.

This isn't sustainable.

I pause as heavy footsteps sound, shrinking back against the wall as a shadow falls over me.

I look up... and up.

A viking-sized alpha towers over me. Light blonde hair is scraped back off his face into a knot, matching the beard that covers his lower face. He blinks down at me as a set of keys jangle in his hand.

Inhaling, his deep green eyes move to mine and widen. "You..." he says in a low voice. "You're the omega from the restaurant."

A terrified whimper erupts from my chest as I scramble up.

Immediately, he takes a few steps back, hands up.

"Steady, now," he mutters. "I'm not gonna hurt you."

He easily could, layers and layers of strong muscles barely hidden underneath the colorful tattoos snaking down both arms. I keep my eyes on him as I reach down, my fingers grabbing for the handle of the duffle bag.

"I didn't mean to scare you," he goes on, gesturing behind us. "This is my gym."

"I'm going," I say abruptly. "Just let me get my stuff, please."

His face tightens as he looks over the doorway. "You slept here?"

Distractingly full lips press together when I stay silent. "It was cold out last night," he says, more gently. "Too cold to sleep outside."

Clothes shoved haphazardly into the duffle, I take a tentative step out of the doorway. The alpha keeps a careful distance, but I can feel the heaviness of his scent, the earthy, resinous scent of teakwood teasing my nose.

"I know." Defensiveness coats my words. "It's temporary."

The alpha nods. "I'm Axel."

He pauses, waiting for me to confirm mine. When I don't say anything, he half-smiles, taking his face from terrifying to devastating in a moment.

Cool it, Gabby. You don't like alphas.

"Nice to meet you. Hold up. I've got some sweatshirts in the back. You'll freeze in that."

My cheeks flush in humiliation. "I'm fine, thank you."

He gives me a look as he moves past me, leaving plenty of space as he unlocks the door, keys jangling. "Stay here for a sec," he calls back as he pushes the door open, vanishing inside.

It's almost a command, his tone deep.

I really should go, but my feet stay stubbornly rooted to the floor until he reappears, dark material bunched in his hands as he holds them out to me. When I reach for them, he holds on for a second, and our eyes meet.

"You got a name?"

I shake my head. Five years ago, I didn't, according to the government.

Just a number. 1028.

Axel slips his hands back into his pocket as I hold the sweatshirts close, a little patch of warmth burning through my stomach.

"You hungry?" he asks. "My packmate makes a mean breakfast."

My already wobbly comfort levels take a nosedive. Axel opens his mouth at the look on my face, but I'm already spinning, walking away.

He jogs up to me, and I flinch away. "Please don't follow me."

He could overpower me easily, drag me into his gym if he wanted to. But I'm grateful when he backs off immediately. "Please come back," he calls out. "If you need anything."

I wave a hand as I pick up the pace. It's surprisingly difficult to walk away, just as bad as the honey-eyed alpha at that restaurant.

I need to get a damn grip and stop letting my hormones take charge with their freaky omega voodoo shit. Still, I can feel his eyes on my back as I walk away. And for the first time, it's not abrasive, or unwelcome.

It's warm.

Stopping to yank the dark green hoodie over my head, I pause at the teakwood scent, clean but very clearly belonging to Axel.

I take a deep breath as I pull the sweatshirt down, lifting the edge to take another greedy inhale.

It's just a nice scent. He probably didn't realize it was his.

I lift the hood up, taking a moment to enjoy the warmth around my face. For the first time in days, I feel like I can actually take a full breath.

"Round three. Here we go."

CHAPTER TEN
HUDSON

My phone goes off, scaring me half to death as I'm leaning over the schedule, trying to rearrange things so I have enough staff to cover today and this evening.

Nate huffs a sleepy laugh at me over his morning coffee as I scramble for my mobile, digging under piles of paper.

"Fuck," I bark down the receiver. "You scared me half to death."

"I found her," Axel rushes out. "The omega."

I blink. "You.. found her? How?"

Nate freezes in his seat, his eyes widening as he points frantically to the phone. I hit the speaker and sit back as Axel spills the story out.

"I knew it," Nate hisses. "She does need help."

He jumps up. "I'm calling Cade."

As he leaves, I switch the speaker off and pull the phone back to my ear. "So?"

"So what?" Axel doesn't give anything away, and my foot taps impatiently.

"Come *on*, Ax. I'm the only one who hasn't met her. What did you think?"

"I... she's...,"

My patience snaps. "She's *what*?" I hiss.

He sighs in my ear. "She's perfect," he rumbles. "But she's gone, Hud. I tried to track her, but it was like she'd vanished into mid-air. Sneaky little cat."

His tone is admiring, rather than pissed off.

Then the fucker hangs up on me.

Huffing in annoyance, I throw the phone down. He's definitely holding out on me. I haven't heard Ax that animated in years.

Nate comes tumbling down the stairs leading off my office to the apartment, throwing out words at a hundred miles an hour. I grab him as he moves to shoulder past me.

"She disappeared," I tell him firmly. "And you need to get to work." His eyes round as he starts to protest, but I hold firm.

"You've got a job. Car's on its way."

Grabbing the phone off him, I push him back towards the stairs. "Dress. Now, Nate."

He growls, but takes the stairs two at a time as I lift the phone to my ear.

"I'm not sure about this," Cade worries. "He's already really attached to this omega and he met her for thirty seconds. She *ran away* from him, me, and now Ax too? Maybe we're doing the wrong thing, trying to track her down."

I start to gather up paperwork, Nate's phone cradled between my shoulder and ear.

"No harm in making sure she's safe," I reason. "She slept in a damn doorway last night, Cade. That doesn't exactly scream safe and secure to me."

I can hear him stressing.

"Calm down," I chide him. "Stop panicking. See if your guy digs anything up, and we'll all keep an eye out in case she reappears."

"Agreed."

And I get my second hang-up in the space of five minutes.

Stomping footsteps announce Nate's reappearance, and he scowls at me as he sweeps into the kitchen, ready to work in a pair of faded denims and a loose white shirt.

"I don't want to work today," he grumbles. "Might call in sick."

"You will not." I point a spatula at him threateningly. "You've been excited about this one for three months. Get your ass into the car. It's outside."

He bares his teeth at me in annoyance. "I hate it when you get all responsible."

"One of us has to be." Hustling him out, I wait with folded arms until he slides into the car, the window winding down as he leans out.

"I want regular updates," he demands. "*Regular*, Hudson. Let me know as soon as you hear something."

I wave exaggeratedly. "Bye, *Nathaniel*. See you later."

The car pulls off with Nate's protests still ringing in the air.

CHAPTER ELEVEN
GABRIELLE

My feet throb inside my battered sneakers as I collapse onto the bench. The evening sky has turned from a dusky rose to solid black. The statues and trees lining the park, welcoming and bright in the daylight, stretch out in menacing shadows.

I *really* don't want to spend the night here.

Biting my lip, I glance up at the deserted path, considering my options.

I could find another doorway. But my body aches, hours of remaining on alert catching up to me. My heart flips over at the idea of seeing Axel again, but I dismiss the idea of going to the gym. He might call someone. He might call the Center.

My chest shrivels at the thought.

They can't force me to do anything. The law has changed.

But it's hard to break the habit of mistrusting a system that hasn't been kind to me in the past.

I know how it starts. Pretty words, fake promises and false smiles, and before I know it, I'll be wrapped up and handed over to an alpha pack with a pretty bow around my neck.

It might not be the harsh constraints of the Omega Compound, but it's still a type of servitude.

The Center isn't an option.

Then I remember the nasally words of the concierge.

There's a place for people like you.

A camp. Under the bridge.

It wouldn't hurt just to check it out. I wouldn't have to stay.

Decision made, I grab my duffle and make my way through the streets to the edge of town, following the path of the river as I get closer.

A soft glow illuminates the darkness as I unsteadily pick my way through the unfamiliar ground, and a hum of voices help direct me as I stumble down an embankment.

Blinking, I take in the dozens of shapes scattered in front of me. Some are real tents, a little battered but standing proudly. Dotted in between are lines of thin rope, holding blankets, bedsheets, various materials scrounged together to create makeshift sleeping areas.

Flickers of firelight appear in between, shadows of people moving between them with the indistinct buzz of conversation and the occasional raised voice.

It's like a really weird, patchwork nest.

Swallowing, I edge a little closer, until I reach the first line of tents.

Picking my way in between, I keep my head down as I walk through, scanning for a potential spot to lay my head down.

The people are mixed. Older, younger, there's no one distinct type, but the one thing they all have in common are their faces.

Weathered, haggard, tired.

They all look broken.

I stumble back as a woman sways into me, her face all too familiar in its slackness.

"'Got a light?" she mumbles, and I shake my head as I back away, my stomach churning.

She moves to follow me, but an arm drops down between us.

"Back off, Sandra," a low voice orders. "She ain't got what you want."

The woman stares at us, before she spins, lilting to the side as she wanders away.

"Damn space addicts," the woman mutters. "You okay, hun?"

She's older, beta, with braided gray hair wrapped up in a bun and a wiry frame.

"Thanks," I say, and she nods.

"Plenty of them around, so be careful. First time?"

When I nod, she cocks her head to the side.

"Best get you sorted out, then. I got a spare blanket you can have."

She clicks her fingers as she moves away. "Come on, gal. No use loitering there."

Hastily stepping over the pegs nailed into the ground, I follow the woman to a small but tidy area. Several sheets hang over the lines above us, and I catch a glimpse of a sleeping bag and what looks like an oil lamp before she tugs a sheet over it.

"Sorry," I apologize in stumbling tones. "I've never… I'm not sure…"

The woman sighs, taking pity on me. "I'm Seek."

"Seek?"

"Aye. Because I find things." She wiggles long, thin fingers at me. "Things that don't want to be found."

My eyes slip to an abandoned stash of wallets on the ground, and Seek tosses a blanket over them.

"First rule of bein' here." She takes a step closer to me,

her voice dropping with a warning note. "Keep your nose to yourself. Got that?"

When I nod furiously, her shoulders relax.

"Here." She throws me a wool blanket before she disappears into her tent and comes back out, a yellowed sheet in her hands. She hands it over.

"Use that to set up," she points at the sheet. "I ain't got a sleeping bag, but I'll keep an eye out for you."

"Thank you. I probably won't be here long, though—"

Seek throws her head back in a loud cackle. "Like I haven't heard that before. Welcome to the dungeon, omega. Watch yourself. There are alphas around."

My flinch doesn't go unnoticed, and she sniffs.

"If I can see it so clearly, they will, too. Most of 'em keep to themselves, so stay outta the way and you should be fine."

Seek vanishes behind her tent, and I wait for a few moments before realizing I've been summarily dismissed. Calling out a weak thank you, I look around, finding a small empty space with an above section of twine.

It takes me a few minutes to throw the sheet over, the cold numbing my fingers and making me fumble. When it's finally up, I spread the blanket over the hard packed dirt underneath and crawl in.

It's freezing, but at least there's some shelter from the wind. Tugging the hood of Axel's sweatshirt over my head, I lie back with my head on my duffle and bury my hands in the pockets, grateful for the length as I suck in another hit of his scent.

The noise of the camp ebbs and flows around me. Hunger claws at my stomach, but I ignore it, shifting onto my side.

My eyes start to flutter, and I stop fighting it.

Please let tomorrow be better.

CHAPTER TWELVE
GABRIELLE

"**G**et outta here."

I slump as the bar door swings shut, jumping back to avoid getting hit in the face.

Six *fucking* days.

Six days of walking every street in the city. Six days of politely asking for work, wheedling, even downright begging.

I don't think there's a single place left to try.

My heart thuds dully in my chest as I turn away, the pulsing music blaring from the bar pounding at my already savage headache.

"Hey, omega."

My shoulders tense as I swing around, arms raised.

The beta takes a step back, hands raised. "Steady. Name's Elliot."

He looks like a creep. Tall, skinny, greasy hair slicked back highlighting the sharp planes of his face. Dark eyes flick over me from head to toe.

He licks his lips as he stares at me.

"I got a job for you," he croons. "Easy money. Big bucks."

It doesn't take a genius to pick up on the underlying insinuation.

"No thanks."

When I turn around, Elliot grabs my arm, sharp nails digging in as I try to pull away.

"Come on, now," he hisses. "What's a girl like you doing out here when you can be making money in there?"

He jerks his head at the door next to the bar. Tucked away, it looks innocent enough until you see the sign.

Knotty Delights.

I shudder as I tug my arm out of his grip.

"Get off me!"

Elliot stays in place as I back away, keeping an eye on him to make sure he doesn't follow before I break into a run.

"I'll be here," he calls silkily. "When you come begging for it. You'll end up on your back eventually, you know. Pretty little thing like you."

My breath seesaws out of me in heaves as I bend over, hands on my knees as his words ring in my ears.

I know exactly what type of place that is.

A place where alphas can get their kicks now the heat nests are closed.

Nausea rises in my throat.

They'd use me like a toy until my batteries ran out, my shine wore off. Use me and dump me, probably addicted to fuck knows what.

I've seen the end results of their offer at the dungeon.

There's not many, but they're there, hidden in the corners. Strung out, empty-eyed omegas, with shaking limbs and dry, cracked lips. Holes in their elbows, between their feet.

Desperately seeking their next fix so they can forget. Offering themselves up to the equally empty-eyed alphas so they can get through the day with a little something *extra*.

The burning behind my eyes intensifies as I walk along, unseeing. My hands shake at my sides.

I'm scared.

Scared of being locked in this cycle. Waking up every morning with numb hands and ears, huddled inside a hoodie that smells less and less like warm, earthy teakwood each day and more and more like desperation.

Scared that one day soon that offer is going to look tempting.

And petrified, because I'm so cold and hungry that right now, the smallest part of me is already tempted. And once it creeps in, it's only a matter of time before that part gets bigger.

And then I'll be on my back, taking a knot from any alpha that wants to pay a few bucks for the privilege just to survive.

My hands bang against the side of a garbage can as I empty the lining of my stomach into it. There's nothing to bring up, just retching until my stomach burns with agony.

People give me a wide berth, muttering to themselves in disgust.

Pulling back, I wipe my hands over the back of my mouth.

I want a shower so badly, but there's nothing around. The best I can do is a quick wash and my teeth in the public toilets. Sharp angles and hollow cheeks look back at me from the mirror, highlighted by the cheap strip lighting flickering overhead.

It's like I'm a ghost. Slowly disappearing.

My feet shuffle along the floor as I walk aimlessly along different streets.

Every bar, every restaurant, every potential opportunity has already said no. What's the point in asking again?

My steps slow as I reach a familiar sight, and my eyes glance up to the sign.

Il Piacere.

Soft Italian music echoes across the sidewalk as I pause, just for a moment, remembering the feeling from the other night.

Warmth. Happiness. Hope.

And the smell of real, well cooked, delicious food.

My stomach twists, the sudden stab taking me by surprise as my breath whooshes out of me.

I can't remember the last time I had anything close to resembling a proper meal.

When I move my eyes to the side of the building, I spot a small entrance, and curiosity gets the better of me.

The opening leads into an alley with a dead end, and I shrink back as a door swings open a few meters down.

A man emerges, cropped blonde hair flashing in the late morning sun as he tosses a trash bag into a large red dumpster with a muscled arm.

My eyes move between him and the trash as he brushes off his hands, heading back inside.

Edging down, I stay close to the wall as my gaze darts back between the dumpster and the door. Revulsion wars with hunger, and the hunger wins out as my hand creeps up to open the lid.

It's heavier than I expected, the black lid creaking ominously. Lifting onto my toes, my stomach churns queasily as I stare in at the bags, the unmistakable scent of rot wafting up.

But there might be something in there.

This feels like... defeat.

But my hand still reaches in, trying to grab at the closest one. It looks like the one the guy threw in. There might be something a bit fresher than the stench burning my nose.

Just... a little... more.

I haul myself up, balancing precariously as my fingers brush the top of the bag.

There.

My moment of triumph is short-lived as I tug the bag towards me and my balance tips. Desperately, I throw my hands out, but there's nothing to latch onto as I tumble head-first into the dumpster.

The bags break my fall, but the breath knocks out of me as I lie there, gasping.

But that's not my biggest concern.

The lid slams shut with a bang, encasing me in darkness.

My breathing speeds up as I sit up, pushing on the lid to open it.

It creaks again, but nothing happens.

My vision narrows to twin pin pricks. My harsh breathing echoes in the small space as I throw all of my meager strength against the lid.

Nothing. It doesn't move.

My hands move to the sides, mindlessly pushing, moving between the lid and the walls.

No, no, no.

The trembling moan bounces back at me from the walls as they close in.

"Help."

My voice is a rasp, panic clawing at my throat as it closes up.

"Help me!"

I curl my hands around my knees and bury my face in them, trying desperately to suck in a breath.

Memories assault me, one after the other, until I can't tell truth from reality.

Get in the hole, bitch.

Stay there until you've learned your place.

A good omega does as she's told.

A good omega follows the Omega Creed.

The terror overtakes me until all I can do is let out tiny, panicked whimpers.

I try in vain to push one more time at the lid, but it remains stubbornly closed.

My nails scratch fruitlessly at the walls, scrambling until they tear.

But nothing happens. Nobody comes.

And the panic becomes all consuming.

CHAPTER THIRTEEN
HUDSON

"Hudson!"

I nearly drop the soap I'm using to scrub my hands.

"Yeah?" I ask, bracing as I turn to my sous chef. Veronica might be a beta, but she's got more alpha energy than most. She plants a hand on her hips, the blonde hair piled untidily on her head bouncing as she gestures dramatically.

"He is in there in his robe again!" she hisses, her face scrunched up with irritation.

"Get him out. The staff can't concentrate!"

Sighing, I dry my hands and brush past her, offering a consolatory pat to her shoulder.

"I'll sort it," I say reassuringly, and she huffs.

Entering the wide kitchen area, my eyes cut straight through the hustle of staff to where Nate is lounging in a seat, coffee mug outstretched with a charming smile on offer for Ella, who's pouring the cup with a delighted smile on her face.

"Nate," I growl. Ella jumps, spinning to face me.

"Hudson!" Her eyes dart from me to Veronica, pure guilt

in them. "I was just helping Mr. Reyne with some coffee."

"How many times have I told you, Ella?" Nate drawls, leaning forward with a slow smile that makes Ella blush from head to toe. "Call me Nathaniel."

"Out!" I point towards the kitchen door as Ella dives past me, her face scarlet. I hear a giggle, and my temper rises.

"If you're not going to help with the lunch prep, then *get out*," I snap. "And stop distracting my staff!" I swing around with a glare, and the huddle of waitresses behind me breaks apart rapidly as they scatter across the kitchen.

Nate pouts, but he slides down from his seat.

"I can help!" he protests as I shepherd him towards the private elevator that connects the restaurant to our penthouse.

Rolling my eyes, I hit the button to call it down.

"You have a job today," I remind him. "The Alexei Monroe shoot."

His eyes widen. "Damn. That's today?"

Thrusting the cup at me, he dives into the elevator, jabbing the button to take him up to our space. Rolling my eyes, I take the cup back with me into the kitchen, handing it to Ella.

"At least try and contain yourself," I say wryly, and she giggles.

"I can't help it," she says with a sigh. "He's just so…"

Yeah, I know. Good job my ego doesn't need stroking, or I might feel a little deflated at the way my staff preen over Nate. But then, doesn't everyone? His face is currently decorating a hundred foot tall billboard across the street, all smoldering eyes and messy bed head as he leans against a wooden bedpost in his underwear.

Waving Ella off, I point towards the rest of the trash, grinning at her dramatic wince.

"Consider it your penance," I smirk, and she groans as she heads over, lifting up the bag with a wrinkled nose.

I'm head down over the schedule for the rest of the week when she reappears, eyes wide and face pale as she yanks my sleeve.

"What is it?" I ask sharply. Nate reappears in the doorway, his hands smoothing down the slightly crumpled white shirt as he glances between us. For once, Ella doesn't even look in his direction.

"There's a *girl*," she says rapidly. "In the dumpster!"

I'm on my feet before she can finish, brushing past her as I dive for the back door. Nate's smoky, charred scent is close behind me as I jump down the steps and lift the lid on the giant dumpster.

"Fucking hell," I hiss, staring down. A small, undeniably female shape is curled up, dark hair spilling out across the filthy bags. "Nate, hold this."

He's already climbing in, boots squishing in the muck as he jumps down with a wet squelch and a grimace.

"She's unconscious," he says hoarsely, holding his fingers to her pulse. Bending down, he gently scoops her up, holding out his arms to me to take her.

She's light as a damn feather in my arms, and my pulse races as I lay her down to the floor.

"Is she dead?" Ella whispers. I glance up, seeing the faces clustered by the door.

"Hud," Nate murmurs. Her eyes are starting to flutter, small noises slipping out as she turns her head, pushing it into my hand.

"Everybody inside, now," I announce. "Ron, get Ella a hot drink and make her sit down."

My sous chef doesn't argue, gently wrapping an arm around Ella's shoulders and leading her inside.

The girl stirs again, her dirty face moving from side to side as Nate and I wait.

"Should I call someone?" he asks in a low tone, and I shake my head as her eyes flutter open.

She blinks blearily, sooty eyelashes sweeping over huge deep blue irises as she focuses on me and Nate. A pure shot of full-blown omega terror hits us like a brick. My spine locks up as Nate lets out a growl of recognition.

"It's you!"

She bolts upright, scrambling away from us on her hands and knees, burnt butterscotch burning my nose. Nate and I exchange glances, and he nods at me.

This is definitely the omega we've been looking for.

"Hey," I say quietly, my hand out. "We just pulled you out of the dumpster. You were unconscious."

Her gaze swings between us and the dumpster as her breath heaves.

"Breathe, kitten," Nate says urgently. He's leaning forward next to me but doesn't move any closer, equally as aware as I am that the omega in front of us is clearly petrified.

"Take a breath now," I coax, keeping my tone low. "One at a time."

She moves that doe-eyed gaze between us, suspicion darkening the blue as she scrambles to her feet. She tilts unsteadily as Nate and I rise slowly, my arm out to keep Nate in place.

"I *know* you," he breathes. "You came here the other night."

The omega's cheeks darken to a deep scarlet as she glances away for a moment, her eyes landing on the dumpster.

My chest tightens with sudden understanding. There's only one reason someone would be rooting around in piles of trash, and my mouth tightens at the realization, taking in her thin frame. Too thin.

"You hungry?" I ask gently. "I can bring you something out."

CHAPTER FOURTEEN
GABRIELLE

Humiliation flushes my skin red hot as I square off against the two alphas in front of me.

The alpha I recognize, the one with the glorious eyes and disheveled hair, opens his mouth, but he doesn't say anything. The silence stretches out for a few seconds, until my traitorous stomach answers for me with a loud gurgle.

My hands wrap around my stomach. "I… I should go."

They're stood between me and a swift exit to the street, both of them watching me closely. The blonde alpha purses his lips, almond-shaped hazel eyes narrowing and crinkling his olive skin at the corners.

God, he's just as good looking as the first one, the one I ran from the other night.

"I don't like seeing anyone hungry," he says finally. "Since you nearly locked yourself into my garbage, I'd like to at least make sure you're fed before you go on your way."

He doesn't miss my nervous look at the door.

"I can bring it out," he says gently. His hazel eyes capture mine, full of understanding that makes my chest hurt.

"Stay?" he cajoles. "Just for a minute?"

When I nod, he moves towards the door, careful not to make any sudden moves.

The other alpha hasn't taken his eyes off me.

"I'm Nathaniel," he says. "Everyone calls me Nate. He's Hudson. What's your name?"

It rises to the tip of my tongue, but I hold back. Nate looks a little disappointed, and I glance down at the ground. My head still feels a little hazy, sickness churning in my stomach from my little imprisonment.

I thought I was going to die. It happens. If they hadn't found me, I might've suffocated. Or the garbage disposal might have come.

My breath jolts out of me in jagged huffs.

The other alpha – Hudson – reappears. There's a takeout bag in his hands, and he holds it out to me.

"There's some meals in there," he says quietly. "Enough to get you by for a few days, at least."

My stomach nearly shrivels in on itself as I stare at the bag, temptation tugging at me to reach out and take it.

I clear my throat. "It's not... there's nothing in it?"

My voice croaks, and Hudson's face tightens in under-standing. "Nothing in it," he reassures me. And even though he could easily be lying, I believe him.

Slowly, I take a few steps forward, reaching my hand out for the bag. He holds it steady, the warmth of his hand brushing against mine as I take it from him.

"Thank you," I whisper. He nods, his eyes scanning my face closely.

I sneak a final look at Nate, who's watching me with his brows lowered.

"Hey," he says quickly as I turn to leave. "You still need a job?"

I pause, my shoulders bunching up.

A job.

Hudson jumps in. "We have a kitchen spot open. Nate didn't know – the other night. You interested?"

The sudden want nearly makes my knees buckle. Am I interested?

But it's tinged in distrust.

"A kitchen job?" I ask, shuffling my feet as I hug the bag to me with one arm. Delicious smells waft out the top, the heat warming my cold arms. Belatedly, I glance around, letting out a little sound of relief when I spot my discarded duffle bag just behind me.

Hudson nods. "It's not easy," he warns. "Big pots, lots of vegetable peeling and running around. But the pay's decent, and you get meals when you're working."

It's clearly a pity offer, but as I hesitate, the thought of heading back to the dungeon, to another night of cold air with no hope, makes my decision for me.

I nod decisively. "I'm interested."

Hudson's smile lights up his face, turning him from interesting to devastating. The laughter lines running from his eyes crinkle.

"Want to start now?" Nate steps forward, and Hudson pins him with a look.

"You," he says pointedly, "need to get to work."

Nate's pout is omega-worthy, but he nods reluctantly before he backs away from us.

"It was nice to meet you," he calls to me. "I'll see you later."

I nod, my eyes flicking from him to Hudson as he waves me up the steps.

"Follow me."

CHAPTER FIFTEEN
HUDSON

Turning my back on the omega, I hold my breath as I walk back inside. Soft footsteps pad behind me, the scent of butterscotch softening from the bitterness of a moment ago. It's still a little sharp, her nerves clear, and I'm careful to keep my distance as relief fills me.

I thought she might run off as soon as I turned my back.

The sheer amount of relief I feel makes me blink as I stop at the door to the kitchen, turning to face her. She stares at me, still clutching her bag of food tightly to her chest.

I'm not actually expecting her to start work right now. I'm not in the habit of forcing traumatized and possibly injured omegas to scrub filthy pots until they keel over.

I just didn't want her to *leave*. But I need to tread carefully, mindful of her skittish movements and the way she keeps glancing towards the door.

Clearing my throat, I think fast.

"We have a stock of uniforms in the staff room," I offer.

The omega bites her lip, her face lighting up briefly before her hands drop to her hoodie. I take in the familiar logo, with a lightness in my chest. She's wearing Axel's clothes.

And he gave her his favorite sweatshirt.

"Laundry facilities too," I add, stepping into the kitchen. Her fingers clench around the little duffle bag she's carrying.

I lead her through the kitchen into the offices, ignoring the eyes on us from my team. Nobody says anything, but the questioning silence feels heavy all the same. Veronica in particular is eyeing me where she sits with a wide-eyed Ella.

Her shoulders are hunched when I turn around.

"They're a good bunch," I say quietly. I've worked very hard to build a team I can trust. "But if you get any trouble, you let me know."

Taking her into the staff area, I point out the break room, the cloakroom where we keep the uniforms, and the laundry area. She absorbs the information quietly, head cocked, hands fiddling with the edge of her dark braid.

I throw my hand towards the back of the corridor. "Shower's over there."

Blue eyes dart to me, the longing there clear enough to grit my teeth.

"Lots of us use it. There's a lock on the door, and you'll find different lotions, conditioner, whatever you need. We all leave things there, so just help yourself."

Pointing her towards the cloakroom, I jab my finger towards my own office. "Take whatever uniform might fit you, and don't rush. I'll be in here, just walk on in. Okay? I mean it. Take your time."

I emphasize the last few words as I take a step away. The omega just stares at me, and I pause awkwardly. I've never dealt with a situation quite like this one. What I'd *really* like to do is take her upstairs, cook her a hot meal, run her a hot, bubbly bath, get her some more of our clothes and make sure she gets some rest. The dark circles under her eyes and her overall condition tell me more than enough about how much rest she's had recently. Very little, if any at all.

I think she'd probably run screaming though. I massage the ache in my chest with my knuckles. Man, alpha instincts are something else. Having never spent any time around omegas before, it feels like getting hit over the head with something heavy. The physical *need* to soothe her is unsettling.

"You okay? Need something else?" My voice croaks.

She clears her throat.

"Gabrielle," she whispers. "That's my name."

"Gabrielle."

Tasting the word on my tongue, I nod. It suits her. "Nice to meet you," I offer with a small smile. I keep my hand to myself, giving her space.

She nods at me, her face drawn and tired as she takes a hesitant step towards the cloakroom, glancing back at me.

"Go on," I urge. "Whatever you need. We've got plenty of supplies and we're always ordering more."

I watch as she ducks into the room, the door closing softly behind her.

I'm barely a few steps down the hall before a stifled sound rubs me the wrong way, my back drawing ramrod straight. Frowning, I turn around and retrace my steps, listening carefully.

The quiet sobbing is muffled, and my heart thumps against my chest as I retrace my steps and knock quietly on the door.

There's no answer.

I wait for approximately half a second before my hand flashes to the handle and I ease it open.

Gabrielle looks up at me from where she sits in the middle of the hard-wearing carpet, her face tear-stained and full lips trembling as she frantically tries to wipe under her eyes. The bag of food sits in her lap.

"So-sorry," she hiccups. "I was just – just—,"

A lump appears in my throat as I take her in. Crossing

the floor between us, I sink down on my haunches in front of her.

"Oh, sweetheart," I murmur. "You've had a hell of a day."

She half laughs, half sobs at my clear understatement.

My hands twitch, and I offer up the only thing I have.

"Want a hug?"

I expect her to refuse, and she bites her lip. But then she's leaning forward, and it feels completely fucking natural to pull her into my arms, wrapping them around her as she cries silent, body-shaking tears into my chest, soaking the cotton of my shirt.

"Shhh," I soothe. "Let it all out."

Rocking her gently, I hold onto her tightly, my hands not moving as she tucks her head underneath my chin. She's a perfect fit against me, like two puzzle pieces with jagged edges slotting together.

The purr rumbles up from deep within my chest, unexpected and sudden. Gabrielle pauses, her tears tailing off.

"Sorry," I whisper. "Didn't expect that. You okay?"

She nods against me, and my eyes flick down to her face. She's nestled against my chest, her cheek against my heart, her eyes closed as her breathing lowers to soft little huffs.

Tenderness, surprise and pure, alpha satisfaction hits me hard.

I hate that she's hurting. It feels wrong, an itch under my skin. But having her in my arms, curled into me?

That feels *right*.

Chapter Sixteen
Gabrielle

I take slow, deep breaths as Hudson rocks me carefully in his arms, solid steel bands encasing me that feel comforting rather than restricting.

His scent burrows into my nose, fresh and sweet, rosemary and basil giving off just a hint of spice. It suits him.

My face turns on instinct as I take a deeper breath, trying to pull it into my lungs. When he freezes, I realize what I'm doing, my nose pressed to the open v of his shirt as I pull it greedily from his skin.

Mortified, I clear my throat and pull away, offering him an awkward smile.

"Sorry," I offer. "I, um, don't normally do that."

I wince at the awkward line, but Hudson just looks down at me, his smile lazy and soft with understanding.

"That makes both of us," he admits. "I've never purred like that in my life."

I stare up at him. "You haven't?"

Why does that make me feel better?

His cheeks tint red. "Never spent much time around omegas," he admits. "Guess we're both on new ground."

His admission makes sense. Most omegas voluntarily

moved into the Omega Center after we were released from the Compound, often living there until they're matched with packs. I've never met an omega aside from the strung out ones hanging down at the dungeon, and most of them are older, discarded by their packs.

"I guess so."

Awkwardly, I pull myself away from him, getting to my feet. He does the same, and I bite my lip. My cheeks feel like they're on fire.

"Thank you… for the hug."

"Of course." He hesitates as he turns to leave.

"I hope you don't feel—," he blurts as he turns back to me. His olive-toned cheeks look as red as mine feel.

"I'd like you to feel safe here," he says softly. "I hope I didn't take advantage."

My mouth drops open. "I don't. Feel that, I mean," I blurt.

Fuck, this is uncomfortable.

He nods. "Good. That's good." He lingers for a moment more, before he spins. "Okay. Going now."

Hudson throws a final glance back at me. "Take your time, okay?"

Taking him at his word, I survey the options in front of me as the door closes. My stomach rumbles, but the urge to get clean is bigger.

Realization hits hard, and I groan as I realize I wrapped myself around Hudson like a pretzel smelling like his garbage dumpster.

Way to make an impression on my new boss.

He's probably gone to wash the stink off. The thought is irrationally irritating as I pick out a pair of pants that look like they might fit, and a matching black shirt. A hint of Hudson's fresh scent lingers in the air, gradually loosening the tension in my limbs as I pull out what I need from my little duffle and store it carefully in a locker.

There's no underwear, but I can make do. Hudson mentioned laundry, so maybe he won't mind if I quickly wash the few things I have stuffed inside my duffle bag later. My spirits lift, buoyed by the thought of clean clothes and an actual hot water flow.

I open the door a fraction, scanning up and down the corridor before I hoof it down to the door marked *Staff Shower*. Much to my relief, there's a lockable cubicle. Various bottles line the metal shelf, things left by previous users. I almost whimper as I spot a shampoo and conditioner with a sizable chunk left inside. My hair is less a sleek, groomed hairstyle and more like a bush after more than a week without washing it.

I definitely whimper when the first spray of hot water hits, my clothes abandoned on top of my duffle outside. Taking my time, I carefully wash away every last trace of dirt and grime, scrubbing my hair for a second time and using some apple-scented body wash to get the smell of the dungeon and the dumpster off as I frantically scrub beneath my nails. The more I scrub, the more I want to feel clean, until my skin reddens under the heat of the water and my frenzied washing.

After tipping my face up to the stream one more time, I turn the knob to halt the water with a hint of regret, but it fades as I wrap myself in one of the big white fluffy folded towels I grab from an overflowing shelf.

Heaven.

Heaven is a hot shower and a fluffy white towel that feels like clouds on my skin.

I purse my lips as I wipe away the steam covering my reflection in the mirror. The lighting isn't great, and I'm not much better.

But I'm clean, and right now it's the best thing I've ever felt.

Biting my lip at having no underwear to put on, I slide on

the new clothes, wriggling in delight at the feel. I stash my dirty clothes inside the duffle, my fingers lingering on Axel's hoodie.

The barest hint of teakwood is still there as I take a deep inhale, but it's mostly covered by rotting garbage. Regretfully, I push it back inside the bag, shoving down the powerful feelings erupting in my chest as the thought of losing his scent altogether. I can't keep it like that, though. I'll have to wash it with the rest of my clothes.

Carrying my duffle and feeling more like an actual human than the trash panda I was half an hour ago, I pad down the hallway, pausing as I come to the door of Hudson's office. The door is wide open, and he glances up from a small desk with a smile as I knock tentatively on the open frame.

"Feeling better?"

I nod vigorously. "Much, thank you."

"I'm glad." He stands and stretches, a hint of muscled olive skin flashing at me from the space between his jeans and shirt. I force my eyes back to his face as he yawns.

"Early start." He gives me a wide berth as he slides past, beckoning me to follow.

"They should be done in the kitchen for a minute. Everyone on the lunch shift starts early to prep, and then they eat and reset the restaurant before we formally open for lunch."

My eyes round. That's generous. I don't think I've ever had free food from any of my shitty jobs. My last employer offered me a burger with all the trimmings in exchange for a blow job.

Anxiety is a lead ball in my stomach as he pushes open the kitchen door we walked through earlier.

I brace myself for an announcement, but it's quiet, the only person in the room a formidable looking ice blonde beta, with her hair tied up in a tight ponytail. She turns to us, pale green eyes scanning me expressionlessly.

"Veronica," Hudson greets her. "This is Gabby. Our new kitchen assistant."

Veronica raises an eyebrow at him, but doesn't say anything as she scans me with pursed lips.

"Got any experience?" she asks.

I catch Hudson's brief look of surprise when I respond. "I've worked in diners for the last few years. Maybe some similar things, but I've never worked in a place like this before."

There's a touch of awe to my tone, and Veronica softens. "You'll get used to it."

Hudson beams. "Go on out and take your break," he tells Veronica. "I'm gonna make some coffee and chat to Gabby here about the job, get her up to speed."

My stomach gurgles again as my chest leaps. *Did he say coffee?*

Veronica gives me a formal nod before she leaves. The kitchen feels huge without all of the people in here, a wide, open space with steel counters lining up in rows and overhead shelves jammed with various pots, pans and instruments. I don't even know what half of them are.

Hudson pulls some stools over to one of the taller counters, pushing a bar stool towards me with his foot. "Have a seat. Want some coffee?"

My mouth waters as he moves over to a monster of a machine that has steam lazily curling out of it, pouring gleaming dark magic into two cups and sliding one over to me with some cream and sugar as he takes a seat.

"I take mine black," he adds. "But my pack are animals and like to cram theirs with cream."

My hand withdraws from hovering over the cream, and he jerks, his eyes widening comically.

"I'm kidding," he says softly. His hand nudges the cream

towards me. "Load yourself up. Even if you are one of those coffee types."

Taking him at his teasing words, I hesitantly top up my cup before wrapping my hands around the warmth and taking a sip.

It takes a lot of effort to stop the moan in my throat from making an appearance. Coffee really is my kryptonite. I can't remember having coffee this good. Ever.

Hudson waits for me to drink, his eyes watching me closely.

"So," he begins, when I set the cup down. "You already have some experience."

I nod, my fingers tracing a pattern over the steel counter. "Some, but the diners I've worked in weren't anything like this. Does it matter?"

I bite my lip, hoping my honesty doesn't put him off.

He smiles crookedly. "Experience is always welcome, but enthusiasm is what I'm interested in here. Everything else can be taught. What do you think of my pride and joy?"

He waves exaggeratedly towards the restaurant, and I bite back a smile.

Thinking on it for a moment, I decide to go with the truth.

"I sat on your steps the other night," I tell him. "I thought it felt like... happiness. Like a moment in time, full of warmth and laughter. I wanted to be part of it."

Hudson swivels back to face me, a hint of surprise in his eyes.

"That was... unexpected," he murmurs. "But I under-stand what you mean completely. Thank you for sharing it with me."

Now I'm embarrassed. I shouldn't have said anything, and I bury my face in my cup to avoid meeting his eyes. "Thank you. For all of this, I mean."

He takes a sip of his coffee, long fingers curling around the cup as he watches me.

"You're not what I expected, you know," he says suddenly.

I blink, confused, and he groans. "That sounded weird. I just meant… Nate told us that he'd met you. He didn't mean to freak you out the other night."

My cheeks flush. "I know. I'm probably a little jumpy." My admission makes him nod.

"That's completely understandable," he says carefully. "Your safety should always be a priority."

He looks like he's about to start asking awkward questions – possibly along the lines of *tell me why you were locked in my dumpster* – so I blurt out the first thing that comes to mind.

"Neither are you. What I expected, I mean."

It's a clumsy confession, but it's true. Alphas have been a red warning sign for me my whole adult life. First through the people that tried to sell me, then at the OC, and then when I managed to break free, alphas were still a danger – maybe even more so, with nothing stopping them from taking advantage. Big, threatening, with the ability to chain my body and force me to do whatever they want with a single bark.

I won't ever live like that again.

Hudson feels different. I'm not on edge, my body relaxed as we talk. I don't know what I expected. But it definitely wasn't this. Coffee, and conversation… even understanding, with this alpha and his knowing eyes.

"I'm not good at this," he says wryly, getting up to refill our cups. "Like I said, I've never spent time around omegas before. So if I do anything to make you uncomfortable, I need you to tell me straight away. I'll never do it intentionally."

Honesty. I like it. "I understand. I'll tell you. As long as you don't use your bark, I'll be alright."

His low growl is furious. "*Never.*"

It feels like a promise, and I relax a little more at his vehement disgust. Maybe this might turn out alright, after all.

As I pile on more creamer, Hudson grabs a folder and slides out a sheet of paper, pushing it over to me. I pause, my eyes flicking over the employment contract and my eyebrows rising as I take in the payment terms.

It's more than I ever made at the diner. Hudson leans forward too, our foreheads nearly touching as we both look at the wording.

He names a figure that nearly makes my eyes bulge out of my head. "This is an old contract, so the numbers are off. That's your hourly rate, plus you get to keep all your tips if you do any front of house work. Free meals when you're on shift, and a thirty minute rest break. How's that sound?"

How does it sound? Like I've won the freaking lottery.

He holds out a hand, and I will my fingers not to shake as I reach out. He gently clasps them, shaking up and down.

"We have a deal, it seems," he says, smiling.

He starts pulling pots and pans out from underneath the counter, setting them out on the side. Uncertain, I shift in my seat. "Um... do you want me to come back?" I ask awkwardly.

Hudson turns to me, raising an eyebrow. "I'm cooking you breakfast, sweetheart. Consider it your welcome to the crew." He mumbles something else under his breath, disappearing through a door as I sit on the stool with a lump in my throat.

He's cooking me breakfast?

Hudson is a whirlwind in the kitchen. He strides from section to section, grabbing what he needs without even looking as he throws together a delicious looking meal in a matter of minutes.

My stomach growls loudly as he sets a plate in front of me, and he winks.

"No empty stomachs in my kitchen. Staff rule."

Staring down at the feast of pancakes, drizzled with syrup and crispy bacon, I sniff. The plate wavers in front of me.

"Gabrielle?" Hudson asks, worry in his tone. "Oh, God. Are you vegetarian?"

I laugh wetly, pressing my hands to my cheeks and shaking my head. "Sorry," I croak. "It's just... this is really nice."

"Oh, sweetheart." Gentle hands cup my cheek as he wipes away a tear. "Where have you been to cry over a breakfast, hmm? Even one as *excellent* as this one."

I snort out a teary laugh, and he steps back as I wipe my face. "I'm so sorry." Embarrassment stains my cheeks, more heat coming off them than the cooker. "I really appreciate it."

"Nonsense." He waves his hand in the air. "Now eat. We've got a busy day ahead."

I dive into the delicious food, struggling not to moan over the feel of the fluffy pancakes in my mouth. The bacon is a lost cause, the first sacrifice to settle my rumbling stomach.

"Oh, god, this is good." The moan slips out. Hudson freezes as I stop, mid-chew.

His scent strengthens as he carries on without saying anything, and I try my best to tone down the awkwardness by stuffing my face as quickly as possible.

I push away my empty plate. My stomach groans from the weight of the food, but I have zero regrets. I'd probably demolish another plate.

"That was amazing, thank you. I don't know what to say—"

"Nothing," he says firmly. "I mean that. You never need to thank me for food, Gabrielle. It was a pleasure to watch you enjoy it."

"It's not for the food," I whisper.

Hudson blushes. I watch in fascination as his olive-toned cheeks tinge pink. He looks even more delicious when he's flustered. Biting my lip, I shake my head to rid myself of the errant thoughts.

Not your alpha, I remind myself. *No. Alphas. Ever.*

But the thought doesn't seem as awful as it used to be. I've never met an alpha like Hudson before. Or Nate – I only met him for a second the other night, and it wasn't great, but I'm feeling more and more like I might have jumped to conclusions. There's no way Hudson can be this nice and the rest of his pack isn't. Right?

Hudson sets me up in a corner with more coffee and flaky perfection in the form of tiny custard tarts as people start filtering back in for the lunchtime shift.

He introduces a few, and they all give me polite nods and smiles before bustling away to their own space. Hudson clearly runs a tight ship, everyone understanding exactly what they need to be doing.

A young beta pauses in front of me, her eyes downcast. "Are you feeling better?" she asks quietly. Hudson leans in, wrapping his arm around her, and I fight back a really fucking irrational burst of jealousy.

Jesus. He's not *mine*.

I force myself to look away, at the beta's face. "I am." My cheeks pink. "Thank you. You found me?"

She nods. "It gave me a fright," she admits, and Hudson squeezes her shoulder.

"Take it easy today," he tells her, and she nods, giving me one last smile before dashing off.

Veronica reappears, and I turn to Hudson uncertainly. He gives me a reassuring look.

"Just watch for now," he urges, his eyes moving to Veronica, who nods. "See how we work, take it all in and finish your coffee before you jump in. I'll come and see you soon."

The urge to follow after him is sudden and a bit unexpected, but I force my body to stay still until I'm completely absorbed in the comings and goings. As customers start to enter the front of the restaurant, waiting staff begin to dart in and out, shouting orders and pinning tiny pieces of paper to a magnetic board, where Veronica rips them off and calls orders to different chefs.

My feet start to itch, the urge to move, to help, starting to nudge me as the kitchen becomes a bustling hive of activity. When Veronica appears, I jump to my feet.

"What can I help with?" I ask her, and she grins, a faint sheen of sweat dotting her brow from the warmth of the heat lamps. "Dangerous questions."

She leads me past a row of chefs working, heat blasting my cheeks from the flames of the cookers, before she shows me to a deep sink absolutely bursting with dishes. A number of steel and copper pots in various sizes are stacked up alongside, jamming the relatively small space.

She looks mildly embarrassed as she turns to me. "Sorry. Zoe quit unexpectedly, so we've been making do."

I'm already rolling up my sleeves. "I'm on it. Where's the washing liquid?"

CHAPTER SEVENTEEN
NATE

"I'm calling it! That's a wrap, people. Pack your shit up."

A whistle sounds, and the set starts to disband, people running back and forth to pack it away for the next booking in the warehouse we're working out of on the outskirts of the city. Max, my director, places his hands on his hips as he wiggles thin dark brows at me.

"Where's your head at today, Nate Reyne?" he scolds.

I offer him an apologetic shrug as I wander over to my station, waving away the hair artist and shrugging on my jeans. The studio bustles with activity around us, photographers and artists dashing around.

"Sorry. Lots on my mind today. Everything okay with the photos?"

Max frowns. "We'll find out in editing, but I think we scraped it. Wasn't your best though."

Wincing, I clap him on the shoulder as I head past. "Sorry, Max. Head in the game for the next one."

Giving easy smiles to the people who stop me, I manage to duck out of the building without too much of a delay. There's a whistle as I look up and down the street, and Axel raises a hand from where he's leaning against his black Ford F-series truck.

"Need a ride?" he calls.

Hell yes.

I slide into the buttery leather with a sigh. Axel gets into the driving seat, his green eyes flicking over me with a hint of curiosity.

"You okay?"

"Have you spoken to Hudson today?" I ask, and he shakes his head, putting the car into drive and sliding out into the afternoon city traffic.

"Been busy," he grunts, braking to avoid an over-enthusiastic cyclist. "Why?"

Looking out the window, I hide my smirk. "No reason."

If Ax doesn't know about the omega yet, then I'm not gonna tell him. His face'll be a picture when we get home.

Assuming she's still there, that is. A trickle of worry worms down my spine at the idea that she might have disappeared. Maybe the job wasn't for her, or she got spooked.

My knee bounces up and down, and I can feel Ax frowning.

"Nate."

"Mm-hmm?"

"Tell me."

His voice is gruff as always, but I can hear the thread of concern, Axel's mother-hen coming out to play.

"All good," I assure him. "It was a rough shoot, that's all."

His face is suspicious, but he drops it, keeping his eyes on the road as we drive through the streets, heading back home. My fingers tap on the side of the door in anticipation as we pull up, Ax smoothly parking in one of our spots outside the restaurant.

"I know something's up," he says, calling me out. "I can

feel it. That's why I came to get you. But keep your secrets, Nathaniel."

I'm practically jigging in my seat. I try my best to pull back on my excitement as I bound up the steps, but my head is on a spin as I slip past the afternoon diners, ignoring the stares and whispers as I duck into the kitchen. Axel follows me, his curiosity leaking through the bitemark on my chest that marks us as pack.

Veronica is first to spot me, her blonde hair plastered to her head as she kneads dough. Her hands flick flour at me as she scowls. "*Out*."

"Ron." I give her my most charming smile, and she snorts at me, unmoved. "I just wanted to check on our newest staff member. She still here?"

Axel's curiosity ratchets up a notch as he lingers at my elbow. "New staff member?" he enquires.

Veronica purses her lips, her gaze flicking towards the end of the kitchen as her face softens.

"Leave her be," she says, a little more quietly. "She's working hard."

"I won't disturb her," I swear, edging past as she glares at me in warning. "Just wanted to check in."

I see her before she sees me. At my side, Axel sucks in a breath, his whole body tightening in realization.

Her dark hair is up in a haphazard bun, tendrils falling down her back and around her face as she darts around the washing up area. Plates disappear into the hot water as quickly as they appear, her brow furrowed in concentration as she stacks the clean ones neatly on the side for drying.

Rosemary reaches my nose as Hudson appears next to me.

"She's still here." I'm watching her greedily, taking in the way she moves around the small space so gracefully, even as more and more dishes pile up.

"She works like a trojan," Hudson mutters, sounding a little exasperated. "Hasn't stopped."

I frown. "Has she had a break?"

"Maybe a few minutes, and then she went straight back to it. Said she wanted to pull her weight."

Hudson shoulders past me as he moves towards her. She turns to him as Hudson gestures, his words too quiet for me to hear over the noise of the kitchen around us. I watch in fascination as her color rises, cheeks flushing a deep raspberry red as he leans in to speak in her ear.

Well, now. That's... interesting.

The omega takes a step back, nodding as she wipes her hands on her apron before wrapping her arms around herself with a glance towards the dishes.

Hud leads her towards us, and I can tell the exact moment she spots Axel at my side. Her foot trips on air, Hudson grabbing her elbow as she staggers.

I can feel Axel's panic. "Would you calm down?" I mutter out of the side of my mouth. He's not exactly giving off calming vibes, his huge frame practically vibrating and his mouth open. I push up his chin and he jerks, scowling at me.

"Thanks for the heads up."

My smirk feels victorious. "Good surprise though, right?"

He jams an elbow into my side before snapping straight as Gabrielle slows, coming to a stop in front of us. I try not to be too insulted that her eyes are focused purely on Axel, her mouth open as she glances between us.

"You... how...?"

"This is Axel," I announce proudly, poking his arm. It flexes under my fingers, the only outward sign of his agitation as he smiles at our omega. "Nice to see you again," he says softly.

Gabrielle looks like she might pass out. "You're all part

of the same pack?" she asks, her tone strangled. "All of you?"

"Cade too," I add. Her brows lower. "I haven't... met him. I don't think."

Axel jabs me again, and a little more clarity filters through. Shit. Maybe I didn't think this through. Our little omega filched Cade's wallet, and even though he's not angry, it'll be more than enough to send her running out the door if we don't handle this right.

Hudson gives me a look that tells me he's got similar thoughts running through his head, and I swallow.

"You'll see him at some point," I say airily, dodging her question and feeling like shit about it. "He's a legal genius, so he only comes out at night."

Hudson groans silently behind her. The little furrow between Gabrielle's eyes only deepens at my truly shitty attempt at a joke.

"Anyway," I clap my hands. "How was your first day?"

She nibbles on her lower lip as she glances between me and Axel, but her eyes brighten. "It's been good. I think?"

She glances at Hudson uncertainly, and he nods firmly. "Excellent."

I swear her back straightens, a hint of pride on her face as her lips twitch upwards.

"But now it's time for dinner," I point out, glancing between them. "Right, Hud?"

I watch the brief glance they share, both of them looking away quickly.

"I should probably get back—,"

"No," Hud interrupts her, hand rubbing at the back of his neck. "You've worked right through since lunchtime, Gabrielle. You need some food."

I bounce on my feet. "We normally eat upstairs as a group," I explain, trying not to sound too eager as she shuffles her feet. Ignoring Hudson's warning look and Axel's ominous silence at my side, I carry on.

"Want to join us for dinner?"

I can see the moment Gabrielle tenses up, her shoulders hunching as she takes a step back.

"Is that what everyone does?" she asks. There's a slight sharpness, a red light for me to back off as her eyes bounce between us with more wariness than they held earlier.

Shit.

"No," I confess. "I just…I wanted to invite you."

She shakes her head. "I'm good, thank you."

She turns back to her station, but Hud stops her.

"No more work until you've had a decent break," he tells her firmly. "All of my team have a break and some food, and that includes you."

He gives me a warning glare as he points her to a bar stool. She gives me a final wary glance before she turns away.

"What the hell, Nate?" Axel snaps at me under his breath. "She's skittish as hell. You really think inviting her to dinner with a bunch of alphas is going to make her feel more comfortable?"

I know he's right.

"Shit," I sigh. "Sorry. Too much."

"Way too much," says Hudson as he stalks past us. I follow him as he grabs a plate, moving around and dropping some fresh pasta and a pinch of salt into boiling water. He crosses his arms as he turns to me.

"Look," he says. His eyes are on Gabrielle. She's looking away from us, watching the kitchen activity as she fidgets with the arm of her shirt.

"I get it," he admits. "I'd like her to eat with us too. But we have to move slowly, Nate. We've just met her, and she doesn't know us."

"So how do we help her get to know us better?"

"*Slowly*." He turns, draining the pasta before swirling in some of the fresh seafood and sauce he's famous for and carrying the plate over to Gabrielle. I watch as she looks down at the plate, all wide eyes and flushed cheeks as he murmurs to her, setting down some cutlery and leaving her to it.

She takes her first bite slowly, cautious as hell. Her eyes widen, and she speeds up until I'm a bit worried she might choke. My chest clenches as she finishes the plate and glances up, a hint of embarrassment pinking her cheeks when our eyes meet and she looks away.

Slowly. I can do that.

Maybe.

CHAPTER EIGHTEEN
GABRIELLE

I can feel eyes watching me, but I don't care as I shovel the steaming pasta into my mouth. It feels like food that should be savored, but I'm too hungry to worry about that as I hold back a moan.

Hudson is one hell of a chef. No wonder we've been so busy for the last ten hours.

Staring down sadly at my cleared plate, I glance up, meeting Nate's honeyed eyes. He's watching me thoughtfully, and my stomach clenches as I remember his offer to eat upstairs.

For a split second, I almost said yes.

Curiosity tugs at me, the urge to find out what their life looks like outside of the little snippet I've seen. Not to mention their mystery pack member.

I can't believe that Axel is here. My heart almost climbed my throat when I saw him next to Nate, his green eyes glittering with familiarity and a matching hoodie to the one I have stashed in my duffle on his huge frame.

My hands drop to the hem of my top before I realize I'm not wearing it. Axel's eyes follow the movement of my hands, creasing a little.

I wonder if he'd consider swapping out. I'd love a top-up of his scent. It's the best sleeping aid I've ever had.

Setting down my cutlery, I consider the three men very obviously *not* watching me as they lounge a little too casually against the wall, chatting. They aren't what I expected alphas to be like. They're not what I know alphas can be.

Dominating. Aggressive. *Violent*.

No, these men aren't like that.

Yet.

The thought doesn't feel right, but I can't let my guard down completely, no matter how nice they've been to me today. Going up to their apartment? Isolating myself with them?

It would be the most stupid thing that I could do. Unfortunately, it also feels like the only thing I *want* to do, which is mildly inconvenient. My hormones are going haywire being this close to alphas, my own body working against me.

Although it's not just me. A number of the girls, and even some of the guys, are shooting flirty looks at the three of them from beneath their lashes, tittering amongst themselves.

I stare down at my feet. I really don't like that.

But I'll get over it. This is the downside to working with alphas. And as things go, it's definitely bearable.

One blonde-haired girl titters at Nate as she sways past him, and he gives her a friendly smile.

Okay. Maybe bearable. Mildly bearable?

Sliding down from my seat, I carry my plate back to my station, determined to ignore the delicious mini pack gathering happening in the corner. More dishes have piled up since I took my break, and I get to work, even though my legs are starting to protest.

The food I've had settles in my stomach, giving me some much needed energy that I've been lacking in the last week or so. Hell, the last five years. I've had the best food of my life today.

Nobody disturbs me, and I lose myself in the reassuring rhythm of washing, rinsing, stacking, until there's nothing left when my hands reach out, grasping at empty air.

Blinking, I turn around, taking in the lack of activity. A few people are still at work, wiping down counters, putting dishes away. My eyes move to the clock on the wall, shocked at the late hour.

Thankfully, the gathering has now dispersed, Nate and Axel nowhere to be seen. The door pushes open and Hudson reappears, a stack of plates in his hands. He moves over to me slowly, setting them down.

"That's the last," he tells me, lips curling up into a smile. "You worked hard today, Gabrielle."

Veronica nods in agreement as she sets down another pot. "You did good."

The praise warms my cheeks. "Thank you."

Veronica nods at me as she undoes her apron, hanging it on a hook. "Same again tomorrow?"

My eyes slide to Hudson. He stares back at me, eyebrows raised in question.

"I'd like that," I say.

As I finish the final few dishes, the kitchen clears out as people head home for the night. Veronica leaves with a wave, the others drifting out in groups as I set the last pot down and grab a cloth to wipe it dry.

A large hand closes over mine softly. "I'll do that."

My mouth seems to have glued itself shut, so I nod like an idiot as Hudson carefully takes the heavy pan from me, wiping it dry before he sets it back in its spot, ready for tomorrow.

"What did you think?" he asks me when he turns around. "I know we kind of put you on the spot earlier, but the job's yours if you want it."

"I want it." The words tumble out of me, and Hudson smiles briefly.

"I'm glad," he says softly. He moves to a till in the corner, pulling out some cash and counting it out. My mouth dries when he slides it into an envelope and holds it out.

"Your wages," he says carefully. His hazel eyes tighten as my shaking fingers close over the paper. "Where are you sleeping tonight, Gabrielle?"

The words make me jolt as I stare up at him. My mouth dries to something resembling a desert, and I try not to choke.

"I… um…,"

"I just want to make sure you're safe," he says gently, but his eyes don't leave my face. "That's all."

My stomach twists as I force a nod. I can't tell them. What would they do, anyway? Ask me to stay? Not likely, and I wouldn't accept if they did.

"I have somewhere," I lie. "It's not an issue."

Hudson scans my face one more time, and I force myself to maintain eye contact. The subterfuge feels sour on my tongue.

I'm not lying, though. It might not be the best place, or conventional, but the dungeon can do for a little longer. I'm not sleeping in doorways where handsome green-eyed viking alphas can coax me with yummy smelling items of clothing. I even have a lamp now.

I squeeze the envelope in my hand. I *could* pay for a motel tonight. Sleep on a proper bed.

But if I do that, I'll keep spending money I could use for a deposit on an actual apartment.

Hudson relaxes slightly, nodding. "You'll tell me? If you need anything?"

I nod, my head feeling heavy as I turn away. I hate that I'm misleading him, but this is for a good reason.

"Nate can be… a lot," he says quietly as my hand lands

on the door handle. "But he has a good heart. The best, actually."

I look down at the floor. "I...can see that."

"His offer was genuine. I hope you'll take us up on it soon."

My heart jumps in my chest as he holds the door open for me as I leave.

"Can I walk you home?" he questions. "Or at least get you a cab?"

Refusing with a shake of my head, I give him a short wave goodbye.

"Thank you, Hudson." My words are earnest, and he smiles at me softly, even though I can still see worry there.

For me.

It warms me from the inside out, even as I make my way through city streets and the muddy riverbank to the dungeon, lighting my oil lamp and curling up on my sleeping bag. I desperately want Axel's hoodie, missing the comfort it's given me since he handed it over, but one cautious whiff tells me that it's in dire need of the laundry facilities at the restaurant.

I keep my wages inside my top, just in case anyone decides to come sneaking around. I'll add it to my hiding place later.

Sleep doesn't come easily, my eyes remaining stubbornly open as I play over the day in my head.

When it finally drags me under, I dream of warm arms holding me and a tempting mixture of honey brown, hazel and bright green eyes.

CHAPTER NINETEEN
CADE

I lean back in my chair as Nate finishes regaling us with what he and Hudson have been doing today.

Hudson is still down in the restaurant, and Axel, Nate and I are settled in the living room, a muted action movie playing on the screen that none of us are paying attention to.

"I invited her to dinner," Nate says, his tone disappointed. "She said no."

Axel looks a little exasperated as he leans back, kicking his legs out in front of him as he crosses his arms. "You steamrolled her. I'm not surprised she backed off."

My nod of agreement makes Nate's shoulders deflate. Wide, frightened blue eyes slide back into my mind, sending my swig of beer down the wrong way as I start to cough.

"We need to be careful," I say hoarsely, as Ax whacks me on the back.

Nate's clearly head over heels already, and it sounds like Hudson is moving in the same direction. I trust their judgment, and it was already clear from our brief encounter that this omega isn't in a great situation. She needs help.

Help that Nate is clearly desperate to offer.

But we can't overstep the boundaries, the lines in the sand set out by our designations. We could easily push her into something she's not ready for purely through using biology, and that's not something I would accept. My pack wouldn't either, but I'm a little worried that Nate might accidentally push this omega into something she isn't ready for without even meaning to.

"I think we need some advice," I offer. "I could call the Center."

Nate frowns. "Why?"

Hesitating, I glance at Axel. He's staring down into his beer.

"We don't know this omega, Nate," I explain. "Not really. If she's on her own, she's not part of the Center setup, and with everything that's happened in the last few years, I just want to make sure we're doing the right thing by her."

And I need to protect my pack.

Nate rolls his eyes at me. "You're always so sensible, Cade. Let's just go with it and see what happens."

I battle the urge to rub the headache that's forming between my eyes, but I don't force the point as Hudson walks in with a cold beer in his own hands. He collapses into a chair with a sigh.

Nate swivels. "Was she okay?" he asks eagerly. Hudson nods, realizing that all of our attention is on him.

"I asked if she had somewhere to go, and she said yes," he rumbles, rubbing at his neck. "I don't know if I completely believed her, but I couldn't force her to stay. She said she's coming back tomorrow."

Nate grins widely. "Excellent."

"Take it easy," Hudson warns him. "She's really fragile, Nate."

He looks unrepentant. "I can do that."

When we all look at him askance, he throws up his hands. "I *can*!"

Axel snorts a low laugh.

"We could give her the spare room," Nate blurts. "It's there to be used."

Axel and I groan unanimously. "Nate." I pinch my nose. "We literally just talked about this."

"I don't mean right now. I just… she was sleeping outside Axel's gym a week ago. Do you really think she has somewhere decent? Because I'm not buying it."

Hudson nods in agreement. "I agree. But, we can't force her, Nate. I think she's had more than enough of that in her past."

Something in his words rub me the wrong way. The others clearly feel the same, Axel leaning forward with his knuckles white around his beer.

"Meaning?" It's a growl, the tension in the room growing.

"I don't know." Hud shrugs, but I can see the frustration in his face. "But it's not like the world has been especially welcoming to omegas, is it?"

Can't disagree on that one. It's only been five years since omegas were locked up, forcibly used as breeding machines for the beta population to tackle the decimation of their birth rate. Nobody knows why betas are no longer able to have children, but it's the omegas who have suffered the most.

My throat tightens at what she might have experienced. I don't think she was part of the OC, though. Omegas generally don't awaken until late teens, so it's unlikely she would have been dragged into that hellhole.

Something to be grateful for, at least.

"She's not ready for that," I tell Nate. "And you will not mention it, Nate."

Nate humphs, but nods reluctantly.

Hudson looks at me. "I like her, Cade. I think you will, too."

"You need to meet her tomorrow," Nate urges. "We could have lunch downstairs. Nothing wrong with that, right?"

I think it over. My pack are obviously very keen to get to know Gabrielle better. Axel is nodding, clearly on board with the idea. It's looking more and more like Gabrielle could be a more permanent fixture in our lives, if she agrees.

An image of her appears in my mind, the one and only time I've seen her. It's in no way enough to get an accurate picture of who she is, but one thing is clear.

She's fragile. Emotionally, physically.

I stifle the little curl of disappointment in my stomach. It was always unlikely that I'd find an omega who'd fit with me in the bedroom. I just need to forget about it.

This isn't about me. My pack are on board. I need to meet her.

"All right. Tomorrow."

CHAPTER TWENTY
GABRIELLE

I arrive at *Il Piacere* early, nervously smoothing down my clothes as I knock on the staff entrance. It's Veronica who pulls it open, her mouth flashing in a quick smile as she beckons me in.

"Busy day," she tells me shortly. "We'll need your help."

I'm immediately thrown into helping with the lunchtime prep, chopping huge piles of carrots, peeling garlic, and making sure everything is set out for the chefs.

I push down the disappointment that there's no sign of Hudson, Nate, or Axel, and keep my head down, following the barked instructions issued by Veronica and the chefs on duty until my head is spinning.

But I can't stop my mouth from stretching into a smile. I feel useful here. Like I'm contributing. Gio, one of the beta chefs, cuffs me gently on the shoulder.

"Good going, new girl," he says, his red cheeks creasing into a grin. "Keep it up."

I take him at his word, moving and ducking between the fast-paced work until eventually, Veronica waves me down and presses a steaming coffee into my hand.

"Break," she orders, eyeing me. "Before you fall over."

I slide into the same seat from yesterday and nibble on a pastry, watching everyone work with my leg tapping.

There's a commotion at the door, and Hudson pops his head around. Straightening in my seat, I watch as he waves down Veronica, murmuring something that makes her scowl and point her finger at him. He laughs, his head thrown back before he ducks back out.

I swallow hard, ignoring the regretful flip in my stomach.

You have a job, I remind myself. *A good job, in a lovely restaurant with people who are actually nice to you. What more do you want?*

Hudson went out of his way yesterday to make me feel welcome. Even to the extent of sitting with me on the floor while I had a breakdown. He doesn't owe me any more than that.

My eyes threaten to sting, and I bite my lip savagely until the feeling disappears.

I take my cup and plate to the sink, rolling up my sleeves to start on the ever increasing pile.

"Brutes," Veronica mutters as she drops off some pans. "Careful, those are hot."

I pull my hand back.

"Is everything okay?" I ask quietly, and she scowls.

"They forget that we have a busy lunchtime rush," she barks, throwing up her hands. "The waitresses go ga-ga when only Nathaniel appears, and now they tell me all four of them are coming in for lunch. Nobody will be concentrating!"

My chest flips over. *The whole pack?*

Veronica sees my expression, patting my shoulder distractedly.

"Don't worry," she says. "You'll get used to it."

She sweeps away as I stare after her in confusion.

Get used to what?

One hour later, I have an answer.

I'm brandishing a mop, wiping up the water I've just tipped down myself and all over the floor when there's a flurry behind me, whispers and giggles until Veronica's voice echoes through the kitchen.

"Everyone, back to work!"

I focus on squeezing the water out into the bucket until a voice distracts me.

"Gabrielle?"

Stumbling, I nearly slip on the wet tiles, but hands appear under my elbows, tugging me into a very male, very broad chest that smells disturbingly like toasted marshmallow. Warm with a hint of vanilla and caramel.

I take a deep breath, swaying slightly as my bones soften.

"Woah," a very male, familiar voice chuckles huskily in my ear. "You okay?"

My eyes fly back open, and I push away from the temptation of Nathaniel's very comfortable chest.

He's staring down at me with the smallest, secret smile on his face when I spin around.

"Hello there," he teases.

My cheeks must be on fire. I can feel the heat and it's nothing to do with the kitchen prep.

"Um… hi?"

He waves a hand behind him. "We thought we might have lunch here," he says with a wink. "Wanted to introduce you to Cade… but I think you may have already met."

My eyes slide behind him. There's no sign of Hudson, but Axel is there, talking to a new alpha watching me with interest, sharply dressed in a dark suit and deep blue shirt.

A terrifyingly familiar alpha with steel blue eyes.

My feet skitter back until my lower back hits the edge of

the metal sink with a crack. My hands fly up as I flinch, and Nate's face changes in an instant, the easy teasing replaced by a rumbling growl.

He takes a step forward, his arm reaching out, but I flinch away. He pauses as a small whine ripples out of my chest.

This is it. I knew it was too good to last.

"Gabrielle," Nate's voice is low. "You don't need to worry. He's not angry at you, kitten."

Axel places his hand on Nate's shoulder. My breathing speeds up as I wait for his face to change, to crease in disgust, for them to throw me out, or call the police.

I don't know what this alpha has told them, but there's no way they'll keep me here.

I'm a *thief*.

My lip starts to tremble. Nate closes his eyes with a grimace, and I brace myself for the inevitable words.

"I'm an idiot," he says quietly. "I didn't mean to scare you, kitten."

My eyes veer between him and the icy blue stare of the alpha from the alley. He takes a slow step forward, his hands up and palms out.

"You're not in trouble," he murmurs.

He's interrupted by Hudson, who appears with a frown on his face.

"Gabrielle?" he asks, his eyes scanning me where I'm frozen in fear against the metal.

"Everyone step back," he barks. "Right the fuck now!"

Nate moves back immediately, the older alpha taking a moment before he does the same.

Hudson appears in front of me, blocking my view as his hands rise up to either side of my face.

"That's Cade," he says firmly. "He's our pack leader. We know about the wallet, and we don't care, Gabrielle. You are *not* in any trouble."

My breath chokes inside my throat as I stare at him, uncomprehending.

Nate's face appears over his shoulder, his eyes worried as he skims my face. "Gabby?"

Hudson growls.

"Nate, I swear to God—,"

Both men cut off, their eyes sliding to me as the whine rolls up the back of my throat.

Too much.

Too many scents, too close, too *alpha*.

Hudson curses, pushing Nate back as he moves away from me.

"God, we're terrible at this," he groans. "Gabrielle, we know that you've met Cade before. We don't care."

Nate gives me puppy dog eyes from over Hudson's shoulder.

"I'm sorry," he murmurs. "I didn't think—,"

"None of us did," Hudson says with a sigh. "Because we're idiots."

Watching them stumble over their words calms me down slightly. The terror gripping my neck recedes enough for me to force out some rational words, even as my body remains stiff against the metal.

"You're not idiots," I mumble.

Hudson frowns. "We'll have to agree to disagree. I meant it, though. We really don't care. We know times have been… difficult. It would be hypocritical of us to judge you for it. Are you okay? Do you need us to go?"

My muscles soften at his words, and I take a deep breath. "I'm fine. So that's… Cade?"

The alpha I stole ten dollars off and hid in an alleyway from steps forward, keeping a distance between us. His icy gaze scans me as I do the same, taking in the broad shoulders hidden behind his crisp blue shirt.

"My apologies," he says crisply. "I didn't mean to scare you."

"I...,"

What do I even say?

Sorry I stole your wallet?

Thank you for not calling the police on me?

Fancy seeing you here?

Swallowing, I blurt out the first thing that comes to mind. "I bought a sandwich."

He blinks at me, a little taken aback. My eyes close in sheer embarrassment.

"Did you need it?"

Unlike Hudson and Nate, this alpha is all command, sharp edges and dominant with the scent of a freshly opened new book hitting my nose. His words penetrate my brain fog of humiliation, and I open my eyes. One sharply defined brow is curved expectantly, and shame curdles my stomach as I nod.

"Well, then." He nods. "We'll say no more about it."

Axel shifts into view, and my hands drop to the hem of my sweatshirt before I realize I'm not wearing it. I'm missing the comfort it offered, swallowing me up and hugging me in his scent. Axel's eyes follow the movement of my hands, creasing at the corners.

He's just as big, if not bigger than I remembered. Whilst Nate is sleek, Hudson stocky and Cade broad, Axel is a freaking *mountain*. Blonde hair pulled up once again into a messy knot, the celtic-looking tattoo that curls around his arm flexes as he crosses them, keeping his distance as he nods.

"Glad to see you again," he says. His words are soft, and I swallow as I take them all in.

Axel. Cade. Nate. Hudson.

This close, it's no wonder the waitresses go *ga-ga*, as Veronica described it.

The combination of their closeness and the tantalizing mixture of scents is threatening to weaken my knees, and I force myself to breathe through my mouth, locking down the urge to offer my neck in submission.

"It's nice to meet you all," I whisper, keeping my eyes on the floor.

Gentle fingers appear under my chin, nudging up my face.

"That's better," Nate says with a smile. "Don't hide that pretty face from us, kitten."

The faintest edge of a purr lingers on the edge of his words, and I'm fairly sure I hear a faint growl as my whole body shivers.

"Enough." Cade's tone snaps me out of my embarrassing omega overload. "Everyone needs to tone it down."

"Gabrielle," he says, his tone a little softer as he turns to me.

"Would you care to have lunch with us?"

I think my hearing might be defective, because I blink at him until those brows drop down in confusion.

"Gabrielle?"

"Say yes," Nate urges softly. "Have lunch with us."

I glance between them. "Why?" I ask, confused.

"Because we want to get to know you."

My stomach flips over at Cade's quiet words.

"And," he adds with a small smile, "I think Nate might combust if you don't."

Nate nods his head vigorously, and I bite back a small laugh.

"I can't," I whisper. "I'm working."

Hudson intercedes, his arms crossed where he's leaning against a wall. "Your boss says it's perfectly acceptable to take your lunch now."

They wait patiently, and I get the feeling that if I say no, they'll back off.

Biting my lip, I consider what I want to do.

And... I do want to know more about this pack.

"Okay," I mumble. Nate grins at me widely.

"Just lunch?" I want to bite the words back, my wariness seeping out into the air.

Ironically, it's Cade who offers the most reassurance. He holds an arm out in front of Nate, stopping him from stepping closer.

"Just lunch," he reassures me. "You'll be back in an hour."

Untying my apron, I hang it carefully over the sink. "All right. I'm not really dressed for out there though."

"I think some fresh air might be in order," Cade says. "How do you feel about Mexican food?"

I wouldn't turn it down, even if I hated it. You don't turn food down when you know what it's like to not have any.

Axel slips in beside me, offering his arm. My hands slip around the familiar softness, and I can't resist rubbing at the material as he escorts me out and the pack follows.

I definitely need to convince him to swap out.

CHAPTER TWENTY-ONE
CADE

We walk down the street, flanking Gabrielle between us as we make for our favorite lunchtime spot. Glancing down, I catch her studying me and she blushes, turning away.

I'm trying to withhold judgment, to be the voice of reason in a group that has clearly already staked their claim on this omega, even if she doesn't realize it yet.

Another alpha, tall and skinny with a weasely looking face, stares at Gabrielle as he walks past. Gabrielle notices, shrinking into me until her sweet scent fills my nose.

So much fucking better than coconuts.

When I glare at him, shifting towards her, he looks away, giving us a wide berth as he scuttles past.

We enter the small Mexican restaurant, making for our favorite booth in the back corner where we can eat undisturbed. It's a little battered, ripped leather seats and graffitied tables, but the food is to die for.

I frown. We should have brought her somewhere nicer than this, but it's too late now.

Gabrielle hesitates, and I nod at the others, all of us

sliding in and leaving the seat at the end free for her. Her shoulders relax before she sits down.

"So," Nate begins. "Do you like Mexican food, kitten?"

Gabrielle worries her plump lower lip with her teeth. "I don't know," she admits. Tendrils of hair hang down from her face, the angle that I'm sitting in hiding her expression from me.

Hudson jumps in, his eyebrows flying up with shock. "You haven't had Mexican food before?"

I frown at him when she shrugs, her hands rubbing at her arms. She doesn't look comfortable.

Flagging down the tired-looking waitress, I order soda for everyone and some water. It comes in a bottle, and Gabrielle offers me a small smile when I pass it to her unopened.

"Thank you," she whispers.

I nod in response. The others settle into quiet chat, allowing Gabrielle to get her bearings as we scan the menu. Her fingers move from the mains to the side orders, moving from one price range to the other.

Clearing my throat, I gently clasp her fingers for a second, and she glances up at me with those damn eyes.

"Lunch is on me," I murmur. "I think we can do a little better than a sandwich this time."

She flushes. "I can pay."

It's Nate who intercedes with an eye-roll. "You'll have to let him. He's a bit of a control-freak."

I drop my hand from hers, the warmth of her hand fading from my skin. Gabrielle glances between us, her lips pursed.

"I may be a little bit of a control freak," I admit, and her mouth twitches upward. "And this lunch is absolutely on me, since we dragged you out of work like Neanderthals."

I'm rewarded with a further tilt, until her lips stretch into a smile. "I said yes to lunch."

"Thank god," Hudson says, his hands on his chest dramatically. "Nate would have been unbearable."

"Hey," Nate complains, poking Hudson in the arm. "You make me sound like a brat."

"You are a brat," Axel rumbles, and Hudson starts laughing as Nate complains.

Gabrielle watches them with that small, hesitant smile still playing on her lips. Her posture loosens until she's toying with a loose piece of hair, winding it around her finger.

After we've placed our order, adding several dishes to make up for Gabrielle's tiny side salad choice, I turn to her, clearing my throat.

"So," I say. "How are you finding working at *Il Piacere?*"

This feels like safe ground. Her whole face lights up.

"I'm really enjoying it," she says shyly. Her fingers trace circles on the table. "The work is soothing."

"What did you do before?" Nate asks, and she tilts her head.

"I waitressed in some diners." She shrugs. "I don't have any qualifications, so there weren't many choices when I got out of the Compound."

All of us pause, and Gabrielle looks between us.

"You were in the Omega Compound?" Axel almost growls the words. "How old are you?"

Gabrielle locks up, like a curtain falling over a bright, sunny day. I can see her drawing into herself.

"Twenty," she whispers. My eyes fly up.

She must've perfumed young, to be in the Compound. They closed it down five years ago.

Hudson hesitates. "Is that why you're not with the Center?"

It's the wrong question to ask. I can almost see her withdrawing, her skin tinting pale as she leans back in her seat, shrinking away from us.

"I don't like the Center," she says quietly.

Our food arrives, breaking the uncomfortable silence. Various plates and sauces are passed around, and Gabrielle picks at her salad.

Hudson gives me a look, but I'm already filling up another plate.

I add some nachos, fajita meat and vegetables, spicy rice and a quesadilla before I place it down in front of her.

"To try," I tell her softly. "Don't worry if you don't like it."

Her hand creeps out, hovering over the quesadilla. When she glances at me, I nod reassuringly, waiting until she's taken a small bite and then another before I start my own food.

We eat quietly, each of us casting sneaky glances at the omega nibbling at her plate of food. She eats the quesadilla, and the fajita meat, but leaves the spicy rice after a tester spoonful. I can see Hudson calculating in his head, and quirk my brow at him.

Gabrielle clears her throat, our attention zeroing in on her. Wilfully, I force myself to relax. It can't be easy being the sole focus of this many alphas at one time.

"Have you known each other for a long time?" she asks softly. Her eyes glance around the table, landing on each of us.

"All our lives," I respond. "We grew up together."

"We couldn't get rid of Nate, so we had to bring him along," Hudson deadpans, and Nate growls at him before biting into yet another fajita.

I've no idea where he puts it, but that man can eat.

Gabrielle smiles. "That must be nice," she muses. "To have friends like that."

"You don't?" Nate asks her.

She shakes her head, her eyes down. "No. It's just me."

There's not a hint of pity in her voice, but my throat tightens up all the same.

"You're not on your own now, you know," Nate teases. "You'll find that we're very hard to get rid of."

Her mouth quirks up, but Nate shoots me a look across the table, and I nod.

I get the message, loud and clear.

After lunch, we walk back to *Il Piacere* slowly.

Nate is walking with Gabrielle up ahead, and I hear a short giggle from her as he goofs off. Axel and Hudson hang back until we're walking together.

All of us are watching her like she's the second coming of heaven. Hudson opens his mouth, and I shake my head. "Later."

He bobs his head, and we join Nate and Gabrielle as they stand outside the restaurant.

She looks around, tucking a wayward piece of hair behind her ear. It springs back into place and she bats it away.

"Thank you for lunch. I...enjoyed myself."

Her words are genuine, and I surprise myself by stepping forward. My voice sounds a little hoarse when I lean in, gently taking the strand of hair between my fingers and tucking it behind her ear, letting my fingers brush the soft skin of her neck. I take the opportunity to snatch a deep breath, soaking in the sweetness of her scent.

"It was our pleasure, Gabrielle. I'll see you soon?"

She stares at me dazedly.

Axel nods at her, and Nate gives a cheery wave before Hudson escorts her inside.

It takes a split second for Nate to blurt it out.

"She's perfect."

Axel chimes in. "I agree."

I shoot him a look and he smirks at me, knowing damn well that he's gone through lunch barely saying a word.

"You'll have to talk to her at some point, you know," I snark. "We won't always be around to be your mouthpiece."

Axel rolls his eyes. "Like I could get a word in edgeways with Nate around."

"Woah. I'm being hit by all sides today. Targeted by my own pack." Nate scowls, but his amusement is light in my chest.

CHAPTER TWENTY-TWO
GABRIELLE

My breathing shoots out of me in short, sharp gasps as I splash freezing cold water on my face. When I glance up, the bathroom mirror still shows bright red cheeks.

Chill, Gabrielle. Jesus.

But I can't.

Cade Reyne is a force. My neck is still tingling where his hand brushed against it. Heat rises on my skin again when I think about it, and I throw more water on my face with a groan.

I need to go back out and work.

I need to focus on getting my own place, not on them.

But it's hard when I keep scenting Cade in my hair, on my skin. When they seem intent on coaxing their way past my defenses, knocking them over one by one like confetti.

What do they even want with me?

The scent lingers for the rest of the day. Doing my best to ignore it, I push the Reyne pack out of my mind and scrub until my hands feel sore. I don't see Hudson again until the end of the night, when he gives me my wages and escorts me to the door.

"I had fun today," he murmurs, holding my gaze as the door opens. "I think we'd all like to do it again."

Chewing on my lip, I throw caution to the wind and ask the question that's been on my mind all day.

"Why did you take me for lunch today?"

His smile grows slowly until it spreads across his face. The look he gives me sends butterflies cartwheeling through my middle as he steps forward until we're close to touching.

"I think you know," he murmurs. Hazel eyes bore into me as he scans my face. "Don't you?"

The butterflies morph into rocks.

"I...," I shake my head. "I don't think I can give you what you want, Hudson."

My breathing speeds up, and he steps back immediately, giving me the space I need to compose myself without his scent clouding my senses.

"We don't want anything you're not willing to give," he responds carefully. "But we'd like the chance to try, Gabrielle. If you're comfortable with that."

Hesitating, I wrap my arms around my waist, my head spinning.

"Slowly," I finally confess. Glancing up at him, his eyes crinkle into a grin as he leans against the door.

"We can work with that."

CHAPTER TWENTY-THREE
AXEL

Hitting the button on the treadmill, I slow down to a walk, blowing out a breath. Sweat is pouring off me, but it's not enough.

Music pounds through my headphones, thudding in time with my heartbeat as I start to run again, pushing up the speed until I'm flat out sprinting. When I finally stop, slipping the headphones down around my neck, I'm gasping.

"Burning off some energy?"

My head turns and I nod at Cade in greeting as he steps up onto the treadmill next to me.

"You could say that," I croak.

He tosses me a bottle of water, and I suck it down gratefully as he waits.

"Want to talk about it?"

Mulling the offer over, I finish off the last of the water and toss the empty bottle into the trash can next to us.

Cade stays silent, waiting me out in that sneaky way he has to get us all to open up.

"Do you think we might be... too much? For her?"

The words catch in my throat as I force them out.

"In what way?"

"In every way. But mainly physically."

I move back up to a slow walk. I always do my best thinking when I'm in the gym. That's why I've spent the last two hours after closing hitting every machine and trying to work off the thoughts I've been having about the little omega we took out for lunch today.

"It's just… we're a lot, Cade. You and me especially. I could crush her with a single finger."

And Cade has his own… *needs*. They hang between us in the air, unspoken but acknowledged.

It's true though. However much I might like her… I'm not sure Gabrielle is for me.

No. That's not right.

I'm not sure I'm the right alpha for *her*. My chest tightens.

I could *hurt* her without even realizing it.

"No, you couldn't," Cade says quietly. "I saw the way you watched her, Ax. I think you need to give this a chance."

He pushes up the speed on his own machine.

"And you?" I ask.

He gives me an exasperated look. "That's different."

"No, it's not. You don't know if she'll be into that."

He looks away. "She's nervous as hell already without knowing about my proclivities. One encounter and she'll run. I don't need it anyway."

Frowning, I finally turn the machine off. "You might not need it, but it's part of who you are, Cade. If she's the right one for us, then she'll be into it, too. Who knows, maybe she's secretly kinky as fuck."

"Oh, fuck off." He throws his wadded up towel at me, and it hits me in the face. Cade raises his eyebrows at me. "Take your own damn advice, will you?"

I snort, but leave him be as he ups his pace.

My pack all have keys to get in and out of this place

whenever they want, so I hit the lights off in the offices and leave the main reception one on for Cade as I leave.

The temperature has dropped again, winter well and truly settling in over the city, and my breath appears in white puffs as I make my way home, mulling over our conversation.

Turning onto the street towards *Il Piacere*, I pause when I see two figures silhouetted in the doorway.

Hudson smiles down at Gabrielle as she lingers on the step, both of them completely absorbed in each other.

Not wanting to interrupt, I loiter awkwardly for a minute or so, until Gabrielle makes her way down the steps. Hudson watches her leave before closing the door, much to my surprise. Then I spot the white wooden slats at the window moving.

I frown. She's walking away, thin arms wrapped around herself as she moves down the street.

On her own.

Late at night.

She doesn't even have a damn *coat* on.

"Gabrielle!"

She jumps a mile, flinching back as she whirls around, frantically searching behind her.

Shit. I didn't mean to growl at her.

"It's me – Axel." I take a few steps forward until I'm illuminated under a streetlight. "Where's your coat?"

It comes out close to a bark, and she shrinks back.

"Sorry." I try to temper my tone. "It's just… it's really cold tonight. And you don't have one."

She glances down, her brows drawing together. "I'm fine."

"You're shivering," I point out darkly. It's true. I can see her trembling from here.

When she shakes her head in stubborn refusal, I shrug out of the sweatshirt I'm wearing. She watches me with wide eyes as I stomp towards her.

"Arms up."

She obeys instantly, and I lose her for a moment as I tug it over her head, concealing her in the fabric before her face emerges, her body swallowed by yards of thick cotton.

The sweatshirt falls nearly to her knees, smothering her in my scent.

She looks good in my clothes.

Swallowing, I nod. "Keep that one, until I get you a coat."

Her fingers emerge from the ends of the sleeves, wrapping around the material.

"I don't need a coat. I seem to be picking up a selection of sweatshirts." There's definite amusement in her words, though, so I figure I'm off the hook for acting like an over-protective bear. Her fingers curl into the material.

"You do." I'm not arguing about this. First thing tomorrow, she's getting a brand new coat. No way is she walking out of that restaurant at night again without one.

"It's too cold to walk around the city without one. And you shouldn't be walking on your own, not at this hour."

She straightens, a hint of indignation on her face. "I can take care of myself."

I swallow down my doubtful response, but I'm pretty sure she can read it on my face anyway.

"Where are you staying?" I ask, glancing at the dark road behind her. "I'll walk you."

It's an opportunity to scope it out. I'm not buying that she has somewhere safe to stay, not when I caught her in the gym doorway not much more than a week ago. Could be a dive, maybe even a shared place. I'm betting that whatever it is, it's not a truly safe option for an omega.

When she blanches, my suspicions are confirmed.

"Ah... that's okay." She skips backward a few steps. "It's actually not far from here. Really close."

I cock my head. "Great. So you won't mind me coming along, if it's not a long walk."

Her huff is actually adorable. "I don't need an escort!"

My temper flares up, and I take a few steps closer until I'm glowering down at her.

"If you think," I say slowly. "That I'm going to stand here and watch you walk off on your own, late at night, then you don't know me very well."

She blinks up at me. "I don't know you at all, really," she points out. "You didn't say much at lunch."

It's a direct hit, and I rub my neck in embarrassment that she's called me out. I have a tendency to rely on my pack too much when we're in groups. Truth is, I'm just not a big fan of people in general. Most of them are assholes.

Although I'll make an exception for her.

"I'm not a big socialiser." Then I gesture. "After you."

I swear she stamps her foot as she turns around, her feet slamming down on the pavement as she takes a few steps.

"You can walk me to the end of my street," she tries to bargain. It's actually pretty cute that she's trying to stand toe to toe with me. "No closer."

Frowning, I consider it. It's a safe call. She doesn't know me, after all.

"That's fair. Lead the way, Gabrielle."

We fall into uneasy silence as we walk through pitch black streets, the only light coming from the occasional streetlamp. Minutes stretch out, and I glance down at her from the corner of my eye. She's chewing her lip as she looks around.

"Really close, huh?"

She flushes. "It's not *that* far."

"'Mmm. Pretty sure we've lapped the city twice by now."

Her lip twitches. "Only another three to go."

My laugh shakes my chest, startling us both.

"Think you'll make it?" I ask, and she glances up at me. "You've got really little legs, you know."

She looks outraged. "I am not *little*!"

"I'm twice your size," I point out. "Need a piggy back?"

She sniffs indignantly. "No, thank you."

"Well, the offer's there."

We reach the river, the streetlights dotting over us casting little sprinkles of light across her face.

"This is home." She points down a street I'm not familiar with. Battered windows hang from broken frames in the house closest to us.

I take a deep breath. Can't push my luck too far.

"How far down are you?"

She points to a spot just beyond my line of sight. "Just there."

I don't like it, but I don't force it. "Okay. I'll wait here for a minute, just in case."

She nods, taking a few steps away from me. My sweatshirt swishes as she turns.

"Axel?"

"Yeah?"

She shrugs. "Thank you. For walking me... home."

"You're welcome, little spoon."

The nickname slips out, and it's completely worth it for the look on her face. Her mouth falls open. "Little spoon?"

I shrug, leaning against a lamppost.

"You would *definitely* be the little spoon."

Nodding my head towards the street, I give her a small smile. "Get home safe. You're not getting any warmer out here."

She bites her lip. "I'll see you tomorrow?"

"Counting on it."

And I'll be bringing a coat with me.

Chapter Twenty-Four

Gabrielle

I wait at the bottom of the street for ages, crouched behind a car in case Axel decides to take a stroll. Pressing the back of my hands to my cheeks, I can still feel the heat coming off them.

Little spoon.

It brings all sorts of thoughts into my head. Thoughts about Axel and the sheer size of him. Thoughts that *definitely* shouldn't be there.

I wasn't expecting him to be so... charming. His bulk might be intimidating, but the alpha isn't. He was quiet at lunchtime, so much so that I assumed he didn't really want to be there. But I saw a different side to him tonight.

And I liked it. A lot.

Finally, I edge my way back up the street, keeping a wary eye out in case he reappears. Tugging the hood up on my newly won sweatshirt, I slip back into the dungeon, avoiding the vacant stare of a young beta woman leaning against the wall.

Orange light from the fires dotted around warm my skin as I make my way to my tent. Glancing over, I look for Seek but her blankets are firmly closed, no sign of movement within. Pulling out the package I brought, I set it down outside her entrance so she sees it when she comes back.

Switching on my tiny oil lamp, I pull out my wages, counting them and adding them to the slowly growing pile. A grunt outside sends me scrambling to hide it, shoving it back into the small hole I managed to dig in the ground and covering it with dirt.

"Thanks for the food, girlie."

Freeing a relieved breath, I don't respond to Seek's call.

I'm not here to make friends. But there's a lot of food that doesn't get used at *Il Piacere*, food that Seek and others here wouldn't see in a month of Sundays. It's such a waste.

After a few days of solid meals, I can feel the difference in my own body. A little of the much-needed weight I've never managed to put on is starting to build, and I feel less shaky. More aware, somehow.

I was definitely more than aware of Axel this evening.

Crawling into my sleeping bag, I stretch out my tired legs with a sigh. The oil lamp flickers and dies, the last of it used up.

At least I can buy some more now.

I might even get myself a couple of toiletries. Maybe a change of clothes.

There's not enough in that hole to cover a deposit, not yet. But if I can just hold on and keep building it up for a few more weeks, I'll be able to get something.

I just need to keep going.

———

Walking out of the department store the next morning, I take sneaky inhales of Axel's teakwood scent, reveling in the freshness of it.

My new clothes are tucked carefully into my duffle bag. Just a pair of leggings, a t-shirt and a pretty camisole and shorts I couldn't resist, but I'm still bouncing with excitement. Between that and the small bottle of body wash I splashed out on, I'm ready to start feeling human again.

Totally worth the glare of the security guard as he trailed me through the aisles like I was going to shove half of the make-up counter under Axel's sweatshirt.

My shift doesn't start for several hours, so I walk aimlessly through the park. Winter sun glints off the sculptures lining the smart pavements as I fill my water bottle from the fountain, taking a seat on a wooden bench.

I settle in for some people watching.

Joggers make their way around the path, skirting in and out as they pass people. Cyclists keep to the side as they ride along on designated paths, sleek and fast in lycra.

Smiling at a cute older couple, I turn to look down the other side of the path, and the breath disappears from my lungs.

An alpha strolls past in a suit, slowing as he approaches me. His nose flexes as he breathes in, his head swinging around. Shrinking back into the bench, I yank my hood as far forward as it'll go and try my best to make myself invisible.

I watch, holding my breath as I swaddle myself in Axel's sweatshirt. The alpha breathes in, his nostrils flaring and brows drawing together before he carries on, glancing over his shoulder.

I only relax once he's out of sight. My hands shake as I push my hood back and raise my water bottle to my lips.

"Gabrielle?"

The soft tone still makes me jump about a clear foot off the bench. My water spills out, spraying me as I cough.

"Shit."

A familiar figure appears in front of me, honeyed eyes peering at me mournfully from underneath a navy baseball cap. "I'm so sorry!"

"Don't worry." I brush at the water. "It'll dry. What are you doing here?"

Nate still looks apologetic as he eases onto the bench next to me. "I didn't have a job today, so figured I'd go for a walk."

The warmth of his body soaks into me where our arms brush together.

"I saw what happened," he says quietly. "With the alpha. Are you okay?"

I swallow roughly. "Yeah."

"Does... does that happen often?"

Shrugging, I tell him the truth. "Often enough."

There aren't enough omegas to go around. Never have been. It was part of the reason the government locked us up in compounds for years, so they could breed us effectively.

Even now the Creed's been disbanded, the world still isn't safe for us. Any omega that isn't behind the walls of the Omega Center is fair game for a lot of alphas.

Nothing's really changed. There's still a collar around my neck, even if it's metaphorical.

"I'm really sorry," Nate murmurs. "I never realized how full on we must be coming across to you. You have to deal with that shit every day."

Startled, I look up at him. He looks stricken.

"I don't mind." The confession slips out of me like a secret shared, dangling in the air between us. "From your pack, I mean. I don't mind."

Nate freezes. "Yeah?"

"Yeah. Just... take it slowly?"

"Always." He turns to me with a smile. "Does this mean I can buy you presents?"

My heart flips in my chest, my breath catching. He studies my expression, grin growing.

"I heard omegas like presents," he whispers conspiratorially. "I have a lot of ideas, you know."

The sudden pang takes me by surprise.

It's true, I do like presents. It's a well-known omega trait. We like shiny, pretty, *soft* things.

That's why we were never allowed any under the Creed. It made us too… omega, I guess. Too tempting for alphas to resist, apparently. Better to keep us tightly contained in case we caused anarchy.

What a crock of fucking bullshit.

My mind skitters back to my little space at the dungeon and I squeeze my eyes shut.

I've never had a present. Not once since I presented as an omega. And definitely not before then, either. My mom wasn't the type of parent who remembered the little things.

Like birthdays.

Nate's smile wavers, settling into softer understanding. "Too much?"

I nod jerkily. "Maybe a little."

Then I bite my lip.

"Maybe one small present?"

Nate throws his head back in a deep, booming laugh. "Let's start there."

Fuck, he's beautiful. His laugh catches attention, two betas suddenly making a beeline for us.

"Nate Reyne?" one squeals. "It *is* you!"

"I'm a big fan," the other gushes, her eyelashes fluttering as she practically elbows me out of the way.

"Have you got something in your eye?" I ask her sweetly. Her mouth draws down into a sneer as she looks me up and down.

"Shoo," she says, actually putting her hands out and flapping them at me. "Nate doesn't have time for dirty little omegas like you."

Wow. Someone's been drinking the pro-Creed Kool-Aid.

The growl that ripples through Nate takes us all by

surprise. The two betas jump back, eyes wide, as he bares his teeth at them.

"Leave," he snarls. "Now."

Stuttering apologies, they nearly trip over themselves as they back away. Nate's arm wraps around my shoulders, pulling me in protectively.

"*Jesus fucking Christ.*" He squeezes my arm. "I'm so sorry, Gabrielle."

I struggle for the right words. "You didn't have to do that."

He frowns. "I did. I wasn't going to let them talk to you like that."

The warmth builds up in my chest, the burning behind my eyes making me sniff frantically.

He *chose* me.

"Hey, now." I'm pulled into strong arms, Nate wrapping himself around me like a blanket as I try not to bawl into his chest.

"I'm Team Gabrielle, you know," he whispers into my ear. I choke out a watery laugh into his t-shirt, and his arms tighten around me.

I think I'm starting to realize that.

"Come on," he says gently. "Let's go."

"Where?" I ask, breaking away and wiping Axel's sleeve over my damp face.

"To get your first present."

The chocolate cupcake shimmers at me, rising up into a mountain of glistening icing that winks invitingly behind the clear glass.

I try not to dribble.

"Nate," I whisper. My hands press against the glass,

undoubtedly leaving print marks, but I don't give a fuck. I'm twitching like a little kid during the holidays.

"Which one, baby?"

His hand briefly traces the back of my neck before it disappears, and I turn to him with a grin.

"That one, please."

"We'll take four, in a gift box, please," Nate says to the scowling beta behind the counter.

I try not to salivate as the cupcakes are placed carefully into a pretty rose gold box and tied carefully with a gold ribbon.

I'm not sure what I love more – the cakes themselves, or the packaging.

My eyes round as Nate passes me the box to inspect.

"These are all for me?" I ask. My fingers tighten around the box as I hold my breath.

"All yours," he confirms with a wink. "Turns out my favorite flavor is butterscotch."

It's cheesy as hell, but I still blush, right down to my toes as he holds the door open for me to walk out with my precious cargo. I clutch the box tightly as we walk along, shielding it from getting bashed.

"Careful, kitten. You're gonna fall on your face if you're not careful."

Nate carefully tugs the box out of my hands, holding it carefully in one hand and reaching out with the other.

His fingers wrap around mine, steady and solid as we stroll along.

It takes me a few minutes to notice the eyes on us, the flash of cameras.

"Nate?" I ask, squeezing his hand as one particularly enthusiastic woman nearly falls into a bush whilst pointing her phone at us. "What exactly do you do?"

For the first time, Nate looks uncertain.

"I model," he admits. His mouth quirks up. "It pays the bills."

I squeeze his hand. "Well, you are *very* pretty."

He barks out a startled laugh. "Speak for yourself, kitten."

We walk up to *Il Piacere*, and Nate turns to me.

"I've actually got a job," he blurts. "This afternoon. Want to come?"

I double-take. "Me?"

He nods, the skin at the base of his throat flushing.

"It'd probably be a bit boring," he says, mouth quirking in a half grin. "Nice to have some company, though."

I glance at the doors of the restaurant, considering.

"It's okay," Nate says quietly. "Stupid idea. You've got work."

"Not until eight. Think we'll be back by then?"

Nate's eyes light up.

"I'll make sure of it," he promises.

CHAPTER TWENTY-FIVE
NATE

Adrenaline surges as we head into the large warehouse. Gabrielle is tucked securely under my arm, her eyes wide as she takes in the hive of activity. People are calling and shouting, and Juan is in full flow, his bellow echoing even above the low pulse of music echoing from somebody's speakers.

Juan is much more active than Max. He's one of my favorite shoot directors to work with and we know each other well, but he can also be a demanding little shit.

"Is this okay?" I ask Gabrielle, belatedly realizing that the hustle and bustle might be a bit much. Cade will tear me a new one if I fuck this up.

She peeks up at me, but she's smiling.

"It's exciting," she admits. She pushes her hair back, her face glowing as she looks around. "Is it always like this?"

"Pretty much." I spot Juan walking towards us and wince.

"Nathaniel," he grits out. "How *wonderful* of you to grace us with your presence today."

I give him my best puppy dog eyes. "Lost track of time. But I'm here now, right?"

"Hmmm." He gives me a disbelieving look before his brown eyes slide to Gabrielle. He takes her in, even backing up a step.

Oh, no. I take a step forward as his face lights up with sheer, ravenous delight. I've seen that face before.

"Juan." My voice is low, and Gabrielle looks between us nervously.

Juan waves me off.

"You, my dear… are *very* welcome. What's your name?"

Gabrielle shyly takes his outstretched hand, and Juan shakes it. "Gabrielle. It's nice to meet you."

"Do you model?" he asks abruptly. "Because you two would look *gorgeous* on camera."

Gabrielle blinks rapidly. "I…er… no."

He clicks his tongue. "Pity. Think about it."

He spins, waving me forward and clapping his hands together. "Come now. We have work to do, Nathaniel!"

I tug Gabrielle with me. She looks a little dazed as I pop her onto a seat where she can see everything, gently nudging the cake box into her hands.

"Oi – Marcus!" I holler. One of the set assistants pauses.

"Get her anything she needs," I direct, my tone firm. "Anything. You get me?"

He nods vigorously. "Of course."

Gabrielle chews on her lip, and I tug it free, my fingers brushing the lushness of her plump lower lip. "You gonna be okay here?"

She nods, her eyes darting around. "I'll be fine."

"I'll be just over there if you need me. Don't worry about interrupting anything."

I dart in, brushing a quick kiss along her soft cheek before I head to get ready. Glancing over my shoulder, I bite back a grin when I see her hand covering the area I just touched. She looks a little dazed.

Game on, kitten.

I'm pushed haphazardly into a chair, the artists hastily applying a touch of bronzer.

Most people think modeling must be glamorous as fuck, but it's mainly a lot of sitting around, and then a lot of staying in the same pose until your limbs are full of cramp while people shout various instructions at you.

"Not too much," Juan warns as he walks past. "I want him natural."

The hairstylist rubs her hands together before tousling my hair into spikes. Her mouth purses in frustration when I lean around her to check on my omega.

She's sat in her seat, hands wrapped around a hot drink. Our eyes meet, and I mouth, *you okay?*

She gives me a thumbs up, and I grin, apologizing to the irate stylist.

When I'm finally made up to their satisfaction, I'm bustled over to wardrobe.

Sascha looks me up and down, popping her gum loudly.

"It's underwear today," she says shortly. "Drop your pants, Reyne."

"God, Sash. At least take me to dinner first."

"You wish you were my type." She gives me the side-eye and I relent, slipping on the white briefs with a robe over the top, leaving it open in the warmth of the lights.

Fuuuck, these are snug.

"Where's this cute omega Juan's waxing on about?" Sascha asks, a glint in her eye. "She single?"

I snap my teeth at her. "Not even a little bit."

She laughs as I stride off, swerving towards Gabrielle. She's watching the team set up, her hands still wrapped around her coffee.

She turns as I whistle, and holy shit, if her reaction doesn't make me preen like a damn bird.

Her mouth parts as she looks down, her eyes skating down my chest and landing squarely on the underwear.

Shit. Did not think this through.

I swallow uncomfortably as my cock hardens, Gabrielle watching with deepening red cheeks as I tug the robe closed.

"Don't look at me like that, kitten," I warn. "I bite, you know."

My words come out deeper than the tease I intended, and Gabrielle twitches, just as I catch the sharpest punch of buttery, warm butterscotch.

"God," I tell her hoarsely. "You're mouthwatering."

Her harsh swallow, fluttering pulse and scent spike all tell me that she's feeling exactly the same as I am right now. Stepping in, I invade her personal space as she tilts her head back to look at me, her neck beautifully bare and open.

The shuddery gasp that comes from her when my hand slides up to gently grip her soft skin nearly undoes me, but I can't carry her off in the middle of a shoot.

However, I can do *this*.

Her lips part beneath mine, her stuttered breaths lost into my mouth as I claim her, my hand around her throat and the other cupping the back of her head. My eyes damn near roll back at the heavenly taste of her.

A tendril of worry snakes through that I've pushed her too far, but Gabrielle sighs, her mouth opening softly under mine as her tongue sneaks out to taste my lips.

Both of us are gasping when we break away. I rest my forehead against hers.

"Kitten," I force out. "Tell me that wasn't in my imagination."

She smiles against me. "It wasn't."

"And tell me we can do it again as soon as we're done here."

Her shy laugh under my fingers is the best thing I've ever heard.

Chapter Twenty-Six

Gabrielle

Well, then.

Feeling the flush of heat across my cheeks as Nate stalks towards the set, I glance around to see if anyone witnessed our little display.

That was… unexpected.

Nate's mouth moving over mine, tasting of warm, slightly charred marshmallows. My tongue darts out as if I can trace the taste of him on my lips.

I expected the shoot to be silent, but the music keeps pumping, Nate bouncing up and down on his toes before he's directed to different places, stretching and moving his body in line with Juan's demands.

And *holy freaking shitballs*, is he good at it.

Pretty sure I have a touch of dribble. More than a touch, if I'm being honest.

Marcus pelts past me every few minutes, only stopping to hand me another steaming coffee.

"He's fantastic, isn't he?"

When I nod, he gives me a once-over, and I brace myself.

"You look good together."

With a quick smile, he's off, dashing towards the set and Juan.

I sit quietly for around an hour, watching Juan become more and more agitated as he paces around Nate.

"Ach!" he bellows eventually, throwing his arms up. "Nathaniel!"

"Yeah?" Nate frowns, stepping down from the wooden frame that he's been resting his arms against. "Something wrong?"

Juan shakes his head. "Not wrong, but… this shoot could *really* use another person."

I freeze when he looks at me.

Nate starts to shake his head, but Juan bounds over to me anyway.

"Gabrielle," he implores. He gently takes my hand, clasping it between his as he stares at me earnestly.

"Just a few quick photos? Teeny, tiny, little photos? And if you're not happy, of course we don't have to use them."

Nate follows him, his hand landing on my shoulder as he squeezes softly.

"Juan," he warns. "Leave her alone. She's here to watch, not to be bullied by you."

Leaning back, I look up at him. "Would it help?"

Juan practically vibrates with excitement as Nate's eyes widen. "Give us a minute, Juan," he says, not moving his eyes from mine.

When Juan backs off, he slides into the seat next to me, taking my hand.

"You want to do it?" he asks seriously. "Or you don't feel comfortable saying no?"

"I… want to help." Shrugging, I glance around. "If I don't like it, Juan won't use them, right?"

He studies me before his face breaks into a grin. "Absolutely. Nothing will happen unless you're comfortable, kitten. Are you sure?"

I'm absolutely not sure that this isn't going to be a fuck-up of monumental proportions, but I give him a nod anyway.

Juan crows when I stand up. "You'll be wonderful!"

He leads me over to the stylists that worked on Nathaniel, leaving me with a delighted grin.

Nate stays close to me as they work, a flurry of brushes and bronzer and who knows what else applied rapidly. The hairstylist sniffs as she picks up my braid, dropping it down so it slaps against my back.

"Tati." Nate gives her a look, eyebrows raised.

"Workable," the beta says grudgingly. Wincing, I decide that I can't blame her. I haven't exactly been keeping up to date with my styling regime recently.

Tati combs out my hair, wrestling with the tangles until it lies smoothly down my back before applying a sweet-smelling spray and brushing it through again.

Juan checks in, nodding happily as his eyes move over my face. "Excellent," he says, beaming at me. "Doing okay, sweetheart?"

I barely manage a nod before they hustle me over to a section filled with portable rails, bursting with various swimsuits and underwear.

The stylist, Sascha, clicks her tongue, her eyes moving over me. "I have just the thing."

She shoos Nate away for me to get dressed, rapidly rigging up a more private section so I'm not flashing the rest of the warehouse.

"Thank you," I tell her. My head is spinning already, and I haven't even stepped in front of a camera yet.

My nerves start to kick in full blast when Sascha passes me a scrap of white material through the curtain. I stare down at it, confused.

"Um, Sascha?" I call. "What's this?"

She just cackles. "That's what we're working with, babe!"

Feeling a little lightheaded, I sink down on the hard floor, taking deep breaths.

I just need a minute.

When Sascha calls my name, I suck it up and wobble to my feet on shaky legs. It takes me a few minutes to wriggle out of my clothes and work out where the various straps go on the brassiere.

There's no mirror, so I gingerly poke my head out, looking for Sascha.

No sign of her, but Nate is leaning against a railing and straightens.

"Kitten?" he asks. He takes a step forward. "You okay?"

Nodding, I brace myself before yanking the curtain open.

Nate goes motionless.

"It's…," I look down. "Is this okay?"

The thin silk bodysuit clings to me like a second skin. Ivory lace panels trace up my stomach and over the cups covering my breasts, held up by a thin halter neck strap that pushes them together.

Nate's throat bobs. "Turn around. Please."

Trembling a little at the growl in his voice, I turn slowly, showing him the length of my bare back. The cool air makes me shiver, and I gasp as the cold is replaced by a furnace of heated, very large alpha.

Nate's chest brushes my back, and I inhale sharply at the feel of him against my skin.

He drops his head, his lips barely brushing my neck and I shake.

"Nate." The whimper falls from my lips, and the growl that ripples through us both makes something clench low in my stomach.

"I want to see you in this again," he murmurs against me. "Lying on a beach, in the sun. On a bed, underneath me. Anywhere, Gabrielle."

I shudder. "Maybe Juan will let me keep it."

"He will." Nate sounds certain. "I'm making sure of it."

The growing sound of voices breaks us apart, Nate's nostrils flaring as he picks up my scent.

Juan claps his hands in delight when he sees us, casting a professional look over me with a firm nod and a smile. "This will be a jewel in the crown of my career," he gloats. "I can feel it!"

Nate's hand slides into mine, and he doesn't let go as we're ushered towards the set. This close, the heat from the lights and the cameras is sweltering, and I'm actually glad that I'm in this and not in something thicker.

My mouth goes dry as Juan directs us both into position.

"Kitten," Nate whispers.

"Eyes on me, okay? Don't think about them."

Easier said than done. But it does help, even as Juan nudges us into increasingly intimate positions until my legs are shaking as I try to keep completely still.

"Nate, lift up her left leg and hook it around your waist. Gabby – lean back, and Nate will hold you. That's it – stay where you are—,"

Nate looks down at me, his eyes heated as Juan works around us. The noise falls away, my awareness zeroing in to where our bodies are pressed together. My chest rises and falls, my breathing speeding up as Nate hardens underneath me.

My lips part as his voice rumbles through me. "Fuck, Gabby."

The thin material between us provides no barrier at all, and the whine rumbles out of me as Nate chokes.

"We need the room!" he shouts.

There's a click, and I hear Juan ushering everybody away, muttering about pheromones. My head feels hazy as I loll back in Nate's arms, my hips moving, seeking.

"Gabrielle," Nate says urgently. "What do you need?"

"I…" My voice almost slurs into the now empty room. "Need you."

Nate curses, and then I'm lifted into strong arms, bundled against his warm chest as he jumps down from the platform. Turning my face, I nuzzle into his chest as he carries me, letting out a plaintive whine as I'm placed down on cool sheets.

"Shhh," he murmurs. "I've got you, kitten."

My head clears a little, and I blink my eyes open.

"Nate…," my voice wobbles. "What's happening?"

He strokes a careful hand over my hair. "I think we may have overdone it, baby. You're all heated up. If we wait, you should calm down."

I shake my head. I don't want to calm down. I want him to finish what we started.

My fingers grasp onto Nate's, and he swallows audibly as I try to pull his hand down.

"Kitten," he whispers. "You're not thinking clearly."

"I am," my voice is throaty, low with arousal. "Make it better, Nate. Please."

Another whine slips out at the end of my words, and Nate is over me in a second.

"Steady," he soothes. "Whatever you want, kitten."

He leans in, his tongue slipping between my lips as I chase his taste before he disappears from my view.

Heated breaths warm the silk of my bodysuit as he moves down my body, and I shiver as his hand traces my side.

"More." It's a demand.

"Yes, ma'am."

He carefully spreads my legs apart, the feel of his eyes on me making me squirm.

"Look at that," he murmurs. "You've made this suit all wet, kitten."

My head throws back against the sheets as he leans in,

pressing a hot, open mouthed kiss to my slit over the silk. When he follows it up with a long lave of his tongue, my whole body jumps up.

"Nate!"

"Fucking divine," he groans into me. "I knew you'd taste like butterscotch."

There's a ripping sound, the tight material parting beneath me as Nate pushes it out of his way.

His arms slide beneath my knees, long fingers sinking into my hip bones to hold me steady for him as he lifts me up.

I drop my head to watch him, his tousled hair giving him a boyish look as he looks up, eyes gleaming.

"Let's get you cleaned up."

And then I lose all sense of myself. My hips buck in his grip as his tongue slides up my folds, over and over again. Nate sucks up every bit of slick my body gives him, drinking it down as he moans.

"Ambrosia," he rasps, before he gently wraps his lips around my clit and sucks, long, steady draws that blur my vision.

"Nate, please," I'm a trembling, shaking mess as he holds me exactly where he wants me.

He blows a cool breath across my heated folds. "Scream for me, kitten."

When his teeth close in the gentlest of bites, the crest overwhelms me, my orgasm coming in never-ending waves that Nate pulls from me as he continues his assault.

When he finally raises his head, pinning me with a slow, devastating smile, his lips are shining.

"Delicious," he purrs. "Such a good girl, staying still for me."

My breathing comes in heavy pants as he crawls over me, his nose brushing against mine as our bodies fit together.

"Still with me?" he asks, pushing back a strand of damp hair.

I can't talk. My bones are mush.

He leans in, dropping a light as a feather kiss against my lips.

"Tell me you're okay," he says, his tone dropping. "Tell me I didn't ruin this."

I blink.

"I'm... good," I gasp out. "Definitely ruined, though."

I think we've just blown the concept of *moving slowly* out the window, but somehow, I can't bring myself to regret what we've just shared.

His smirk is a beautiful thing as he rolls onto his side next to me, blowing out a breath.

"I could do that every day," he says dreamily. "Breakfast, lunch and dinner."

I choke. "I don't think I'd live past lunchtime."

Nate's delighted laugh warms my skin. A slight breeze brushes over us, making me shiver as I realize that my lower half is pretty much completely bared to the elements, thanks to Nate's overzealous approach. I cover my face with my arm as I groan.

"We broke the bodysuit. Juan definitely won't invite me back."

Nate chuckles as he sits up, carefully lifting me as he squeezes me into him.

"I broke the bodysuit." His words are mischievous. "And I wouldn't be so sure."

As it turns out, Nate is right.

Once I'm dressed in my normal clothes and Nate has let everyone back in, Juan waltzes over with a smile.

"Darling," he purrs. "You were an experience. Alpha and omega pairings are a *dream*. Just look at these!"

My chest flutters as I glance down at the camera screen, taking in the shots of Nate and I together.

"The pheromones were flying," Juan crows. "And it shows!"

Nate grunts, and Juan flaps his hand.

"Come back anytime," he tells me. "Anytime at all. I might even be in touch, if there's anything I think might fit. I'll send the paperwork to Nathaniel, for you to have a look at."

My head is still spinning as Nate leads me out into the street, hailing down a cab.

"Am I late for work?" I ask blearily. I've absolutely no idea what time it is.

Nate shakes his head. "Plenty of time to get back and ready before you start. I think Hudson would let you off, though, if you wanted to continue our…earlier conversation."

He wiggles his brows at me, making me laugh.

"I'd like to, but I won't let him down."

"Rain check, then," he decides, tucking me underneath him as the cab trundles through the streets. My muscles slacken, my breathing evening out as my eyes drift closed.

"Sleep," Nate murmurs. "I've got you."

"I know."

It's the last thing I remember before I doze off in his arms.

CHAPTER TWENTY-SEVEN
CADE

I'm pulled away from my laptop by low, hissed voices.

When I duck out of our kitchen, I stop short at the sight of Nate, with an unconscious Gabrielle against his chest.

Axel is hovering around them with a frown.

I'm across the hallway in a second.

"What the hell?" I hiss at Nate. "What happened?"

He widens his eyes at me. "Will you *shut up*? She's *sleeping*. Could you be any more dramatic?"

I deflate, but follow them, Axel next to me as we watch Nate set Gabrielle down on one of the leather couches in the living room. She grumbles slightly as she turns over, and Nate drapes a throw over her before we back away.

Crossing my arms, I give him a pointed look as he gently closes the door.

"Where have you been?" I demand.

"Work." He shrugs, but his ears turn bright red.

"And?" Axel stands next to me, both of us watching Nate squirm.

"I took her with me. Juan asked her to take part."

"He *what*?"

Nate straightens, glaring at me. "She wanted to, Cade. Nobody forced her, and I was with her the whole time."

My hands flex. "What kind of shoot was it?"

Nate frowns. "Underwear."

My growl takes us all by surprise.

"You let her take part in an *underwear* shoot?" My voice raises.

"Nobody *let me* do anything," a voice mumbles. We all whirl around to see a sleepy-eyed Gabrielle in the doorway. She yawns, and Nate half-shoves me out of the way as he pulls her into a hug.

I watch with slight disbelief as she curls into him, setting her head against his chest with a contented sigh. Nate raises his eyebrows at me, and I make a concerted effort to close my mouth, pressing my lips together.

Nate and I will be having words about this.

"Did you enjoy today?" Axel asks, and she nods blearily.

"Need to get ready for work."

She takes a shuffling step away from Nate before her face scrunches. She glances around and then back at us.

"Where are we?" she asks. Nate winces as I turn to give him a *look* for bringing her here without her permission.

"Our apartment. It's right above *Il Piacere*. Stairs are there." I point to them immediately, and she relaxes.

"Sorry," Nate says apologetically. "It's just... you were sleeping really deeply."

Gabrielle nods, a touch of color rising on her cheeks. "It was a busy afternoon."

Suspicion rises at the look she slides Nate from under her lashes – a look that my pack member is returning. I clear my throat and they both look away from each other.

Definitely suspicious.

"Do you want to get ready here?" Nate asks eagerly. "You can use my room."

Aaand the evidence is mounting.

She shakes her head, sidling towards the stairs. "Downstairs is fine. I… thank you for today."

She glances at Axel and I awkwardly.

Nate laughs. "Let's do it again. Tomorrow?"

Her cheeks flush full-blown scarlet, the color dropping down her neck as she backs out of the hallway without answering.

Axel and I wait a whole four seconds before we round on Nathaniel.

"Explain," I demand. "Right the fuck now, Nathaniel."

He rolls his eyes at me before he responds. "We got a bit carried away. Turns out they don't exaggerate about alphas and omegas and all the hormones. Had to take a break."

"And?"

"And, she's entitled to her privacy." He frowns at us. "I'm not going to brag to you all about what happens between us."

So something did happen.

The envy takes me by surprise, and I bite back the instinct to demand more information.

"Fine." I turn, intending to leave them to it, but Nate calls out.

"I want her for our pack, Cade."

He looks determined, and I nod, slowly.

"We agreed," I remind him. "We all need to get to know her, and she needs to agree to all of us, Nate. That's the only way this'll work."

The sarcastic little shit raises an eyebrow at me. "Better get moving then, old man."

Growling, I slam the door shut behind me.

CHAPTER TWENTY-EIGHT
HUDSON

I'm elbow deep in flour, throwing out instructions to the sous chefs when Gabrielle ducks into the kitchen, her eyes skittering to where I'm standing.

When I smile at her in greeting, she glances away, grabbing her apron from the hook and fastening it around her waist as she ducks into the dish station.

Frowning, I keep an eye on her as I finish up with my crew and wash up at the sink, brushing off Veronica as I weave my way around various people to get to her.

"Hey," I say, rubbing my neck when I reach her.

She barely glances at me as she plunges her hands into the hot soapy water.

"Hi, Hudson."

I rock back on my heels.

"Ah… is everything alright? You seem a little…"

"Everything is fine."

At least I get a small smile this time.

"You promise?" I ask, searching her face. "Anyone upset you?"

She shakes her head vigorously, her cheeks pinking. "No."

"Okay. You'll let me know if you need anything?"

When she nods, I relent, backing away as we throw ourselves into the rush of a busy service. The waiting team duck in and out, shouting orders and grabbing plates from under the heat lamps to carry through.

I divide my time between checking dishes, tasting sauces and making tweaks in the back, darting out into the restaurant to shake hands and say hello.

But my mind doesn't stray from the omega who is very determinedly avoiding my eye.

In a spare moment, I duck outside, shooting off a text.

Anyone seen Gabrielle today?

Cade's short response comes through seconds later.

Ask Nathaniel.

Worry furrows my brow for a brief minute before Nate's reply comes.

She's fine, Hud. We had a busy afternoon.

Another message comes through.

Take it easy on her.

Well, okay then.

When I finally close the door on the last customer, I flip the sign to closed and head back to the kitchen. Gabrielle is still determinedly washing up, some of the team grabbing cloths to help dry the dishes as they come through.

Coming up behind her, I nudge her out of the way, grabbing one of the bigger pots that are absolute shithouses to clean.

I can feel her frowning at me. "I can do that."

Shaking my head, I point to the table.

"Sit down," I say firmly. "I've got this."

She flops into a chair, glowering at me, and I stifle my grin as I scrub.

"This is my job," she says quietly. "I'm not a little weak omega, Hudson."

My chest constricts, fingers flexing on the metal in front of me.

Shit.

"I know that." Placing the final pot on the side, I take a seat next to her.

"Sometimes it's just about helping out," I say gently. "I know you're capable. You're the best dishwasher I've ever had, Gabrielle. That doesn't mean I enjoy watching you lug around pots bigger than you are when you've been working your ass off all night – *without* a break."

She winces. "You noticed?"

"I notice every single thing about you."

She turns to me at my admission. "You do?"

I clear my throat.

"You like too much creamer in your coffee, but you hate sweetener."

She blinks.

"You actually enjoy washing dishes. It's not a job for everyone, but you genuinely find pleasure in it."

I cast a glance at her. "Am I right?"

She nods. "What else?" Her tone is cautious, curious.

"You collect pretty rocks."

Now her eyes round, her mouth falling open. "How could you possibly know that?" she demands, but there's a hint of laughter in her voice.

Pursing my lips, I pull the small bag I've been carrying around for the last two days from my pocket, handing it to her.

"Sometimes you put one on the ledge when you're working. It's like you're a magpie," I tease.

Gabrielle shakes open the small blue bag, the small stones tinkling as they fall into her palm.

Her mouth rounds at the pretty colors.

"You got these for me?" she asks.

I can feel the blush crawling up my skin.

"Actually, they're mine," I admit. "I have quite a few. But these, I wanted you to have."

She looks aghast. "I can't take them if they're yours, Hudson."

"They're not mine. They're yours, now." I nudge her shoulder.

Her fingers close around them. "Thank you."

We sit in silence for a moment.

"What else do you know?" she whispers.

I mull it over for a moment before I answer, my words softer than before.

"You're scared of the dark."

She flinches. "Lots of people don't like the dark."

"I saw your face," I say quietly. "When we first met. And it was... I never want to see that look on your face again, sweetheart."

Her arm trembles slightly against mine.

"I'm not going to ask," I say gently. "But if you ever need to talk, I'm a pretty good listener."

Her head dips in acknowledgement, a chunk of hair falling down to hide her face from me.

Jumping up, I eye the last of the clean-up. Most of it's done, just the bigger pots that held tonight's pasta dishes left. Lifting the lid, I take in the amount of food that's left with a frown.

When I get out a bag, Gabrielle's buttery scent washes over me.

"What are you doing?" she asks.

Shrugging, I move to scoop the leftovers into the bag. "Getting rid of the waste. These are the last pots, and then we're clocking off for the night."

There's no answer, and I glance around to where Gabby is standing, her face creased into a deep frown.

"Do you know how many people would love a meal like

this?" she says hesitantly, sweeping her hand to indicate the four pots sitting there.

"I know. I hate wasting food."

She shakes her head so forcefully that her braid nearly smacks her in the face. "You don't have to," she blurts.

When I glance at her, she shifts from side to side awkwardly.

"What do you mean?"

She chews on her lip for a moment. "There's a whole group of people on the river who'd love a meal like this one, Hudson."

My brows fly up. "You talking about the homeless encampment?"

When she nods, realization hits me.

Oh, Gabrielle.

Scanning the shelves, I point to a pack of take-out containers.

"Get those for me, Gabby."

The shortened version of her name slips out without thinking, but her eyes widen as she looks to where I'm pointing.

"You mean it?" she asks.

Nodding, I grab the pot. "It's a great idea. Wish I'd thought of it sooner."

Her face spreads into a smile, starting at the edge of her mouth and growing until she's grinning at me. "Thank you!"

"Don't thank me," I say softly. My hand brushes hers as she hands me the containers. "I should've thought of this years ago."

Working in quiet partnership, we get all of the remaining food parceled into the containers.

"Twenty-seven…twenty-eight…twenty-nine!" Gabby bounces on her toes as I seal the final lid. "This is fantastic."

Her excitement makes me smile, softening the churning thoughts that have absorbed me for the last few minutes.

If Gabrielle knows about the dungeon, the likelihood is that she's stayed there before.

And if she has... my mouth tightens. It's not a good environment for anyone, but especially a small omega with zero defensive skills.

There's a knock on the door, and Cade strides in. His eyes move straight to Gabrielle before roving over the containers lining the counters.

"What's going on?"

"We're taking the leftovers from tonight down the dungeon." Gabby is placing some of the containers into bags, completely missing the *oh hell no you're fucking not* look Cade shoots me.

Pressing my lips into a thin line, I give him a flat stare back.

Join the fucking dots, Cade.

"I'm coming with you." Cade's tone is deep, and Gabby pauses, her hand outstretched in mid-air.

"Oh- well—,"

"I insist," he says smoothly. Reaching around Gabrielle, he grabs several bags and raises an eyebrow at her. "Shall we?"

She swallows, shooting an uncertain look at me before she picks up a few bags and makes her way to the door.

CHAPTER TWENTY-NINE
CADE

"What exactly is our plan here?"

My words pierce the silence blanketing the car. Gabrielle jumps, her cheeks flushing in the brief flashes of street lights shining into the car as she turns to me.

"Our plan?" she asks.

Cocking my head, I tap the bags that sit between us on the seat.

"For giving out the food," I clarify. "Is there a set distribution area?"

Hudson's eyes meet mine in the rearview mirror, his lips turned down.

Gabrielle looks startled.

"I... no, I don't think so."

"So we just turn up? And hand it out?"

She starts to fidget, her hands yanking her sleeve down as she fiddles with a loose black thread on the cuff of her black shirt. "I guess...,"

She visibly deflates in front of me, and I sigh.

"We'll have a look around," I say more gently. "It's just... the dungeon isn't a nice place at night, Gabrielle."

Her lips purse, but she nods as she looks away from me. Hudson rolls his eyes at me in the mirror, widening them enough to make me frown.

I'm right, though.

I've been to the dungeon before, part of volunteering days I run at the office. It's a hive of bustling activity, a sea of makeshift tents stretching out for over a mile. The people are a mixed bunch of betas, alphas, and even some omegas around the edges.

My shoulders stiffen. The closer we get, the more I think that this isn't a good idea.

Hudson pulls the car to a stop a few minutes' walk away, twisting in his seat to smile at Gabrielle.

"You ready?" he asks. She slides a nervous look towards me before she nods.

She takes off with more assurance than I expected, weaving her way down towards the flickering lights. Hudson and I hustle after her, our hands filled with bags.

"I'm not happy about this," I mutter to him as we follow her.

"You think?" his voice drips with sarcasm. "But she's right about wasting food. And I think she's more familiar with this place than you realize, Cade."

Blinking, I nearly stop. "You think she's stayed here before?"

Hudson shrugs. "Maybe."

I chew on the thought as we start to duck between tents, Hudson and I spreading out on either side of Gabrielle and making sure she's between us.

Our omega moves with purpose, making her way in a set direction.

She's definitely familiar with this place.

My hackles rise. I don't want her anywhere near it, the instinct to bundle her up and take her back to the car biting at me.

"Gabrielle," I call in a low voice. "Where exactly are we going?"

She stops short, turning to face us with a look of apology on her face.

"Sorry. I… know someone here. Someone who can help."

Hudson's face looks relaxed, even as his shoulders are stiff as a board. "Lead the way, Gabby."

We follow her footsteps all the way to a small clearing.

A trail of solar-powered fairy lights twinkle above us, strung between poles that hold up sheets and materials, creating several tents. A small fire is burning right in the center, and there's a beta lounging next to it.

She springs to her feet when she sees us coming, her eyes moving suspiciously between me and Hudson.

She doesn't look surprised to see Gabrielle in the slightest.

"What're you doin', girlie?" the beta rasps. Her hand flips a watch in her hand, moving it between her fingers with surprising elegance.

Gabrielle looks back, her eyes colliding with mine as she pauses. I let her see the promise in my own – I want an explanation when we leave.

She swallows, turning back.

"Seek," she says. "These are… friends of mine. Cade and Hudson."

The beta looks us up and down. "Got yourself a pack after all, then? They from here? Don't dress like it."

My lip curls at the suggestion that we're anything like the alphas from the dungeon. I've seen enough to know that none of them are alphas I'd care to call a friend.

"We're not from here."

Gabrielle frowns at me, but the beta cackles. "Didn't think so. Dungeon alphas don't dress in designer suits, sunshine."

Her voice lowers as she leans forward. "Puttin' a target on your back, coming here with them, girlie. Watch yourself."

Gabrielle flinches, but she holds up a bag. "We brought some food. What's the best thing to do with it?"

Seek flicks a curved eyebrow upwards, the small silver ring glinting in the light of the fire.

"Set it down there," she gestures to a space, and Gabby sets her bags down. "We'll get it out."

Hudson and I place our bags down. As soon as my hands are free, I move closer to Gabrielle, my hand landing on her shoulder.

"We should go," I murmur in her ear.

She glances at Seek again before she nods.

"I'll... see you soon?" she asks, her voice high-pitched.

Seek's eyes move across us, and she grins. "Maybe, girlie."

As we turn to head out, Seek stops us.

"Gabrielle," she calls, her voice low. "Want me to put you one of these in your tent?"

Gabrielle sucks in a breath as Hudson and I stop dead. Realization steals over me, clenching my jaw so tightly the tendons jump out on my neck.

Hudson swings around to Seek. She eyes us carefully, her body coiled as though she's bracing herself to run.

Gabrielle is still frozen, her shoulders hunched close to her ears. I take another step closer to her, battling to keep my composure as I lean down and whisper in her ear.

"*Your* tent?"

Her mouth drops open, her eyes flicking around as she searches for a response.

Her eyes land on one space as she grapples with her words, and I'm across the clearing before she can do more than blink.

"Cade – wait!"

But I'm yanking across the thin curtain, staring in disbelief at Gabrielle's home.

Her scent is saturated within the space, the warmth of her
butterscotch perfume contrasting harshly with the meager
contents.

There's a thin blanket on the floor, a navy sleeping bag
rolled up and tidily placed into the corner. A tiny lamp sits
alongside it, and I spot Axel's sweatshirt folded up neatly.

That's it.

This is where she lives?

This is her *nest*?

My mouth dries as I turn back to her. Something stabs
deep inside my chest.

"Gabrielle."

She's shaking, her whole body rolling in tremors as she
hugs her arms desperately to her sides. Her eyes stay fixed to
the ground.

"*Gabrielle*."

Hudson swears quietly behind me as he gets a look
inside.

My hands land gently on her cheeks as I tip her face up
to mine. My eyes search hers, those deep blue depths swimming as a tear falls down her cheek.

"Why didn't you tell us?" I breathe. "How long have you
been here?"

Her lip wobbles, but I keep her face tilted up.

"A few weeks," she whispers shakily. "I lost my job. And
my apartment."

My stomach turns over. "And you've been here since?"

She nods, her small face fragile between my hands.

"I'm getting somewhere else," she mutters, her eyes
sliding down. "I've been saving."

Hudson appears at my side, his arms folded. I can feel
the tension sliding from him, flooding into our pack bond.

Nate and Axel must be wondering what the hell is going on.

"Axel walked you home," he says quietly, and she flinches. "He said your street seemed quiet. A little run down, but decent."

She shrugs. "I hid until he was gone."

My eyes slide shut briefly. Axel is not going to be happy.

"You're coming home with us."

The words trip straight off my tongue, and Gabby blinks, startled, as my hands fall to my sides.

"I… what?"

Hudson nods firmly. "You're not staying here, sweetheart. Not for a second longer. Pack your stuff."

Gabrielle's eyes close for a moment, and when she opens them, they're full of determination.

"I can't."

"You damn well can," I interrupt. "We are not leaving you here. Get your things."

She looks between us, her head shaking. "You already gave me a job. You don't need to move me into your home, too."

I take another step until my chest brushes against hers, and she shivers.

"There is not a single part of me," I breathe, "that is willing to let you stay here, Gabrielle. There are alphas prowling this area that look for omegas just like you. You want to know what they do?"

Her eyes spark fire at me, her chin lifting.

"I know what they do," she says in a low voice. Her hands tighten into fists. "A lot better than you do, Cade."

My head jerks back, my mouth drying. "Have they… has anyone hurt you?"

I'll rip them apart.

She shakes her head, and my shoulder relax a smidgeon.

"It's not forever," she says in a low voice.

"It's not for a second longer," I shoot back, my tone flat.

"Get your stuff, Gabrielle. Or I swear to god, I will carry you out of here over my shoulder. I guarantee you that nobody will stop me."

Her mouth falls open as Hudson's hand lands on my shoulder.

"Please," he implores her. "We can't leave you here, sweetheart. We have more than enough room, and you can have all the space you need. A bathroom of your own, even. It doesn't have to be forever. Just until you get back on your feet."

Objection rises on my tongue, but I bite it back when Gabrielle hesitates.

"Just for now?"

My head jerks in a nod.

Her hands twist. "And I can pay rent?"

The *fuck no* is about to come out when Hudson nods. "Whatever makes you feel comfortable."

Choking back the denial, I fold my arms. "Need a hand getting your things?"

She glances at me from under her lashes as she ducks into the tent. "I'm good."

Hudson turns to me as she disappears from view. His lip is curled, on the edge of a growl.

"For fucks sake, Cade," he snaps. "Will you tone it down?"

A bark of laughter interrupts us. Seek is watching avidly from her seat next to the fire.

"Best entertainment I've had all year," she remarks.

"Seek."

Gabrielle ducks out of her tent, arms clutching material that Hudson gently relieves her of.

I watch as she moves over to Seek, the two of them exchanging a few words before she walks over to us. Her feet stamp just a little, enough to tell me she's not completely happy with this arrangement.

For a second, I wonder if we're doing the right thing.

But then my eyes slide right back to that tent. Imagining her coming back here, night after night, curling up on that threadbare fucking blanket in the cold...

My nostrils flare, and I take a deep breath.

"You ready?" I ask her. I'm more than ready to get her away from this place.

Gabrielle looks at me, her face suddenly seeming older than I've ever seen it as she sighs.

"I'm ready."

CHAPTER THIRTY
GABRIELLE

My head reels as I slide back into the car, this time with the rest of my stuff.

I can't believe I'm leaving here.

What the hell was I thinking, bringing them here?

I didn't expect Seek to even be there. I was planning to drop off the food and leave. No questions asked.

But she dropped me in it instead.

"Why'd you tell them?" I ask her softly.

Seek's face looks hollow, the lines on her forehead more prominent this close up.

"This world... it'll chew you up and spit you out, girlie. Ain't no help for most of us. Those alphas... they're good people. Let 'em help you. Gawd knows most of us would bite off their hands for an opportunity like this one. Don't throw away a chance in life just because it doesn't fit your margins."

My hand rubs nervously over my trousers, over and over again. A large hand settles over mine, flattening my fingers.

Cade stares down at me, his blue eyes darker than I've ever seen them.

"I'm glad you came," he admits, surprising me. I was

readying myself for another *me Tarzan, you Jane, get on my shoulder, wench* discussion.

"Did I have a choice?"

His lip twitches. "It probably doesn't seem like it, but yes."

I raise a sardonic eyebrow at him, and he twitches. "Maybe. Half a choice."

My snort of laughter slips out, and Cade looks down at our hands. The warmth from his palm soaks into my cool skin, and I keep it where it is.

"My pack likes you," he says. His eyes remain on our hands.

My mouth dries up. I'm trying not to think about the fact that on the same day I had my first sexual experience with an alpha, I'm moving into his apartment.

Honey, I'm home.

"But," Cade continues. "I'm not going to let them steam-roll you into anything. I just wanted to be clear. Nobody expects a single thing from you, Gabrielle."

His voice is low and firm, ringing with absolute sincerity.

I should feel reassured. I do. But the smallest, tiniest part of me feels a little… sad.

"You don't want me?" The words slip out, followed by mortification.

Cade stiffens as heat rushes to my cheeks. I can't believe I just said that.

"I mean," I stutter. "I didn't mean…"

Oh, dear lord, someone save me.

Thankfully, the car stops, saving me from myself. I feel Cade's eyes on me as I quickly yank off my belt and slide out, but he stays quiet as Hudson takes my things.

"You good?" he murmurs, his eyes trailing over me.

"I'm fine," I assure him. Pretty sure my cheeks are the same shade as the center of the sun, but Hudson doesn't call me out on it. Heading through the darkened restaurant, he leads me to where the elevator is. I can feel Cade's presence behind me, silently observing.

"It's a private key," he explains, showing me. "We'll get you one tomorrow, but it means that only pack can come up here."

My shoulders relax a little. Just them. I can deal with that.

I *can*.

But as the elevator rises, Hudson and Cade's scents locking around me in the small space, I take tiny breaths and try not to panic.

I can leave if I want to.

The doors slide open with a cheerful ping, and I take in the hallway I saw earlier. It feels like this afternoon happened days ago.

God, this has been a day.

The hall is brightly lit with overhead lamps, the light wooden floors and white walls giving it a fresh feel. I glance around as Hudson leads me down the long hall.

It's… a little empty. There are no paintings, no decorations.

"Have you lived here long?" I ask, and Hudson laughs.

"A few years," he admits, glancing at me over his shoulder. "I know, it's a bit bare. We keep meaning to decorate, put some pictures up, but we never seem to have time."

"It's lovely, though."

It is, the high ceilings and ornate lighting continuing as Hudson points to different doors.

"Living room," he explains. "Television, games, books – that's where you tend to find us."

He points out their bedrooms, several bathrooms.

"This is Cade's office," he says, jerking his thumb at a closed door. "He's very precious about his space."

Cade steps up behind me, his heat soaking through the thin shirt I'm wearing.

"You're always welcome," he murmurs. "Hudson is exaggerating."

Hudson whistles. "Open invite. Somebody likes you."

He moves on without acknowledging my blush, pushing open another door.

"This will be your room," he says softly, stepping back so I can look in.

I take a few steps forward, pausing at the entrance and glancing down at my old sneakers.

Toeing them off, my steps are hesitant as I pad into the bedroom. The plush cream carpet sinks beneath my toes as I take in the delicate white furniture, the gilded mirror, the cozy armchair that looks made for cuddling.

The bed, though. It's a four poster, sheets draping every side and above to create the perfect small space for curling up.

My breath catches. This isn't a spare bedroom.

This is a room made for an omega.

My breathing speeds up, and Cade's voice comes from the doorway.

"No expectations," he reminds me softly. "The room is here, Gabrielle. We want you to be comfortable."

By giving me the room that's clearly meant for their future omega. My chest aches at the thought, even as I turn and offer them a shaky smile.

"It's perfect," I assure them. "And too much. Thank you."

"Pfft," Hudson waves off my thanks. "It's a pleasure to have you here. There's no ensuite, but the bathroom on your right isn't used by anyone in the pack, so consider it yours."

My own bathroom.

My lips part, a true smile lifting them.

I could feel safe here. *Truly* safe.

"Thank you," I breathe. "I won't be any trouble."

"I love trouble," Hudson declares. He smiles at me.

"You're very welcome. Settle in, and get some sleep."

"Help yourself to anything you need," Cade says firmly. "Kitchen's always stocked, courtesy of our resident chef here, and there's normally something to snack on in the refrigerator."

When I nod, they both hesitate.

"Is there anything you need?" Hudson asks finally. "Anything at all we can get you?"

I survey the room around me.

"This is more than I need," I say softly. "Truly."

It's more than I've ever had.

"In that case, we'll let you get some sleep. Call if you need us."

And with that, the door closes softly.

I take a few uncertain steps, before I settle gingerly on the edge of the bed.

It feels like a cloud.

My hand traces the silver embroidery on the silky smooth blanket that sits on top before I pull them away.

I don't feel clean enough to get in, even though the urge to crawl under the covers and cocoon myself is pulling at me.

Instead, I move to the door, peering out.

My things and my duffle sit just outside, and I smile a little at the reminder of Hudson's respect for my boundaries. Neither he or Cade took a step into the room, making it very clear that the space is a private one.

Gathering up the items, I settle down on the floor and look at what I have.

One sleeping bag. One blanket. Two sweatshirts, courtesy of Axel. A few items of clothing.

Pulling out my rock collection, I glance around. There's a window opposite the bed, large panes of glass overlooking the park opposite the restaurant where I saw Nate this morning.

Gently, I place them across the windowsill. Hudson's gifts go in the middle, the pink quartz having pride of place as I step back.

Grabbing a camisole and my hair products, I pull the door open and peek outside.

The hall is deserted, the faint sound of a television echoing from the living room they pointed out earlier. I wonder if Nate and Axel are here. What Hudson and Cade will tell them about this evening.

God, Axel is going to be so angry at me for lying.

Cringing, I sidle out and make a beeline for the bathroom next door, slipping inside and resting my back against the door.

My mouth parts.

Gleaming blue and gold tiles line the far wall, artfully shaped in curved lines like a mermaid's tail, framing a huge floor length shower with a gleaming golden head. The white bathtub with golden feet has matching taps, a dark wooden shelf placed carefully across it.

It takes just a few minutes for the tub to fill, steam swirling from it in lazy whirls. Sniffing one of the tubs lined up on the wooden counter, I pour a healthy dollop of bubble bath in, breathing in the scent of raspberries.

The feel of my feet sinking into the blissfully hot water draws a groan from my lips. It bounces around the room, echoing slightly in the space as I sink beneath the water.

Heaven. This is absolutely what heaven looks like.

Forget the harps, the angels, the pearly gates. Heaven is a steaming hot bath after the longest day in history.

Reaching for the shampoo, I lather up my hair, rinsing it with the showerhead helpfully connected.

For a pack of bachelor alphas, they sure are set up for everything an omega might need.

Selecting one of the gigantic fluffy towels from a wicker basket, I dry off my hair and wrap it around myself before I carefully make my way back to my room, keeping an eye out for wandering alphas.

Once I'm ensconced, I slip on the camisole and brush out my hair, tying it back into a sleek braid before I slip under the thick covers of the bed.

Oh. *Oh.*

I'm cocooned in warm silk, the gauzy curtains above me creating the sensation of an enclosed space. The only thing I can hear is my quiet breathing as I sink into the warm sheets.

It feels like how I always imagined a nest might feel.

I've never had one before. Never been able to make one. First by law, then by circumstance.

But this… my toes wriggle happily against the blankets. This, I could get used to.

But it's only temporary.

The thought threatens to jar me out of my peaceful snuggling, but the events of the day are catching up to me. Hell, the events of the last eight weeks are hitting me like a sledgehammer.

Yawning widely, I let my eyes slide shut.

That's definitely a problem for tomorrow's Gabrielle.

CHAPTER THIRTY-ONE
AXEL

"She *what*?"

My arms twitch at my sides, shock flooding me as Nate and I jump to our feet.

Cade's mouth is turned down in a frown, Hudson next to him as he explains how they found out Gabrielle was living at the fucking *dungeon*.

Nate starts to pace. "She's been on her own, all this time?"

I can understand his anger. I feel the same way.

How did we *miss* this?

"I walked her home." My voice is hoarse as I try to understand. Cade gives me a pitying look, but I can see my frustration mirrored in his own eyes.

"She hid," he says, almost gently. "When you waited at the end of the street. Waited until you were gone."

Well, fuck. So much for keeping an eye on her.

The dungeon is full of everything society likes to pretend doesn't exist. Drugs, sex trade, illegal trafficking – you name it, that's where you get it.

And she lived there. In a shitty little tent that would have been as good as useless if one of those fucker alphas had scented her.

I make a beeline for the door, and Cade steps in my way.

My lips curl back in a growl. "Get out of my way, Cade."

He shakes his head. "I promised her we wouldn't steamroll her. And you, in this mood? That's not happening, Ax. Tone your shit down before you go anywhere near her."

My breathing heaves as we stare each other off, and Cade lifts his chin as our gazes lock.

I'm not strong enough to challenge him, so when I drop my eyes, I turn and drop into a seat, crossing my arms. "So what now?"

Hudson steps in, his gaze moving between me and Cade. I stubbornly refuse to look in his direction.

Am I sulking? *Abso-fucking-lutely.*

"She's staying with us, temporarily."

Nate's brows drop into a frown. "Temporarily?"

"For now." Cade's voice is firm. "Unless and until we can persuade her otherwise, but this makes things more difficult, not less, Nate. The last thing we want is for her to feel pressured by us because she's staying here."

I swallow back my protests. He's right. We need to take it easy.

"Okay," Nate reasons. "But she and I spent today together. I'm not pulling back from that unless she wants me to."

Cade nods. "Just be aware of how you're acting."

Nate runs his hand through his hair. "I still can't believe she's been living like that."

Hudson winces. "She said she lost her job, and her apartment."

I ponder his words. Life is hard for any omega not under the wing of the Grey pack and the Omega Center. Despite the Creed being abolished, I'm well aware that the world isn't overly kind to a designation many still see as responsible for declining beta birth rates. Not to mention that since the Creed was abolished, there's a growing section of the population who feel strongly that omegas should still be forced to bear children for adoption through the government.

I purse my lips. I've never bought into that shit. Omegas are built differently, pure and simple. It's not their fault that betas can't have kids.

Alphas can father kids, something that seems to fall under the radar, all of the hate and anger focused on the omegas. But we're much harder to take down in a fight.

"What do we know about her background?" I ask.

Nate shrugs, his mouth thinning. "Not much. She said she was in the Compound."

The Omega Compound.

My fists clench again at the thought of her in that hell-hole. We watched the press coverage of Ava Grey speaking up about the abuse she endured – that all omegas endured.

Hudson is clearly thinking along the same lines.

"She needs care," he says, crossing the room and taking a seat next to Nate. "She needs to be treated like an omega should be."

"Like a fucking queen," Nate mutters.

None of us contradict him.

Our silent agreement rings through the room. I can feel it in my chest, the pack bond that ties me to the alphas around me. We're all completely on board for some omega spoiling.

A hint of worry snakes through. I'm not charming like Nate. Never have the right words to say, unlike Hud. And Cade? He's got it all.

I'm not about to admit that I don't have the faintest idea what omega spoiling looks like. If there's someone to punch, I can do that. Keep someone safe? No problem.

Things like bonds, and gifts, and *nesting*, definitely aren't part of my vocabulary.

I need to do some research.

Standing up, I throw a hand up to them.

"Going to bed."

Heading out on the chorus of goodnights, I'm deep in thought as I head down the hallway. It's when I pass a certain door that I stop short.

A full hit of hot butterscotch hits me straight in the nose. But it's not the scent I recognize.

No, this scent is sharp. Acrid. Bitter.

Then the quietest moan filters in through the door.

The scent of an omega in distress.

I'm through the door before I can think about it. The four poster bed is moving, thrashing shapes appearing in the murky darkness.

"Gabrielle?" I call her name quietly, not wanting to freak her out by looming over her.

"Please," she whimpers. "Please let me out."

The terror dripping from her words makes me bolt around the room, ripping open the curtain as I look for her.

She's curled up in a ball, her arms shaking, back covered in sweat as she rocks herself.

My chest caves in.

"Gabrielle."

My tone is rough, but she doesn't flinch, doesn't move – just continues to rock, her small sobs breaking my damn heart.

"Please," she begs again. "I'll be good. Just let me out."

Chest constricting, I consider what to do. There's a noise at the door and then Cade is there, his hand reaching out as I yank him back.

"What is it?" His voice comes out deep, guttural, picking up on the acrid change in her scent as easily as I did. It feels like a direct punch to the throat.

"She's having a nightmare," I say, my mouth dry as my lips form the words.

I don't know what to do. I'm torn between respecting her space and wanting to shake her awake.

Cade freezes where he is, his uncertainty similar to mine. Nate or Hudson would be much better in this situation, but there's no sign of them.

Gabrielle twists, letting out a heartbreakingly quiet cry.

Brushing past Cade, I prop one knee on the bed as I reach out, carefully placing my hand on her arm.

"Gabrielle?"

She flinches away from my hand so hard that she nearly falls off the end of the bed.

"Little spoon." I keep my voice as low as I can. "It's not real, sweetheart. You're safe."

"Fuck," Cade whispers, and I can't disagree with him. I've never seen night terrors as strong as these.

"There's nothing to be afraid of," I murmur, my throat tight with emotion. "You need to come back to us now."

She twitches again, rolling over to face me. Her face is twisted, silent tears falling from her closed eyes.

Reaching out, I carefully wipe one away. "Little spoon."

My words are slightly louder this time, and her twitching stops, her breathing coming in harsh snaps as her eyes creak open.

"There you are," I murmur. "You were having a nightmare."

It takes a moment for her to come around, the drowsiness leaving her eyes and replaced by awareness.

She licks her lips. "Axel?"

"Mmhmm." I keep my voice low, soothing. "You're alright now. Just a bad dream."

Her eyes flicker from me to Cade. "Was I loud?"

Cade hesitates. "No. Your scent – you perfumed quite heavily."

Her eyes squeeze closed. "I'm sorry."

"Nothing to apologize for. We'll leave you in peace."

I stand up, but her breath hitches again. When I glance down, she's chewing on her lip. Her eyes dart towards the door.

"I can stay," I say gently. "Just for a little while, until you go back to sleep."

Lips parting, she nods soundlessly. Cade gives me a nod, a final smile for Gabrielle before he turns to leave, leaving the door ajar.

I settle down with my back against the side of her bed. There's movement above me, a slight shuffling as Gabrielle rearranges herself.

"Thank you," she whispers.

Tipping my head back, I glance at the dark ceiling. "Anytime, little spoon."

We stay in silence for a few minutes, Gabrielle's breathing still a little harsh. My chest aches, wanting to tug her into my arms, curl myself around her so she can hide from all of her nightmares.

Gentle fingers slide over my shoulder, and I blink at the small hand that appears, fingers outstretched.

When I take it, interlacing our fingers together, she sighs, long and deep.

Neither of us say anything, but I cradle her hand carefully with mine as her breathing slows and deepens.

She doesn't have any more nightmares.

CHAPTER THIRTY-TWO
GABRIELLE

The lack of noise is what wakes me.

There's no shouting, no hustle and bustle of the dungeon as it bursts into life to eke out another day. Just peaceful quiet.

My eyes blink open, seeing gauzy white above me instead of the stained green sheet of my tent.

There's movement to my left, and I turn my head on the soft pillow, taking in the sight of the alpha leaning against my bed, his head slumped slightly to the side as deep breathing breaks into the silence.

My heart constricts as I realize my fingers are still gripped gently in his hand, held firmly against his chest. His heartbeat pulses under my palm.

He stayed. All night.

My eyes burn, and I blink the tears away as I take him in.

There's a brief glimpse of memory, and I cringe as I realize what they must've heard from me last night. The darkness of the hole threatens to swallow me up again, and I take a deep, shuddery breath.

Axel's fingers close against mine.

"Little spoon?"

Turning my head, I give him a watery smile. "Good morning."

"Mornin'." His green eyes peer into mine, his face sleepy and rumpled. "How'd you sleep?"

"Fine," I whisper. "Better when you were here."

He winces. "Stupid question. Sorry. I'm not good without coffee in the morning."

Coffee.

He must see my eyes light up, because he offers me an adorable half smile as he unfolds his bulk from the floor, towering up above me.

He seems even taller from this angle.

He holds out a hand to me. "Cade makes really good coffee."

I take his hand without thinking, letting him pull me out of bed. It's only when I'm standing before him and he swallows that I realize I'm dressed in a camisole and not much else.

"Ah." He whirls to face the door, a flush rising up to cover the back of his neck.

Diving across the room, I burrow myself in the safety of his sweatshirt before I slip my hand back into his. Startled, he looks down at me, but entwines his fingers with mine as he leads me out of my room.

"I like that shirt on you."

His words are slightly gruff, and I smile down at the Alpha Gym sweatshirt. "It's my favorite, actually."

His fingers tighten around mine.

The kitchen is quiet when we enter, and I glance around in wonder, taking in the gleaming black marble counters, the overhead brass lamps dropping from driftwood fittings and the vast array of cookware stacked everywhere.

Axel squeezes my hand again before letting go. "This is Hudson's area," he tells me, moving around to grab us cups.

I watch avidly as he pours delicious smelling black coffee into them from a pot on the side. "We try not to get in his way, but—,"

"But it seems to happen anyway," a voice deadpans. Hudson's scent ghosts across my back before his lips press gently to my cheek. "Morning, sweetheart."

I flush. "Morning."

My mouth dries as I take him in. Deeply defined muscles ripple along his back as he turns away from me, reaching for a cup in one of the cherry-colored wooden cupboards sitting above the counter.

His back flexes, muscles running down to show two dimples just above the gray sweatpants covering his ass.

I swallow down a choked breath as he turns around, frantically swinging my gaze to somewhere else. Anywhere else.

Unfortunately, that just happens to be another delicious male chest, this one a little more familiar as smoky vanilla-scented arms wrap themselves around me.

Tucking my head against Nate's chest, I take a sneaky inhale, my mouth watering. "Nate."

He pulls back, his hands cradling my face as he scans me with concern, pushing some hair back.

"You look good in our kitchen, kitten."

He finishes off with a wink as Axel slides me a huge cup of coffee in a pink teacup, decorated with vibrant blue and purple swirls.

My hands wrap around it as I tug it closer, examining the painted pattern. It's so *pretty*.

Wait – why do they have a mug like this? It's not exactly screaming alpha male.

When I look up, all three men suddenly busy themselves. Definitely avoiding my gaze.

Hesitantly, I tap Nate's arm. "Did you get this for me?" I ask, holding up the mug.

I feel stupid as soon as I've said it. Of course they didn't. I only arrived last night.

Nate's honeyed skin darkens with a golden hue.

"Ah... I thought you might like it," he mumbles.

Hudson snickers behind him.

"Don't listen to him," he tells me. "Nate likes his own cup and he had a panic that you might be the same, so he went out this morning and bought you one."

My hands tighten around the ceramic.

Nate bought this for me. Picked it out so I'd have a cup of my own.

My whole body warms.

Nate shoots Hudson a smug smile. "Told you. She likes it."

"We can always exchange it." Axel clicks his tongue.

"No!" I yank the cup away from any grabby alpha hands, biting my lip as they look at me with varying degrees of amusement.

"I mean... I like it. It's beautiful. Thank you, Nate."

Cade strolls in, saving Nate and I from any further blushes. His eyes move straight to mine, dropping to the cup in my hands. His mouth quirks up in a smile as he moves towards the coffee pot, checking it.

"How did you sleep?" he asks me softly, leaning on the counter next to me.

The sleeves of his smart double-breasted gray suit brush my arm as he leans in, my head swimming as I'm hit with his ink and paper scent.

"Good," I manage as he hits me with a full, mildly disarming stare. "Ax stayed with me."

"Good." He repeats the word back to me as his hand reaches up, gently cupping my cheek.

"Take it easy today."

There's a thin layer of command underneath his words, the tone of an alpha used to being obeyed.

"I'm working," I point out. Cade shakes his head, but I hold up a hand.

"You've been... very kind to me. And I do appreciate it. But I need to work, Cade."

His mouth presses together, and he nods.

"You're not working until later, right?" Nate asks, balancing his hip against the counter on my other side. His soulful brown eyes peer down at me hopefully.

When I shake my head, he grins.

"So, we can go shopping?"

Three mutual groans ring out around the kitchen, Axel, Cade and Hudson all rolling their eyes.

"Shopping," Axel mutters in disgust.

I try to stifle my laugh. "You're not...uh, fans? Of shopping?"

All three of them shake their heads violently like little boys.

"I don't mind it," Cade admits. "But Nate is on another level."

"Philistines." Nate sniffs. "You're all impeccably dressed because of me."

My eyes slide back to Cade's suit, taking in the perfect tailoring that stretches the material across his chest, teasing the defined muscle underneath.

Flutters appear in my stomach as a finger slowly pushes up my chin, closing my open mouth. "See something you like?"

Flushing, I duck my head from Cade's smirk, clearing my throat. "That's a very nice suit."

My mutter is low enough that only Cade hears it above the ribbing Nate is getting from Hudson and Axel, and he leans down to whisper in my ear.

"I'm very glad you like it."

His hot breath caresses my skin, sending a shiver up my back as Cade presses a soft kiss to my cheek.

"Have a good day," he tells me. "Don't let Nate drag you around fifty different shops."

Nate pulls a face behind him, and I bite my lip to stave off the laugh as Cade leaves.

"He's such a heathen," Nate says affectionately. "Don't worry. It's just the one place, I swear."

CHAPTER THIRTY-THREE
NATE

"This is… a really big shop."

Snorting back a laugh, I grab Gabrielle's hand and tow her along with me as she chews on her lip.

"Come on, kitten," I cajole. "We don't have to stay long."

We're outside the biggest department store in the city. Heaven has everything anyone could possibly need to furnish a home – or a nest.

It's damn time someone showed our kitten how it feels to be treated like a queen, and today? I'm at her service.

Tugging my cap down, I stop pulling her along like a toy train, slowing down and winding our fingers together.

As we enter through the ornate double doors, Gabrielle glances around, her eyes wide as she takes in the billowing jeweled sashes draped strategically from the ceiling, creating the feel of a circus tent.

"What do you need to get?" she asks me as I steer us towards the home décor section.

"Just browsing, really."

We wander around for a few minutes, and I keep a close

eye on Gabrielle, taking in what she looks at for a little too long, where her fingers move and pull back.

When we reach the section I'm looking for, she stops short. "Nate."

I can't really hide it when the sign spells it out in giant, illuminated letters.

Omega nesting.

When I turn to Gabrielle, the teasing smirk on my lips slides away. "Kitten?"

She's pale as fuck, staring up at those letters like they're about to jump off the wall and eat her. "Why are we here?"

Spotting a display chair, I gently take her shoulders and steer her towards it. Once I've nudged her into sitting down, I drop to my knees, taking her cold hands between mine.

"You've never had a nest before, have you?" I murmur.

It doesn't take a genius to work it out. She's been working her ass off just to survive, and before that nests were strictly outlawed by the Omega Creed.

Fucking assholes. What the fuck does a fluffy blanket have to do with birth rates?

It was all control.

And even if she doesn't realize it, my kitten is still being controlled by them.

"I'm not going to force you to go in there," I murmur. "If you want to leave, we'll walk out right now and go for another cupcake."

Her eyes move to mine, the slight shimmer grabbing at my heart and yanking it.

"But," I breathe, "I'd really like to take you in there and spend a few hours learning exactly what my kitten wants in her nest. Think of it as useful research."

She blinks, her voice wavering. "Research?"

"For your nest," I say softly. "At home."

A tear trickles down her cheek. "I don't *have* a home, Nate."

Fuck. My fucking heart.

"Oh, Gabrielle."

Ignoring the scowling saleswoman watching us from the other side of the room, I lift Gabrielle and slide into her vacated seat, adjusting until she's curled up on my lap, her head tucked underneath my chin.

Her light breathing fades in and out against the skin at the neck of my shirt.

"Does this feel right to you?" I ask her quietly, running my hand up her arm. She nods, her hair brushing against my other arm as she rubs her cheek into me like a cat.

"It feels right to me too," I whisper. "I know we haven't known each other long, kitten. But sometimes, you meet someone, and you just know that you work better together than you do apart."

She sniffs. "I don't understand why you'd want me, Nate. I'm a mess. And you – all of you—,"

"Want *you*." My words are firm, cutting her off. "All of us want you, Gabrielle. Without question."

When she stiffens, I panic for a second that I've fucked up, shown our cards too early.

Cade will be livid when he hears about this conversation, but I don't care. I'm not about to play coy and let this omega believe that she's alone in the world. Not for another damn minute.

"I don't need your secrets, Gabrielle."

Softening my tone, I stroke my thumb across the softness of her cheek.

"Not if you're not ready to share them. But right now, I want to see you give the proverbial middle finger to everyone who told you that omegas couldn't nest, and I want to help you pick out all of the pretty things you need to design a nest that's perfect for you."

Her fingers clench on my arm. "I want that," she whispers.

It's a confession, dropping into the quiet like the first breath after being underwater.

"I just... I don't know *how* to have it, Nate. Where do I even begin? How exactly do you build a nest?"

"Now that is the magic question, kitten," I say, keeping hold of her as I stand up. She squeals, hooking her arms around my neck.

"Luckily, you have a master to help you."

Who's laughing now, assholes?

I've been prepping for this day on every single shopping expedition we've ever been on, and I didn't even know it.

CHAPTER THIRTY-FOUR
GABRIELLE

Nate's words play on a loop inside my head as he carries me towards the doorway.

All of us want you, Gabrielle. Without question.

This pack… wants me.

Permanently.

It should feel petrifying.

I never wanted a pack.

I ran from that possibility the second they set me free from the Omega Compound, literally running from my supposed rescuers, from their pretty promises about omega choices and bitemarks and helping omegas to find the pack that was right for them.

I didn't want to listen, too afraid of my own shadow and too angry at everyone who contributed to what we went through by doing *nothing*.

I never thought any pack would be right for me. But these alphas are slowly creeping their way into my heart, sneakily worming their way in through kind words and kinder actions.

My rambled thoughts scatter apart as Nate sets me down,

sliding my body against his until my feet are resting on the floor, his large hands spreading over my hips to hold me steady when I wobble.

He rests his chin on my head as I stare at the open space in front of us.

"Wow."

They have everything here. Everything that could possibly be used to make a nest.

My heart twitches. I never dared to think I'd ever be able to create a nest of my own. I've never felt safe enough, not since my very first day as an omega, when I awakened in a violent burst of pheromones and ended up in a cage for my trouble.

Blocking out the memories, I lean back into Nate, feeling his warmth soak through my back. "Where do we start?"

It's all so... overwhelming.

Nate clasps my hand in his.

"We'll start at that end," he points. "Work our way around? We can have a look first, think about what you'd like, and then pick anything up on the second run."

My mind goes to the small wad of cash stuffed into my trouser pocket.

I'm so close to being able to afford my own deposit.

Maybe I'll just pick out something small.

We walk over to the first aisle, and I take a deep breath as the conflicting scents of thousands of candles hits me in a rush. Coughing, I take a few more breaths until my head stops swimming, the immediate bombardment dying down.

Nate's not much better, his eyes watering.

"Well, this is a good start," he jokes as we start to stroll. A variety of options greet us, from tiny tea lights to candles in tins and gigantic pillar candles.

My hand reaches out and Nate nearly collides with me as he puts his hands on my shoulders.

"You like this one?" Nate asks, as I look at the label.

The bookshop.

Cracking it open, I take a sniff and my eyes widen. It smells just like Cade, his unique inky paper scent bottled and placed here for smelling *any time I like*.

My fingers tighten around it.

Just one candle. One little candle won't hurt.

But a few steps later, my eyes are drawn to another one.

Rosemary and Basil.

It's not an exact match, but it's close enough to Hudson's fresh, almost minty scent that I add it to Cade's.

Chewing my lip, I start to scan the shelves.

It takes me a few minutes, but I manage to find some teakwood-scented tealights, the earthy, rich scent an exact replica of Axel.

When I turn, Nate catches my eye. He's stayed back, giving me space to hunt down the scents I need. His grins at me, eyes sparkling.

"You don't need those, you know," he says. Embarrassment flushes my neck red, until his lip twitches.

"You're laughing at me," I say primly, "but I haven't found yours yet."

And I'll be really, irrationally annoyed if I can't find a candle that smells like toasted marshmallows.

Nate pushes himself upright, sauntering towards me. I keep my feet steady as he leans in, his cheek running against mine and giving me full access to his neck.

"You," he purrs, "have a constant supply on hand."

I swallow, nearly dropping the candles in my hands when he steps back, a satisfied smile spreading over his face. Reaching forward, he takes them from me.

Narrowing my eyes at him playfully, I turn back to the shelves. I'll admit that having my own toasted marshmallow-scented alpha on hand might be handy, but he won't be with me all the time.

I'm pushing aside a selection of truly disgusting

pineapple candles when I pause, my hand hovering over a selection of wax burners.

"Kitten?" Nate's voice sounds behind me.

I'm acting like a bitemarked omega.

I'm acting like *their* omega.

And whatever Nate says about all of them wanting me, I only have his word for it. What if he's wrong? What if the others don't feel the same?

What if this isn't real?

"Stop it," Nate says firmly. He turns me to face him, and I stare at the middle of his chest, the cotton blurring.

"Whatever self-destructive thoughts you're having," he says quietly, "I want them to stop, Gabrielle. You were having fun, and I was having fun watching you."

He taps my temple gently. "Don't let them win."

"It's hard, Nate," I admit. "Every piece of happiness I've ever had has been taken away."

"Not this time, kitten. I won't let that happen."

Swallowing, I try to soak in his confidence, steal a little of it for myself. Steeling myself, I step forward and wrap my arms around Nate's waist, giving in to the instinct to bury myself in his chest and suck in that delicious toasty scent.

His hand strokes over my hair, soft as a feather.

"There we go," he says, his face soft with understanding as I pull back. "You ready?"

Nodding, I dash a hand across my damp eyes and take a deep breath.

"Say it," he coaxes. "What do you want?"

"I want a toasted marshmallow candle," I say firmly. "One that smells just like you."

Nate's full lips stretch into a smile. "Come on then, kitten. Let's find one."

Once my candles are stored safely in Nate's arms, we move on to the next aisle. Nate snags a trolley despite my protests, leisurely rolling it past stacks of different lotions and oils and looking far, far sexier than any alpha has a right to when they're cooing over marshmallow-scented bubble bath.

I wait until he's not looking before I slide it into the trolley.

A beta eyeballs him opposite us, her hand pausing in mid-air as she drags lascivious eyes up his body. The sudden jealousy pooling in my stomach takes me by surprise, even as I step forward, blocking her way and baring my teeth.

Blonde hair bounces around her shoulders as she hastily drops her lotion into her basket and scurries off.

Embarrassment flares hotly in my chest as I turn away. God, I can't believe I just did that. But when I turn around, Nate is full-on laughing, his shoulders shaking as he inspects the back of a bottle a little too closely.

"Stop it," I chastise, biting my lip as amusement bubbles up. "I think she thought I was going to eat her."

Nate gives me a dramatic look, clasping his hands over his chest. "That was the best moment of my entire life. You growled and everything, kitten. Promise me you'll growl for me when we're in bed."

I drop my face into my hands to hide my flaming cheeks. "Nathaniel!"

I'm assaulted by images of a sexy, warm Nate with mussed hair and heated eyes. My core clenches at the thought, and Nate pauses, his nostrils flaring.

"Rain check," he grumbles. "We're not leaving here without making sure you're all stocked up."

Nate coaxes me into inhaling various scents, watching me to see which ones I like and throwing them into the trolley. I give up on mentally tallying the total after the fifth, resigning myself to building my emergency fund back up.

There's time, I tell myself. And if the thought feels a little empty, I ignore it.

When we reach the end of the never-ending lotion line, I stop. "What's this?"

Soft furnishings.

My breath catches as I take in the hundreds, if not thousands, of different shapes and materials. All colors, from the palest, shimmering pink to vibrant jeweled emerald green beckon me, all soft and warm and silky.

I walk through in a daze, my fingers gently tracing fabrics.

For the first time, I start imagining what I'd like my nest to be. What I need it to be.

Bright. Soft. Enclosed.

Safe.

My hand reaches out as I grasp a delicate purple blanket, the amethyst color calling to me like a beacon. Then a deep, midnight blue velvet that shimmers with golden stars.

Nate quietly relieves me as my arms become full, but I keep hold of the starry blanket, holding it to me as it's joined by a beautiful silver furred throw and a crimson silk sheet that shines in the overhead lights.

Blinking, I realize we've reached the end of the aisle. My arms are overflowing again when I look down and then sheepishly at Nate.

"Beautiful," he says, taking some and adding to the pile in the trolley.

"I can't wait to see your nest," he says. "I hope you'll invite me in."

"Maybe I will," I tease lightly, "maybe I won't."

He growls, a loud, rippling pretend roar that sends me pelting up the next aisle with a giggling squeal.

I can feel the eyes, disapproving looks, but I don't care. The only person I care about in this space is the alpha who directs the sales assistant to load up my purchases before pushing away my cash with a snort.

"No good alpha would let his omega pay for this," he tells me firmly. "This is my privilege, to do this for you."

The sales assistant's mouth falls slack, her eyes sliding to me. She tilts her head towards Nate, her wide eyes sending a very clear message.

Why are you complaining? You freaking idiot.

Frowning, I stuff the small wad back into my pocket.

"Thank you," I say, as we're wheeling the cart back out to the car. "But I don't need you to pay for everything for me, Nate. I have money of my own."

He nudges my shoulder. "Indulge me. You're used to doing everything on your own. I get that. But you're not *on* your own now, sweetheart. You have us. It's alright to lean on that."

I'm about to reply when my neck prickles. Spinning, I take in the busy parking lot. People duck and weave between cars, piling in groceries and shopping. Two betas shout at each other, arms waving out of their car windows as they argue over the same space.

Nobody is paying attention to us. There's nothing to explain why I can feel *eyes* on me. It feels… oily. Wrong.

"Gabrielle?"

Nate has stopped, his posture tense as he moves closer.

"Everything okay?" He follows my eyes, his carefree expression melting away as he picks up on my unease.

My hand reaches up to rub at my neck. *Stupid.*

Now I'm imagining things.

"Everything's fine." Blowing out a breath, I scan the lot one more time before sliding into the car.

Nate's words linger in my head as he drives us back, one arm slung comfortably over the back of my chair as he hums under his breath. His fingers stroke across the back of my neck with light strokes.

It's peaceful. Soothing. So much so that my eyes start to

drift closed, too many weeks of light sleeping and abrupt awakenings catching up with me.

Maybe it's time to stop resisting, I think drowsily. Nate's hand smooths over my hair.

"Sleep, kitten. I'll wake you when we get back."

I fall asleep with a warmth in my chest.

It feels a lot like *hope*.

CHAPTER THIRTY-FIVE
AXEL

Gabrielle stirs, sleepy eyes blinking up at me before they widen.

"Oh."

"You want me to put you down?" I ask.

When Nate pulled up, I was the only one home to pick up his message and come help shift an absolutely ridiculous number of parcels from the car upstairs.

But I snagged the best one first.

"No," she mumbles drowsily. A hand reaches up to curl into my shirt as she rubs her cheek against it.

"You feel like pillow."

Choking back a laugh, I carry her into the apartment.

"Where to?" I ask Nate, and he jerks a thumb in the direction of her room.

"The nest."

With a slow nod, I carry her down, toeing off my shoes at the doorway before stepping into her bedroom. It's already drenched in her scent, and I breathe my fill as Nate slides open the doors.

"She hasn't seen this yet," I tell him. "I don't think so, anyway."

Excitement lights up his eyes as he glances down at Gabrielle.

"Kitten?"

"Mmph."

"Time to wake up."

"Hmm?"

When her eyes flutter open again, I carefully set her down, holding onto her as she catches her balance.

"Ready to see your nest?"

Sleep clears from her face as she turns to me, her face twisted in curiosity.

"I thought this was the nest?"

Nate laughs. "This is your bedroom. But this—" he gestures through the double doors, flicking on the overhead light, "—is your nest."

Gabrielle's body turns to stone against mine.

I take a breath, bracing myself and exchanging a look with Nate.

Gabrielle has never had a nest of her own before. But we know from our time at the Omega Center how important this is.

Gabrielle's nest should be her safe space, her retreat, her rest area, her comfort.

And if she can't settle... then it's because she doesn't feel safe enough.

With us.

I peer over the top of her head. It's an empty canvas, but the bones are there. Low ceilings, no windows, one exit point. The floor is a soft, built-in mattress, with wooden shelves lining the area to hold any objects she wants to include.

If our omega likes it, then she'll nest.

I don't even realize I'm holding my breath until she takes a step away from me.

"This is for me?" She doesn't look away from it as she

speaks.

"It is," I say awkwardly. "If you want it?"

"You don't have to—,"

"I *love* it."

Nate's panicked burbling nearly drowns out her awed whisper.

My shoulders sag, relief loosening my bones.

"You do?" I ask. "Are you sure? We can change it around—,"

"No. It's perfect as it is."

Gabrielle spins to me. And her face splits into the most perfect, heartbreaking grin.

My heart nearly stops when she throws herself into me, her arms wrapping around my neck as she hugs me tightly.

I've barely caught my breath when she releases me to do the same to Nate. I wonder if I look like I've been whacked over the head, because he sure does.

"No arguments?" Nate asks suspiciously. "Not even a little?"

Gabrielle smiles.

"I've decided to try it your way," she tells him. "A little hope never hurt anybody."

Nate beams, running a hand through his hair. "So... you're sticking with us?"

My head swivels to Gabrielle so quickly I think it might actually fall off. She bites her lip, giving me a shy look from under her lashes as she nods.

"I think so," she whispers. "If you're sure, Nate. If you're *all* sure."

I lift her chin with my finger, my hands sliding up to cup her cheeks.

"You'll stay." My voice rumbles in my chest. "Here? With us?"

With all of us?

Her face dips up and down between my hands as she nods jerkily.

Then she pushes herself forward, and I'm captured in a kiss so soft it feels like feathers brushing against my lips.

I stay still, accepting the precious gift I've just been given. My hands curl into tight fists as I battle the urge to take control, to show Gabrielle exactly how much I want her.

There'll be time for that. For all of it.

My heart skips inside my chest as Gabrielle grabs my hand, tugging me forwards.

"Nate," she calls. "Can I have my blankets?"

"You can have anything you want, kitten."

I lean against the wall as she bounces on the mattress, her laughter ringing out as she chides Nate about some pineapple candle shit he's slipped into one of the bags. One hand rubs at my chest.

Gabrielle... she fits here. Like she was made for this room, this nest, this pack.

Ours.

She's ours.

And despite her brave words today, I know she's not there yet. But it feels like we've taken a huge step towards a future that seems impossible just a few days ago.

"You look good in this space, little spoon," I tell her. "It suits you."

A light pink tinges her lips as she nods, her hands gripping a dark blue glittered blanket tightly.

"I think it does."

She darts out, reappearing a moment later with her hands cupped together. She carries something over to the shelves, kneeling down and placing several items down.

Rocks?

"You collect these?" I ask, curiosity thrumming through me at this new peek into Gabrielle.

Leaning back on her heels, she nods, reaching out to straighten a smooth gray rock.

"I always did," she says. "When I was a kid, I used to carry them around in my pockets."

I smile. "Bet that drove your parents mad, always digging them out."

Her shoulders tense, giving me the first sign that I've said something wrong.

"I…" Stopping, she coughs lightly. "It was just my mom. I never met my dad."

Surprise lifts my eyebrows. Gabrielle is young enough that the birth rates would have been dropping rapidly when she was born. It's unusual that her father wouldn't have wanted to be involved in that.

"You never met him at all?" Nate asks softly. He takes a seat next to her, stretching his legs out.

"My mom was an addict." Gabrielle picks at a loose thread on her knee. "I guess he was someone she used to feed her habit. A one-nighter."

Oh, little spoon.

She stares down at her now-empty hands. Then she takes a deep breath.

"My mom… she sold me."

Shock renders me immobile for a split second. Then roaring, pulsing fury hits me like a sledgehammer, roaring in my ears.

"She *what*?" I growl.

Tell me I didn't hear that correctly.

"When I awakened. The Creed… it said I had to go to the Omega Compound. But she thought she could make a few bucks. There was this gang that trafficked omegas under the radar. Renting them out to alphas."

Bile stings the back of my throat. Nate is pale as he watches Gabrielle.

"And your mom sold you to them?" He asks her softly.

Swallowing, she nods. "Nothing really bad happened," she whispers, her voice almost expressionless. "I was with them for a few nights, and the Government found me. That's how I ended up in the OC."

She sniffs, letting out a watery laugh. "Sorry. There I go again, ruining the moment."

"Stop that."

My growl takes everyone by surprise. Gabrielle jumps as I crouch down, holding her gaze.

"Stop sugarcoating your emotions for us, little spoon. None of us want that. We're not just here for a good time. We're here for you. I want every single piece of you. And if any are broken, then I'll help you glue them back together. But you are not an inconvenience to us. You get me?"

She blinks watery eyes. "I get you."

Then she holds out her arms.

It takes seconds for me to lift her into me, sinking down onto the soft floor with her curled up in my arms. Nate watches us solemnly.

"I'm so sorry that happened to you," I say hoarsely.

Nate nods. "A parent should put their child above everything."

"I know that now," she says with a sigh as she nestles into me. "It took me longer than it should have to realize it, though."

She climbs off my lap, reaching for one of the bags and digging through it as I get to my feet.

I lean down, giving her shoulder a soft squeeze.

"We'll give you some space," I say, jerking my head at Nate. "Take however long you want, and call if you need any help."

"Or if you run out of candles," Nate quips.

That's not possible. There are dozens of candles in there.

How many candles does an omega need?

CHAPTER THIRTY-SIX
GABRIELLE

Glaring at the empty bag, I blow out a frustrated breath.

I ran out of candles.

But my whole body tingles in glee as I look around the room.

It feels like an honest-to-god, bury-me-in-blankets-and-tuck mc-in-like-a-burrito *nest*.

My lotions and candles are carefully arranged on the surrounding shelves, interspersed with my rocks, artfully arranged in little sparkling circles. Something in my chest settles as I look at them.

The blankets I picked out are scattered across the floor, deep greens, purples, reds, blues mixing together. Then there's the cushions.

So. Many. Cushions.

Lying back, I burrow myself into a particularly soft, floppy pillow and stare up at the ceiling.

"Gabrielle?"

I jerk at the sound of Hudson's voice, sitting up to see him lingering by the door.

He gives me a small smile. "Hey, you."

"Hey." I suddenly feel inexplicably shy, curled up here in my nest with an alpha at the doorway. He holds up a bag.

"Bought you something."

My fingers twitch. "You did?"

He doesn't move, and we end up in a weird stand-off until I slap my hand over my eyes.

"Sorry," I mumble. "Of course you can come in."

He whistles. "Thank god for that. For a moment there I thought you'd left me hanging."

Handing me the bag, he takes a step back. The brown paper rustles under my hands as I open it up. It takes me a moment.

Then I pull them out, and something in my chest tugs hard.

Swallowing, I run a finger over the plastic. "Glow in the dark stars?"

"So you'll never be left in the dark again," he says quietly.

My vision blurs. "Hudson... this is really sweet."

He's been so good to me. They all have.

The sudden one-sidedness of all of this hits me, and I frown sightlessly at the wall.

I want to do something for *them*.

A growling noise punctuates the silence, and Hudson laughs when I turn to him. "Sorry. Drawback of a busy lunch session. No time for food."

He pats his stomach, a mournful look on his handsome face. "Don't worry, buddy. We'll get you fed soon."

Inspiration hits, and I scramble to my feet. Hudson follows my lead.

"You okay?" he asks me, but I'm nodding absently.

"Can I... could I use your kitchen? To make something?" I ask.

His eyebrows fly up. "Of course. Are you hungry? Because I can—,"

"Nuh uh." I shake my head. "It's my turn to feed you."

Hudson tips his head to the side. "You been holding out on me, sweetheart? I'm intrigued. I didn't know you could cook."

———

I… can't cook.

As in, I should be barred from going anywhere near any cooking facilities for the rest of my life.

Staring at the solid black burnt mass stuck firmly to the side of Hudson's lovely ceramic dish, I poke it mournfully as he peers over my shoulder.

"Gabby," he whispers, his hand caressing my shoulder soothingly. "I think it's done, sweetheart."

There's a choking noise, and I swing around to see Cade swinging an arm across his face as he walks in, his face scrunched in disgust.

"What," he sputters, "is that smell?"

"Cade," Hudson says in a suspiciously cheery voice, "Gabrielle is cooking dinner for us!"

I roll my eyes at the clear *shut-up-you-idiot* vibes he's broadcasting.

"I think the salad is okay," I say woefully. "I didn't have to cook that."

Hudson seizes on it with a bright smile, grabbing a tomato from the top.

"This is perfect." He tosses it into his mouth, and I watch in growing horror as his throat bulges. "Hudson?"

His jaw is making some seriously weird gurning motions, and Cade and I watch in stunned silence as Hudson battles through, swallowing loudly.

"Lovely." His voice croaks.

I pull the bowl towards me, staring down at it.

How the hell did I fuck up a salad?

"What's wrong with it?" I ask weakly. Hudson shakes his head, and I pin him with a glare.

"Don't make me eat it," I beg. "Just break it to me."

"Ah." He rubs the back of his neck. "Did you put in salt, by any chance?"

I nod. "You don't like salt?"

He grimaces. "I love salt. But, um... that's sugar, sweetheart."

Oh, for the love of actual fuck.

Throwing up my hands, I turn to face them both. "Okay, so I can't cook. I just wanted to do something nice for you, but I have no skills whatsoever. I can't even do a salad right."

My lip wobbles, and Hudson looks between me and the salad desperately.

"You know, it's not that bad," he says quickly. "I kind of like it."

Sniffling, I wipe my nose. "No, you don't. Nobody likes sugar on their salad, Hudson."

"It's growing on me." Before I can stop him, he takes a huge piece of pepper and bites into it.

"Mmm. Cade," he mumbles, "try it."

Cade tugs at his collar as he eyes the bowl like something's gonna crawl out and eat him.

"Try what?" Axel's hand cups my neck in an already-familiar caress. I bite my lip, leaning into him as I watch Cade struggle. A hint of amusement starts to grow as Hudson slides the bowl forwards.

"Gabrielle made us a salad," he tells Axel.

To his credit, Axel doesn't bat an eyelid. "Thank you, little spoon."

My amusement grows into choked back giggles when he spoons a big helping into a bowl. Hudson pulls a face at me when Ax turns away to grab a fork. Plopping himself down on a seat, he glances around, fork poised.

"You're not eating?" he asks.

"Already ate," Cade says smoothly.

We all watch as Axel takes a huge bite of a salad leaf. His eyebrows scrunch together as his chewing slows, eyes glancing askance down at the bowl.

It's too much. My laughter erupts at the panicked look on his face.

"Stop," I say, confiscating the fork. "Please. For everyone's sake, back away from the salad. I think we can all agree that cooking is not my strong point."

Axel protests half-heartedly as Hudson steps up behind me and slides his arms around my waist. "I'll teach you," he murmurs into my ear.

"I'm a *very* thorough teacher."

I have a feeling I might enjoy Hudson's lessons.

"But right now, I have to get downstairs."

Before he leaves, he presses a long, hot kiss to my neck. My toes actually curl as my head lolls to the side.

"So responsive," Hudson murmurs. "Isn't she, Cade?"

My eyes flash straight up, meeting icy-blue depths fixed firmly on my face.

"She is," Cade agrees.

For a moment, I wonder what it would be like. Feel like, to be pressed in between them both, covered in their scents and their bodies.

"You're getting all worked up," Hudson notes, the rasp of his stubble brushing against the back of my shoulder as he breathes me in. The scent floods the kitchen, the sweetness cutting through the acrid burnt smell of what was *supposed* to be lasagne.

"No time for that," Cade scolds lightly, but there's heat in his eyes as he watches us across the table. "We have plans this evening."

A little moue of disappointment flickers in my chest, but I belatedly catch on when he glances at me. "Me?"

"If you're available to join me."

A mixture of apprehension and curiosity causes a whole flock of butterflies to take flight in my stomach.

I haven't spent any time with Cade alone. Truthfully, he feels so aloof sometimes, it's like he's unreachable in a way the others aren't. I twist away from Hudson, needing to clear my head of his fresh scent so I can think this through.

"Where are we going?" I ask. Cade grins.

"Somewhere I think you'll like."

CHAPTER THIRTY-SEVEN
CADE

Apprehension curls in my chest as we pull up to the gallery.

The ride over has been silent, Gabrielle deep in thought that feels too important to interrupt. Her eyes keep sliding over to me and away.

I run a hand down my casual shirt, smoothing away any creases as I open her car door, holding out a hand.

She exits, brushing off her dark denim jeans and tee as she stares up at the imposing building in front of us.

"What's this?" she asks me.

"You'll see." I hold out by hand in a silent question, and she reaches for it, our fingers curling together as I lead her inside.

"Good evening! Do you need any – oh! Mr. Reyne!"

"Rebecca." I give the beta my most practiced smile, aware of Gabrielle tensing at my side.

I wonder if she realizes that territorial instincts are typical omega mating behavior.

My shoulders deliberately relax as I pull her closer. "This is Gabrielle."

Rebecca's shoulders slump in the corner of my eye as I

smile down at the omega at my side. A true smile, not the practiced public puppet smile I gave before. Gabrielle's shoulders relax, and we continue on.

"You come here often?"

I shrug. "A fair bit. I'm a patron – I gave some money to the museum in return for a lifetime membership."

I feel her smile. "You like art?"

"I do. If I hadn't gone into law, I would have been an artist, I think. Likely not a very good one."

Her light laugh trails off as we turn the corner, her breath stuttering into a gasp. "Oh, Cade."

"It's beautiful, isn't it?" My eyes aren't on the installation. They're on her.

She stares up at the six-hundred and eighty-seven glowing lanterns above our head. The room around us is pitch black glass, making the pink and violet lighting mirror beneath our feet until it feels like we're surrounded by light in every direction.

"Careful," I warn, keeping a hold of her hand as she spins to look down the room. "It can be disconcerting at first."

She takes an unsteady step, wobbling until she finds her footing with a delighted laugh.

"This is… I've never seen anything like this."

A heaviness in my chest lightens at her words. I wanted to share this with her, this private part of myself. "This isn't everything, you know."

She turns to me, her eyes shining with the shimmering light of the lanterns above us.

"Show me?"

Such a simple request, but it hits hard. As I stare at her, both of us bathed in warm light, the realization hits me.

I'd do anything this omega asked me to do. *Anything*.

"Cade?"

Snapping out of it, I clear my throat and steer us through.

The lantern show is just the first part of what makes this one of my favorite places. Gabrielle laughs in delight as the next room reveals itself as an immersive aquarium, walls, ceiling and floors alive with the blue of the sea and filled with thousands of fish and plants.

We walk through slowly, stopping at nearly every section to take it in. Gabrielle reads every single display with intense concentration, her forehead creasing as she repeats the words back to herself.

And I just watch, soaking in her enthusiasm, thirsty for every excited squeak, every word, every glance she gives me, every tug on my hand.

And then we get to the final exhibit.

Gabrielle falls silent when I push open the double doors.

Her hand falls from mine as she drifts forward, her head craned up.

The night sky twinkles above us, the stars enlarged to glowing balls overhead, the planets on full display.

"It's like we've just walked into space," Gabrielle whispers.

Taking her hand again, I gently steer her to the area I arranged earlier. There's only a handful of other groups here, the space more than large enough for privacy as she takes in the heap of blankets, the bottle of wine chilling in a bucket, the glasses.

"This is for us?"

"For you."

She sinks down onto the blankets and I pour us a glass each as she continues to take it in.

"They built the planetarium a couple of years ago. This is my favorite part," I admit.

"I think it's mine too." Her voice is full of wonder.

"Just wait." Checking my watch, I relieve her of her glass, encouraging her to lie back as I do the same. We wait in comfortable silence, the quiet of the space around us broken by Gabrielle's soft breathing.

It only takes a minute before the first shooting star barrels across the sky. Turning to Gabrielle, I watch the show in the reflection of her wide eyes, her lips parted as star after star cascades in a shower of golden light, building until the sky above us is lit up with hundreds of sparkling bursts.

I feel her fingers brushing against mine, the gentle nudge of her hand.

Entangling our fingers together feels as natural as breathing.

When the show ends, she rolls onto her side instead of sitting up, and I follow suit. We watch each other in the darkness, the brightness of the shooting stars replaced by the muted light of the planets around us.

"Where did you come from?" The wondering words slip out, and her mouth stretches into a smile.

"I should be asking you that question. This doesn't feel real."

"It's real. I promise, Gabrielle."

She hesitates. "And... you want me too?"

The vulnerability in her questions shakes me. Prompts me to give her my own honesty back.

"I do. But... I'm not entirely sure you'll want me."

Her eyes widen. "Why not?"

Gathering the courage she's shown me, I tell her. "Because the things I like to do might not be what you enjoy."

I can see the confusion, then realization, the slow blush stealing over her cheekbones evident even in the partial darkness.

"Do... do they hurt? These things?"

A shadow flits over her face.

"No." I shake my head vehemently. "That's not my thing, sweetheart. I don't get off on hurting women."

"Okay." She bites her lip.

Deciding that I've pushed her quite far enough for one evening, I reluctantly roll to my feet, helping her up.

She's quiet as we leave, the late evening breeze cool enough that I slide my jacket around her shoulders. Her hand remains tightly gripped in mine, the other clutching the jacket as we drive home. I don't push her, content to give her space to think before this goes any further.

Before I can't let her go.

Although I'm starting to think it's far too late for that.

CHAPTER THIRTY-EIGHT
GABRIELLE

I throw my covers aside with a huff.

Hours of tossing and turning have left me a tired, grumpy omega. There's an itch running under my skin, something crawling in my veins that's leaving me unable to stay still.

My feet pad lightly on the wooden floor of the hall as I make my way down to an unfamiliar door.

Swallowing, I knock lightly. When I hear footsteps, I second guess my decision, my feet suddenly itching to race back to the safety of my bed.

The door swings open, my eyes meeting the warm tones of a bared torso. Axel blinks down at me, his hair mussed and eyes heavy from sleep.

"Little spoon?" he asks, his gaze sharpening. "Are you alright?"

My agitation is growing worse. Ducking under his arm, I make straight for the bed, breathing in Axel's earthy scent as I burrow myself under the covers. Breathing deeply, I belatedly realize how it must look and pop my head out sheepishly.

Axel perches on the side of the bed, eyeing me.

"Couldn't sleep?"

When I shake my head, he pulls back the covers, waiting for me to nod before he slides in next to me. His body feels like its own type of blanket, the heat radiating from him enough for me to snuggle in, my cheek resting against his chest and my leg slipping between his. Once we're completely pressed together, my body goes slack, the tension leaving it in a sudden burst of relaxation.

Sighing, I rub my cheek against Axel, listening to the faint thump of his heartbeat.

It sounds a little fast.

When I cock my head up, Axel is staring down at me, his mouth slightly open. My whole body flushes with embarrassment.

Holy shit. What am I *doing*?

I move to pull back, an apology on my lips, but Axel wraps his arms around me like steel bands.

"What are you doing, little spoon?" he murmurs.

Swallowing, I struggle to meet his eyes.

"Sorry," I whisper. "I – I don't know — ,"

I don't know what just happened.

A little furrow appears in Axel's forehead.

"So this is an omega thing, then?" he asks carefully. "Not a Gabrielle thing?"

Grateful for the easy out, I'm about to blame it all on my pesky pheromones when I pause.

"Not… not just an omega thing," I admit.

Axel feels safe. They all do. But anyone outside of that… my palms start sweating at the thought of it.

This can't be an omega thing. Because surely, any alpha would do.

And the only alpha I want right now is in this room.

Avoiding his eyes, I lean back against his chest, my voice muffled. "Not an omega thing at all, actually."

Axel's hand strokes down my hair, the gentle caress at odds with the sheer size of him.

"Sleep then, little spoon," his voice rumbles in his chest. "I've got you."

And just like that, my eyes drift closed as if the last few hours never happened at all.

There's something digging into my butt.

Something big.

My eyes fly open as Axel's breathing rumbles in my ear, my body becoming absolutely still. He grumbles in his sleep, his arms banding around my waist and tucking me into him, his body curving over me.

His hand closes firmly over my right breast.

And his dick slips straight between my cheeks.

The sensation sends a tremble through my whole body. A deep, clenching tug of need comes directly from my lower half.

If I was half asleep before, I'm well and truly awake now.

The steady breathing behind me hitches, the drowsy voice behind me full of pure alpha male.

"What are you doing, little spoon?"

I freeze.

"Nothing," I whisper. "Why?"

He nuzzles into my neck. "Your scent."

Within seconds, there's more deep breathing as he drifts back off to sleep.

The tugging doesn't go away. If anything, it's getting worse, that clawing need from last night building back up in my veins, making me twitchy. Axel's hand on my breast feels like a brand, but I need more. His cock is still rock hard against me, pushing into me but not moving.

I need to *move*.

My hand creeps down, towards the edge of the sleeping shorts I'm wearing.

Maybe I could just... take the edge off?

My breathing speeds up, aware of the alpha curled around me.

What if he wakes up?

What if he doesn't?

My body makes the decision for me, another thirsty pull pushing my hands down underneath my shorts. I slip my fingers through my curls, an embarrassing amount of wetness making me wonder if this is actually a good idea.

But the first stroke of my fingers makes my eyes roll back in my head, my fingers circling my clit, pressing and flicking it until a low, heavy whine draws from my throat.

I pause, holding my breath.

And then a heavy hand slips over mine.

"Keep going," Axel murmurs. "I'm enjoying the show."

Oh. My. God.

Kill me now.

I stay completely still, hoping for a thunderbolt or lightning stroke or some other act of God to storm down and save me from the humiliation.

"Little spoon."

Axel's coaxing tone makes me squeeze my eyes closed, because that damn voice is not helping in my current, very sticky situation.

Please go back to sleep, please go back to sleep...

"You know I can hear you, right?"

Oh fuckety fuck fuck.

His body shakes. "That too."

Bracing myself, I acknowledge that I will actually need to respond properly to this situation.

"I, er, was just... taking the edge off."

"Oh?"

Axel's fingers trace a circle over the back of my hand, which is still pressed firmly against my clit. I make a concentrated effort not to shift my hips.

"Need any help?" He purrs into my ear, turning my bones to mush. "To take that edge off."

His hand squeezes my breast, and I push it into his touch with a silent demand for more.

"Talk to me, little spoon." His voice drops, deeper than I've heard it. "Tell me what you want."

I wet my lips. My whole body is trembling, and Axel holds me steady.

"Touch me."

The second the words fall from my lips, Axel's hand slips beneath mine, hot skin possessively cupping me. His palm grinds against my clit and I throw my head back against his chest at the sensation.

"Do you know what you do to me?" He murmurs. His hand continues to move, gently abrasive as it rubs against my sensitive skin.

"Do you know," he continues, "how fucking hot you looked, rubbing that needy little clit?"

Oh, sweet lord.

His fingers curl up to circle my entrance, and the keen that pulls from my throat is loud enough to wake the dead.

"Please." It's a moan, my body moving for him.

His dips just the edge of a finger in, pulling it back and forth, driving me insane.

"Axel!"

"Have you ever had a knot, Gabrielle?"

My mind short circuits as his finger surges inside me, the slick on his fingers more than enough to smooth his way. He pumps it in and out, curving his fingers slightly and pressing against something that makes my legs thrash.

"No," I pant.

He kisses my shoulder, even as his hand continues to move.

"I've thought about how you'd look, with my knot buried inside you. This little pussy, wet with your slick, taking me in and me filling you up."

His filthy words whispered in my ear make me see fucking stars.

"Yes," I gasp. "Yes to the knot. I want the knot!"

Give me aaaaall the knots.

He slows a little, and I nearly sob for the need that comes over me. "Soon, little spoon."

He's saying *no*?

"Not soon," I snap.

I'm done with tiptoeing around how much I want them.

"Now, Axel. I *want your knot*."

I groan as his fingers leave me, and then he's rolling me over, his face appearing over mine.

"You want it?" he asks softly. "Are you sure?"

Instead of answering, I wriggle, tugging him until my legs are wrapped around his waist, his cock pushing against the wet material of my shorts.

"I am sure. I want you. Right now."

When he thrusts against me, his eyes tracing my face, I'm unprepared for the sensation, the tantalizing tease of pressure that pushes against me.

"Yes," I murmur, winding my hands into his hair. "More of that, please."

Instead, he drops his face to mine, his lips moving over mine in a soft caress.

"Have you ever done this before?" he asks me, pulling back.

My skin sizzles with sensitivity as he moves across my neck, dropping little kisses against my skin. "No. But I'm sure."

His hand curls around my waist, his arms braced on his

elbows as he continues his slow assault on my body, his mouth tracing over my light camisole.

Fingers tracing the thin lace at the bottom, he glances up at me. "Take this off for me?"

Wriggling, I tug at the hem as he helps to push it up my body, slowly revealing my breasts to him. My nipples peak in the cool air of the early morning, and he reverently strokes his finger over them.

"Luckiest alpha on the planet," he murmurs. "Look at these pretty breasts, Gabrielle. These nipples, little and pink and needy."

I nearly lift off the bed when he sucks one between his lips, the pulling sensation unlike anything I've felt before.

"Axel!"

He releases one, his tongue dancing over it before moving across to the other.

My head tips back against the pillow as I push myself into him, wanting more.

I want to be *consumed* by him.

It feels like he's everywhere, but it's not enough, the empty feeling inside me growing into a clenching in my abdomen that borders on pain.

"Please," I half moan, half sob. "More."

"I've got you, baby."

He moves away from my breasts, continuing down my body, pressing his lips to my navel and moving down until my abdomen flutters underneath his soft administration.

When his fingers hook into my shorts, I impatiently shove them down, hastily kicking them off when they catch on my ankle.

He gives me an admonishing look. "So impatient."

Staring down at him, my heart pulses at how *much* he is. Leaning on his elbows, his head between my legs, this alpha with the huge body and even bigger heart.

I fight not to blush when he drops his head, looking straight between my legs.

"Beautiful." His throaty growl ripples between us. "You're so beautiful, Gabrielle. Everywhere."

I feel it, when his hands are constantly touching me, worshiping me, everywhere I need them to be. Touching, stroking, pinching.

My slick pulses from me, a steady stream demonstrating how wet I am for him. How much I need him.

Axel sits upwards, his eyes on me as he pushes his boxers down.

His cock springs free, and my eyes bulge at the sheer side of him. Thick, defined, it juts out proudly, a thick vein running down the side.

"You... definitely in proportion," I croak, blinking.

That is absolutely not going to fit.

He laughs, a low, breathless sound before he presses more kisses to the inside of my thighs. His finger traces me again, circling before sinking into me.

"So wet for me, little spoon." He adds another finger, then another, scissoring them until I feel myself stretching, my body accommodating everything he gives me and still leaving me wanting more.

He climbs back up my body, settling in, his face leaning over mine as he kisses me again, angling himself so he nudges against my entrance.

I gasp into his mouth, and he smiles against my lips. "Breathe for me, baby."

When I suck in a shuddery breath, he sinks in a single slow, torturous inch, then another, my body welcoming him with only a slight burn. It's so much more than I expected, as though he's slowly branding me from the inside.

"That's it," he praises, wiping damp strands of hair from my face. "You're taking me in, Gabrielle. Pulling me into that perfect little pussy of yours. Feels like you were made for me."

We both groan, our foreheads resting together as he pushes in further, until there's nowhere left to go.

Something pushes against my entrance. Something bigger than his cock.

"You're going to look perfect with my knot buried inside you," Axel promises.

"Look at me."

When my eyes lock on his, my breathing shuddering between us, he pulls himself out before coming back, surging against me as he finds a rhythm between our bodies.

And all the while, he watches me, his face taking in every little change as he plays my body like a damn virtuoso.

"It feels... like you were made for me," I breathe. He nods, both of us sucking in our breath as he grinds himself against my clit, his hand dropping to my breast and squeezing.

"Ours," he grunts. "You're ours, Gabrielle. Say it."

"Yours." The cry falls from my lips as his thrusts become faster, impossibly deeper. "Yours, Axel!"

My pussy muscles clench around him, and he drops his forehead to my shoulder as he swells inside me.

"Take the rest," he coaxes. "Feel my knot pushing inside you, Gabrielle. Can you feel it?"

Holding my breath, I keen as he stretches me impossibly wider, his knot demanding entry.

"Made for me, baby." It's a demand and a promise as his knot pushes inside, an impossibly full sensation.

It tips me over the edge, my cry throaty as my muscles clench, over and over again until I'm shaking against him. Axel roars as he pulses jets of hot fluid into me, mixing with my slick until I feel it seeping around his knot, locked firmly inside me.

Keeping us connected, locked together until it loosens.

It makes me feel…protected. Owned. Conquered.

And I want to do it again as soon as possible.

Axel's thrusts slow to gentle nudges as he eases me down from my high, moving more slowly until he stills. His shoulders tremble as he presses a shaking kiss to my lips.

"You are…," he breathes. "God, you look perfect with my knot buried inside you, Gabrielle."

I wriggle against him experimentally, but I'm very much not going anywhere until he softens.

My smile breaks across my face, starting slow and growing until I'm beaming.

Axel kisses the corner of my turned-up lips, before he wraps his arms around me. I yelp when he rolls us over, keeping me tight against him until I'm sprawled over him, my legs wrapped around his hips, his knot still tight and hard inside me.

"Oh." Wriggling, I test this new position. Axel looks like a Greek God as he lies back, his hands still tracing over my body as if he can't stop touching me. I take in the light pelt of golden hair covering the thick muscles of his chest and stomach.

Is that a *ten-pack*? Is that even a thing?

Seeing Axel like this, all delicious and warm and messy, makes my pussy give another little clench.

"I like this position," I decide. "We'll do this next."

Axel chokes. "Next?"

Leaning down, I rub my nose against his, my heart feeling light, and full, and happy.

"Unless you think you're not up to it," I tease. "How old are you, anyway?"

He snaps his teeth at me playfully. "I'm thirty-two, and I'm pretty sure I can fuck you more than enough to keep you happy, little spoon."

My squeal trails off into laughter as he rolls us back over, his mouth moving across my skin until my laughter trails off into trembling moans.

More than enough, indeed.

I'm humming as I pour myself a glass of water in the kitchen. My hair trails down my back in tangled wet curls that will be a nightmare to comb out, but I can't bring myself to move as I sit down at the table, sipping from my glass.

It turns out that Axel is very focused on keeping his promises.

Very focused.

My fingers tangle in the edges of Axel's shirt, stolen from his closet. It smells even better than his sweatshirt.

"Well, hello there."

Swivelling, I offer a smile to Nate. His eyes linger on my bare feet, traveling up my body and taking in Axel's shirt with a low whistle.

"You look damn good in our clothes, kitten."

He strolls forward, dropping into the chair next to me and leaning his arm across the back of my chair. Then he pauses, his nostrils flaring as he takes a deep breath. He turns to face me, his eyes lingering on my face.

"All okay?" he asks.

I swallow down my embarrassment that apparently, everyone in this apartment will know that Axel and I did the dirty because I'm smothered in his scent.

"Fine," I whisper, then I panic that it sounds like I hated it. "It was lovely."

"Just lovely?"

"He was… very good."

Oh, god. Blood rushes to my face as Nate throws his head back with a roar of laughter.

"Very good?" he leans in closer, his scent tickling at my nose. "Surely we can do better than that, kitten."

I'm saved from further blushes by Axel entering the kitchen. He swats Nate on the back of the head as he passes, his hand cupping the back of my neck possessively as he gives me a long, lingering kiss.

"Well, now I'm jealous," Nate complains good-naturedly before he jumps up.

"Wait – I actually meant to show you something."

Axel strokes his thumb across my skin as Nate comes skidding back in, holding an envelope.

"Juan sent the photos over," he says, wiggling his eyebrows. "I wanted to wait for you before we looked at them."

My heart thumps inside my chest as I stare at the innocuous brown envelope. It feels like ages ago instead of just a few days, memories of Nate and I curled up on the bed making my chest pound.

Nate slides it open, spreading the photos out on the table as Axel and I both lean in to get a closer look.

My breath catches in my throat.

"Oh, I want this one on my wall." Nate picks up a photo of the two of us. My back is curled over Nate's arm and he's holding me up, my leg hitched around his waist.

But it's his face that holds my attention. He's staring at me like I'm the only thing in his world.

His eyes darken when he looks down at me.

"See that?" he says quietly. "This is how I always feel when I look at you."

His hand curls around mine, squeezing gently as I try to catch my breath.

This pack is going to be the death of me. I'm feeling more and more certain about it.

I disappear to get ready for work, but not before sliding the photo off the table.

Nate says nothing, but I can feel his eyes on me as I leave. Back in my room, I place the photo of us carefully in my nest, positioning it until I'm happy.

Then I peel off Axel's shirt, adding it to my little pile of alpha-scented clothing.

Hmm. I prod it at, irritation prickling at me.

Not right.

Not *enough*.

Poking my tongue into the side of my cheek, I push away the feeling as I get ready.

Just a typical omega thing. It doesn't *mean* anything.

CHAPTER THIRTY-NINE
HUDSON

After fucking up the fourth order of the day, Veronica not-so-gently shoves me away from the serving station. Wincing, I rub at my arm as she pins me with a dark look.

"What the hell is the matter with you?" she asks. "You've been off your game all damn day."

"Sorry."

I don't offer her an explanation even as I throw down my serving towel, stalking away and pushing open the back door to grab a deep breath of fresh air.

Truth is, I can't concentrate. Gabrielle is in there, working her ass off at her station and determinedly avoiding my gaze.

It... hurts. And I get it completely.

I was so eager to have her here, close and safe, that it didn't even occur to me that I'm her boss, for fucks' sake.

I don't blame her for keeping a distance, even though all I want to do is eat up the space between us, stop her from having to scrub those massive fucking pots that are almost as big as she is, and make sure everyone in this restaurant knows exactly who I belong to.

But I'm guessing that's exactly what she doesn't want.

So I stay outside, trying to clear my head of sweet, hot butterscotch until the lunch rush is over, mulling over the best way to approach this. When I finally stick my head back inside, Gabrielle's shift is over.

"She went up a while back," Veronica says shortly as she passes me. "Don't think she was feeling well."

That's all I need to bolt from the kitchen area. Too impatient to wait for the elevator, my steps pound up the stairs. I'll give her all the space she wants at work, but I'm not staying away if she's not well.

"Gabrielle?" I call when my feet hit the wooden slats of the hall.

Listening, I pick up the faintest noise from the living room. When I push the door open, I'm not prepared in any way for a weeping omega, Gabrielle's face tear-stained as she covers it with her hands.

I'm dropping down next to her in a second, my hands reaching for her automatically, the need to comfort her hitting me like a brick. When she flinches, a low whine in her throat, I stop short, my heart in my mouth.

"Gabrielle," I coax. "Sweetheart. What's the matter?"

Sniffling, she opens her hands. A cascade of colored cards scatter to the floor, one landing near me with a familiar unpleasant scent.

Coconut.

The scent cards sent to us by the Center lie around us like an omission of guilt. Gabrielle turns her face away from me.

"Is this why you asked me to stay?" she asks numbly. "Any omega will do, right? Pick one out of a catalog, pick one out of a dumpster. What's the difference?"

Her shaky words hit me straight in the chest.

"No, baby, no." I reach for her but she recoils, her blue eyes darker than I've ever seen them.

"I was so stupid," she whispers. "Nothing this good can be real."

I swear my heart cracks in two. Panic trails up my throat in a blaze as she starts to climb to her feet.

"Gabrielle." I grab for her hand, and when she tugs it away, I refuse to let go.

"Listen to me," I beg. She shakes her head.

"I need to go. I need to get my things."

"This is not what you think. We did contact the Center a while back – but it wasn't right for us."

She's not listening to me, her shoulders tight as she withdraws into herself, her eyes closing off to me like blinds over a window.

"Stop it," she says, louder now. "I don't need to hear it!"

"You do!" My temper snapping, I get in her way as she makes for the door.

"None of them were you!" My voice rises in a shout, and she stops.

"None of them held a candle to you," I say, more softly now that she's actually looking at me.

"We didn't expect to find you, Gabrielle. You are not a substitute."

Her eyes search my face, so fucking vulnerable that my fists clench at my side with the desperate need to draw her closer.

"So what am I?" she asks quietly. "What am I to you, Hudson?"

"Everything," I say hoarsely. "You're everything."

Her hand reaches up to rub at her chest, the uncertainty in her eyes gutting me. I don't ever want her to feel uncertain about us. I risk taking a step closer.

"I am in love with you, Gabrielle."

The words slip out so easily. Her mouth opens, and I hold up a hand.

"Let me get this out," I beg. "You're ours. But we're yours, too. All of us."

She looks at the floor. "But you haven't…"

The vulnerability in her words hits me hard.

"I didn't want you to feel pressured," I explain, feeling like an absolute moron. "I'm your *boss*, Gabrielle. That gives us a dimension that the others don't have. I never wanted you to feel that your job here was at risk."

Relief burns through my chest as realization lights up her face. She chews on her lip, her eyes falling on the cards.

"They don't mean anything," I murmur. "I swear to God, Gabby. You are the only one we want. The only one *I* want."

I wait, as thoughts flit across her face too quickly for me to read.

I'm completely unprepared when she steps forward, her body brushing against mine as she tips her face up. We watch each other, our breathing mingling together.

"Don't you break my heart, Hudson Reyne," she whispers. "Don't you dare."

And then she kisses me.

Her hands slide up and around my neck as my arms wrap around her, holding her to me as she explores my mouth gently, her soft touch almost undoing me.

When I can't take any more, my arms tighten and she squeaks into my mouth as I take over, tasting the hint of butterscotch on her lips, drinking her down like the finest wine.

She's better than any wine I've ever tasted.

The cards crunch under our feet as we stumble backwards, my arms shooting out to protect her back from slamming into the wall. The shelf next to us wobbles, a plant crashing to the ground as I hoist her up, her legs wrapping around my waist.

"Don't hold back," she begs. "No more, Hudson."

"No more."

It takes seconds for me to undo the row of buttons lining her shirt, Gabrielle's fingers stumbling as she does the same to me. Holding her up with one arm, I help her push the sleeves down, shrugging off one arm at a time before my mouth drops, tracing a line up her skin.

Now that I'm tasting her, touching her, for the first time?

It's better than I ever imagined.

She cries out as my teeth bite gently into her throat, leaving just the edge of my teeth. Nowhere near enough for a bitemark, a bonding bite, but a promise.

Mine.

Her hands roam across my chest, raking across my nipples as I tug the band holding her braid free, releasing her hair in a cloud of black waves that falls around us.

"I want you to grow old with me."

Her eyes widen at my words.

"I want to sit with you, with our pack, on a porch somewhere. Cook good food. Drink wine. Laugh. And I want to watch you every single day, until this beautiful hair turns silver. And you'll be just as beautiful to me, Gabrielle."

"Every day," she whispers. Her eyes mist, a single tear dropping that I kiss away.

"Every day." It's a vow.

Our hands fumble, clumsy in our desperation as we explore each other.

She breaks away from our kiss, her pupils blown wide.

"Nest," she breathes. "Take me to the nest, Hudson."

I turn, keeping her locked around me as I stride out of the room and down the hall. It feels like an eternity as I carry her into her room, past her bed and to the double doors, pushing them open with a single hand.

When I lay her gently down on a midnight blue blanket, she reaches for me again. "*Closer.*"

It takes me a second to kick off my shoes before I ease

down on top of her, her arms tugging at me until every inch of us is pressed together.

Her scent rises up, hot, sweet, fucking delicious butter-scotch that makes my mouth water with need.

"Are you sure?" I ask, kissing her neck.

"Yes." It's a moan, her hands pushing at my trousers until I help her, unbuckling my belt, slipping free the button and shucking them down.

She's doing the same, and my eyes take her in, her pale skin shining underneath the dim lighting.

"You're a fucking vision," I breathe. "Fuck, Gabrielle." Helpless to resist, I go to her. Her legs wrap around me, my cock nudging against her opening as we both inhale sharply.

"No more waiting," she whispers. "Now."

As I push into the soft, enticing heat of her, my eyes slide shut.

"Gabrielle," I groan. She lifts her hips, helping me to push until I'm buried to the hilt deep inside her. We both let out a long breath.

It feels like coming home.

My thrusts start out slow, wanting to keep the sensation for as long as possible, never wanting it to end. But she bucks, demands for more falling from her lips until we're moving together in a sinuous rhythm, our bodies undulating, the air heavy with our mingled scents.

I want her smothered in my scent. I want to brand it into her skin so everyone knows that she's *ours*.

"Never letting you go."

She shakes her head, dark curls dancing around her head like a halo as she cries out. Her pussy clenches, muscles tightening around my cock, my knot pulsing at the base and demanding entry *right fucking now*.

Her body opens for me, my knot slipping securely inside her as I pulse, our releases hitting at the same time. She keens, my name on her lips more than enough to finish me off with a roar as I empty myself inside her, her greedy pussy wringing every single drop until I'm completely spent.

Bodies shining with a light sheen of sweat, we're both breathing heavily when I lean in, stealing a lazy kiss from her lips.

"I've wanted this since the first day we met," I admit. "I never thought... shit, Gabrielle. You're everything I never even knew I wanted."

She buries her face in my neck, and we stay wrapped up in each other, whispering promises and future memories until well after my knot has loosened inside her.

And when she falls asleep, nestled securely in my arms, I take a deep breath, my eyes on the stars glowing across her ceiling.

"You're my forever, Gabrielle."

CHAPTER FORTY
GABRIELLE

I wake up to not one, but *two* alphas in my nest. Hudson's chest presses up against my back, soft breathing punctuating the air in huffs that send hairs flying across the top of my head. His arm is banded possessively around my waist, keeping us pressed together.

With a smile, I stretch my toes out.

"Good morning," I whisper to Axel. He gives me a sweet smile back, his green eyes flashing.

"Couldn't sleep," he admits. "Wanted you."

My heart melts when he leans in, giving me a soft kiss.

"Is this okay?" he asks. "That I came in?"

I nod. "More than okay."

I feel secure with them both here. I'd feel better, though, if Nate and Cade were here too. Chewing on the inside of my mouth, I contemplate how I could bring that up in conversation.

Needy omega alert.

The thoughts that have been bandying around my mind since my trip to the museum with Cade kick back in.

Axel raises an eyebrow at me as I stare at him. "What is it?"

Wetting my lips, I ask. "Do you know what Cade is into?"

Axel grins boyishly. "I do. You should ask him yourself, though."

"I did," I mutter. "He said I wouldn't… like it."

Axel's face grows serious. "It's not that bad. He just worries. He'd never hurt you, little spoon."

That just makes it even more mysterious.

It plays on my mind throughout breakfast, Axel making me coffee in my now favorite cup and Hudson cooking the most delicious stack of pancakes I've ever tasted.

But there's no sign of Cade or Nate.

"Nate is on a job," Axel tells me. "They wanted a sunrise shot. But Cade's in his office."

I glance at the clock. We're all up early. "Already?"

Hudson puts yet another pancake on my plate. "He's a workaholic. He'll do a few hours here and then head to his actual office in the city."

Frowning, I glance at the stack of pancakes. Making a decision, I jump up, getting a plate out and loading it up, adding some fruit on the side. Hudson and Axel watch me, Hudson snatching away the salt cellar when I reach for it by mistake.

"We need to label those," I grumble, heading out of the kitchen to the sound of his laughter.

The nerves kick in as I make my way down the hall.

Maybe he's busy.

Maybe he doesn't like pancakes.

Maybe he doesn't want to see me.

I've just about talked myself out of the whole thing when I arrive at his door. The dark wood feels imposing, and I swallow, shifting from foot to foot as I debate it.

Holding my breath, I tap lightly on the door.

Maybe he won't even hear—

"Come in."

Well, shit.

My hand curls around the door handle, pushing it down as I keep the plate steady in my hand.

"Gabrielle?"

I keep my focus on the plate as his footsteps round the desk ahead of me, soft thumps on the thick blue carpet before a finger tips up my chin. Cade stares down at me, already impeccably dressed for the day in a smart gray suit, his navy tie neatly tied against his white shirt.

His full lips twist up. "Is this for me?" he asks, pointing to the plate.

When I nod, he takes the plate from me, setting it down on the desk behind him. "Thank you."

"Did you… ah… make these?"

Amusement flickers in my chest. "You're safe. Hudson made them. You have him to thank for there not being a shaking of salt over the top."

I fidget in place as he takes his seat behind the desk.

"Do you want to sit down?" he asks me gently. Nodding, I fold myself into a seat and clasp my hands together, watching as he takes a bite.

"Delicious. As always."

I feel a little like a naughty schoolgirl, swinging my legs as I wait for him to finish eating.

When the plate is empty, he puts it to one side with a smile. "Thank you," he says earnestly. "Time got away from me this morning. What can I help you with?"

I bite my lip. He seems so formal here. Nothing like the Cade I saw at the gallery, and my nerve wavers, before it disappears entirely.

"It doesn't matter." I jump up from my seat, my feet turning towards the door. "I'm sorry to have disturbed you."

He catches me as my hand reaches for the handle, his hand wrapping around mine. "Wait."

I wait, feeling the brush of his suit against the soft cotton of my tee.

"Talk to me," he coaxes. "Something is bothering you?"

His hand threads with mine as he tangles our fingers together. The movement relaxes me, recognizing that this alpha is still *Cade*, even in his suit and tie.

I draw on my courage.

"I wanted to continue our conversation." Turning to face him, I keep my eyes planted firmly on his chest. "From the other night?"

"Oh?"

I swallow. "About your… tastes."

Cade stills, stiffening against me. "I see."

Turning, he leads me back to his desk, prompting me to take a seat with his hand nudging my shoulder. Settling himself in his leather chair, he leans back, icy blue eyes watching me keenly as I struggle for the right words.

Giving up, I just throw it out. "I want to know," I blurt out. "What you like. To see if I might like it too."

Smooth, Gabrielle. Real smooth.

He hesitates, and my mouth kicks into autopilot.

"You said you don't like pain. Axel told me the same thing. So it can't be that bad, Cade. And I just… I want to know you. All of you."

He swallows, a hand lifting to his tie and smoothing it down.

"I see you, Cade." It's almost a whisper, dropping into the air between us. "I don't want you to hold back."

His eyes move to mine, holding my gaze as he pushes his chair back slightly.

"All right." Victory leaps in my chest. "But if you don't like it, if this makes you feel uncomfortable, I need you to tell me, Gabrielle. Do you understand?"

Trying to hide my suddenly shaky hands, I nod.

"I need your words," he says gently.

"Y-yes. I understand."

"Good girl."

The moniker makes me shiver, my stomach flipping as Cade gestures me towards him.

When I move around the desk, he positions me directly in front of him, his hands holding my hips in place as he maneuvers me between his legs. They feel like a brand through the thin material of my shorts, and as he slips them around my body to cup my ass, my body sways.

My breathing is already embarrassingly loud in the quiet of his office, the uncertainty sending a thrill through my entire body as I stare at him, waiting for instructions.

He continues to caress me, his hands moving slowly over my cheeks, massaging and tugging at the skin until I'm biting my lip in an effort not to move.

The front of my shorts grows damp with my arousal, Cade's nostrils flaring as he picks up on my changed scent.

Then he stops, leaning back in his chair and watching me for a moment, his eyes gleaming. I'm shaking under his gaze, my hands by my sides.

"Take this off, please." He points to my camisole.

With trembling hands, I peel it over my head and drop it to the side. My nipples peak in the cool morning air, my breasts completely on display for him as he traces every inch with his gaze.

When he leans forward, I can't suppress a gasp as he runs his finger straight through the dampness at the front of my shorts, rubbing exactly where I need him to through the thin silk.

"Cade." It's a moan, and he pulls back immediately.

"Now these."

I hook my fingers into the waistband, sliding them down until they pool at my feet.

My slick is coming through so strongly that I can feel wetness on the inside of my thighs.

"Excellent," Cade praises, his voice deeper than I've ever heard it. "You're doing so well, Gabrielle."

His praise makes me stand a little straighter. I'm desperate to please him.

"I have a lot of work to do today," he murmurs. "You're awfully distracting."

Work?

"I'll need to make sure you can't distract me too much."

When he begins to undo his tie, my vision short-circuits, various scenarios running through my head. My abdomen flutters as he runs a soothing hand across it.

"Turn around." He watches me closely, his words a dare, almost as if he thinks I won't do it.

Turning slowly, I push my arms behind my back, holding them together.

"Very good." There's a smile in his voice as I feel the brush of silk, Cade wrapping his tie around my wrists and securing it until I can barely pull them apart.

The sensation is… disconcerting. And exciting.

His hand slides up my back, pushing me forwards until my cheek is pressed to the cool oiled wood of his desk. My breathing heaves, the papers next to me fluttering.

Hands wrap around the inside of my thighs, tugging them apart until I'm completely exposed to Cade, fully at his mercy as I lie bound over his desk.

Holy *fuck*. Why did we wait so long to do this?

I wait, the anticipation only building with each silent breath Cade takes. I hear him settle back in his chair, the squeak of the wheels as he rolls forward.

Hot lips press against my spine, and my back bows.

"Down," Cade says firmly, and I push my head back against the desk.

A finger swirls through my slick, gathering up the fluids on my thigh.

There's a sucking noise. "You taste so sweet, Gabrielle. Did you know that?"

When I shake my head, I jump as his finger appears, rubbing along my lips. "Taste it."

My pulse spikes as I open my mouth and he slips his finger inside, my tongue swirling, taking in the taste of my own slick.

It's as sweet as he promised it would be, and my eyes meet his as I wrap my tongue around his finger and suck.

His hands smooth back my hair. "Fuck, you're doing well, baby."

My body shifts as he pulls away from me.

There's silence before his fingers suddenly slide into me without warning. My legs nearly buckle as I cry out, shaking as he curls them inside me.

"Shhh," he murmurs. "Now, then. You're going to do exactly as you're told, Gabrielle. And if you're a good girl...," he pauses. "You'll be rewarded."

My choppy breathing turns ragged as he pulls his fingers away, hooking them around my wrist and urging me upright.

He turns me back to him, his eyes scanning mine.

"This okay?"

I'm a shaking, trembling, shivering mess of an omega, but I want more.

Cade sits back in his chair, spreading his legs wide. "On your knees."

I blink, the gruff command taking a second to work through the hazy arousal in my brain.

My knees hit the carpet with a dull thud, my tied hands making me clumsy, and anticipation makes my heart pound as I stare up at Cade.

His hand moves down, unbuckling his belt.

"Have you ever sucked a cock, sweetheart?" he asks conversationally, like we're discussing the weather.

"No." My eyes are wide, focused on his hands undoing

the buttons on his suit trousers and revealing a hint of black boxers.

"Good. I want to be your first. But we're not doing that right now."

"We're – we're not?"

Confused, aroused and slightly nervous, I watch as he tugs himself free. His cock juts out proudly, level with my eyes, giving me a brief glance at his already swollen knot.

It's bigger than I thought it would be, and I gulp.

I've got this. It's not like it's the first time I've taken a knot. Axel and Hudson have given me a pretty thorough introduction.

As I work through my little internal pep talk, Cade's strong wrist wraps around his length, flexing as he drags his hand slowly up and down, pumping his cock once, twice.

"You're going to take me in your mouth, Gabrielle."

Another push of slick, making me a little worried about the condition of his carpet when we're done here.

"And you're going to stay still until I say you can move."

"Stay still?"

He nods. "You're going to hold me in your mouth like a good girl, and you are not going to move. Understand?"

Curious, I nod. Cade pushes himself forward until his length brushes my lips. His other hand gathers my hair behind me, holding my head still.

"Open."

His cock pushes into my open mouth, silk over stone as he gently presses my head forwards.

"That's it," he coaxes. "Taking my cock so well, Gabrielle."

My eyes water as he nudges the back of my throat, my mouth coming to a stop with his knot firm against my lips.

"Such a good omega," Cade praises. I stare up at him, my cheeks flushed, my hands still tight behind my back.

Completely at his mercy.

His hand cups my throat gently.

"One day," he tells me, his fingers massaging the skin. "I'm going to knot this beautiful mouth. Keep you locked onto me, my cum flowing down your throat."

My groan vibrates against his shaft, and he grins.

"You like that?"

His hand moves to my head, stroking over my hair as I work on my breathing.

"Remember what I said. Stay still, and you'll be rewarded."

I blink heavy eyes as his hand pulls away. His scent, his taste is everywhere, my mouth full as I watch him. Saliva begins to collect in my mouth, the urge to suck, to move, growing.

Breathing deeply, I force myself to stay still.

Cade looks down, an approving look on his face when his phone rings.

My eyes widen when he answers it, leaning back in his chair.

"Morning, Mikhail."

I twitch, and he leans down, continuing his stroking over my hair as I sit, listening to him discuss a complicated legal case with a colleague.

Holding his cock in my mouth.

As the minutes tick on, I adjust to his weight, laying my head on his thigh to keep my balance. The more he ignores me, the more that clenching, clawing need in my stomach grows, begging for him to touch me.

Every part of my body feels sensitive, my cheeks growing warm as he finishes his call and starts typing something on his laptop.

He doesn't look down, and eventually, I start to relax, my body softening and my mind drifting into a half-doze.

In a weird way, this feels… comforting?

I jolt when Cade's hand cups my breast. He rolls my nipple between his fingers, tugging it gently.

"Still awake down there?" he teases, a curve to his eyebrow and a satisfied smile twisting up his mouth.

My affirmation is muffled.

"You've done very well, Gabrielle. I think you enjoyed this. Am I right?"

My nipple twists, and I moan.

"I bet you're soaking wet," he growls. "All ready to be filled."

My pussy flutters in a definite *yes*.

Cade slides himself out of my mouth, and I work the kink out of my jaw as he lifts me. My legs threaten to fold as he bends me again over his desk, his hands petting down my back.

I let out a half-scream, half-moan when his cock rubs up and down my slit, gathering slick.

When he pushes inside me, burying himself to the hilt, my legs lose control completely, and his hands curl under my thighs, holding my feet off the ground as he stays still.

"*Cade.*"

"Flawless," he murmurs. "I've been dreaming about you for days, Gabrielle." He thrusts, my whimper swallowed against his desk.

"The reality is better than I ever imagined."

I wait for him to speed up, but Cade maintains his steady thrusting, never changing his pace until I'm mewling, twisting underneath him.

"Please!"

I'll beg. I'll do anything, as long as he speeds the fuck up. He pauses, leaning forward to speak quietly in my ear.

"The next time we do this, I want you to sit on my lap, hold my cock inside that perfect pussy. Will you do that for me, Gabrielle? I think the others would enjoy the show.

Maybe I'll take you to the theater, and you can sit and watch the show with my cock filling your cunt."

My mind threatens to short-circuit at the image he presents. Fuck, I think I might have a little voyeurism kink because the idea of having to sit completely still, holding his cock between my legs in the middle of a packed theatre makes me *melt*.

"Anything," I answer desperately. "Anything, Cade."

He slaps my ass, the movement pushing me forward, and then finally, he moves.

With my hands still bound, all I can do is lie there, each thrust drawing a cry from my throat as Cade takes me, owns every single inch of my body.

And he's a fucking master at it.

My release crests over me, wave after wave clenching my muscles around him tightly. Cade thrusts one last time, his knot effortlessly pushing through my entrance as I open up to him, sealing us together as Cade groans, hot pulses of seed jetting into me as I gasp for breath.

"We're making a mess of your desk," I say finally, when my vision clears.

"Worth it, baby."

My body is mush. I'm never moving again.

I barely feel Cade undoing my binding, lifting me in some sort of complicated move that positions me on his lap with my back pressed against his clothed chest, my legs spread and his knot nestled inside me, the position spreading me open for anyone who walks in to see me. His breathing seesaws in my ear as I lay back, my head lolling against his neck.

He kisses my damp skin, hands tracing my arms, running up and down, paying particular attention to my wrists.

"How do you feel?" he asks, smoothing my hair back. I manage to muster up the strength for a slight grunt. He's fucked the energy right out of me.

"I need a nap," I manage to squeeze out. "Will you... come with me? To the nest?"

His hands clench on my hips, and I ready myself for rejection.

"Of course," he says softly. "Give it a few minutes."

He strokes my hair, lulling me into a light doze until his knot finally loosens enough for us to break apart. I expect him to put me down, but Cade lifts me instead, carrying me out of his office and down the hall.

Exhausted and sated, I'm very happy to do nothing but rub my cheek against his chest.

I'm asleep by the time we get there.

But when I wake up, that peaceful feeling is well and truly shattered.

Chapter Forty-One
Nate

B ounding up the steps to *Il Piacere*, I'm whistling when there's a prickle of warning at the back of my neck.

Turning, I frown as I slow, my head turning to glance up and down the street.

It's the same feeling I had in the parking lot, when I was with Gabrielle.

When nothing jumps out, I slowly make my way inside.

Maybe I have a stalker.

Wouldn't be the first time an overzealous fan started following me around. I'll have to be more careful for a while, especially if I've got Gabrielle with me.

Meaning to talk to Cade, I stick my head inside his office when I get upstairs.

The scent hits me like a fist to my stomach, the scattered papers giving me an idea of what's been happening here this morning. Slamming the door shut, I take deep breaths, trying to force my suddenly half-mast cock to take a chill pill.

My feet turn towards Gabrielle's room, but I pull myself back. If she's with Cade, she probably won't welcome me sticking my nose in.

A little ball of envy forms in my stomach.

I've been tied up for the last few days, pulled all over the city on jobs, so I haven't really had chance to spend much time with our omega. I've had to rely on updates from my pack, and they are not the best at communicating.

As if on cue, my phone goes off in my pocket.

Cade: Nest. Code red.

I stare at the message.

Code red?

We have codes now?

Another message comes through.

Cade: Hurry.

My feet start moving before my brain has fully caught up, and I push through Gabrielle's door without asking.

The doors to her nest are open, and Cade spins to me.

I take in his disheveled state.

Cade is *never* disheveled.

His unbuttoned shirt is half-tucked in, his trousers loosened at the top.

"Why are you only wearing one shoe?"

Even his hair looks wild, sticking up all over the place as though he's run his hands through it a dozen times. He barely looks down, gesturing towards the doors of Gabrielle's nest.

"Get in here," he snaps.

Then I hear the sniffle, and I take off, pushing past him as I find an omega-shaped lump of blankets in the center of her nest.

Cade follows me in, and I give him the side-eye, mouthing *what's going on?*

He shrugs helplessly, his eyes panicked.

I clear my throat. "Kitten?"

The blankets freeze, and I hear a muffled sob.

"Nate?" Gabrielle's voice shakes.

"It's me. Won't you come out?"

The blankets move in a pattern that I'm pretty sure means she's shaking her head.

Cade crouches next to me. "Whatever is wrong with the nest, we can fix it."

Another sniffle.

"What's wrong with the nest?" I cast my eyes around, taking in the little touches that Gabrielle has made since our shopping trip. Her glow in the dark stars are scattered right across the ceiling, the floor covered in various blankets, cushions.

The blankets move, and finally, Gabrielle appears, tear-stained with her hair everywhere.

She looks adorable. And frustrated.

"It's a stupid omega thing," she grumbles.

Pounding footsteps appear down the hall, and Hudson skids to a stop in the doorway.

"Sweetheart?" he asks, his gaze landing on Gabrielle. "What is it?"

She chews on her lip. "Is everyone coming?"

Cade gives her an apologetic smile. "I thought it might help you feel better."

She nods slowly. "It… it does, actually. Thank you."

"So what can we do?" I ask her softly. "Whatever you need."

Her eyes skitter past me.

"Axel will be here soon," Cade says, tossing his phone down. "He was at the gym."

She covers her face with her hands.

"I'm sorry. I'm a mess. I don't know what's going on with me."

"You have instincts," I say gently. "There's nothing wrong with that. It comes with the territory, kitten."

She throws up her hands. "But I don't know anything about them!"

We exchange looks. "You've never learned?" Cade asks her. "About what it means to be an omega?"

She shakes her head. "It wasn't something I thought about when I was with my mom. And after... well, the OC taught us their own crap, nothing about any of this."

They wouldn't have.

"What about the Center? They have open sessions for omegas to go and ask—,"

She's already shaking her head, face paling as she recoils back into her blankets. "I don't want to go there."

"Steady," I soothe, my hand out. "You won't go anywhere you don't want to, kitten. In this case, we'll just have to follow your lead, okay? So tell us what you need."

The urge to soothe her draws my voice low, the barest edge of a bark making her sit up straight.

"*Ineedyourscents.*"

I blink at the blurted words. "Our scents?"

Her fingers twist into the blanket. "There's a little in here, but it's not enough. I woke up and I had... a bit of a meltdown."

"Okay." Hudson settles himself down. "So how do we do this?"

She bites her lip. "Could I... have some of your clothes?"

Her eyes slide to Axel's hoodie.

"And maybe a pillow?" she asks forlornly.

Oh, kitten.

"You can have whatever you want," I say firmly. "Come on."

Holding out my hand, I pull her up when she takes it. Keeping her hand wrapped around mine, I walk her out of the nest and to my room, Cade and Hudson trailing behind us.

Pushing open my door, I spread my arm out. "What

would you prefer?" I ask her. "Want me to pick, or would you rather choose?"

Her fingers twitch as she steps forward.

"I can choose?" she asks me hesitantly.

"Anything you like. Whatever will make you feel better."

I watch as Gabrielle sidles in, glancing over her shoulder at us uncertainly before she moves over to the bed and picks up my pillow. She sniffs at it, before she wraps her arms around it and turns to me.

"This one?"

"Definitely." I lean down, picking up the shirt I wore yesterday. "What about this?"

Her eyes lock onto it, and she makes grabby hands that makes someone cough behind me to hide their laugh.

We follow her from room to room, watching in growing amusement as Gabrielle slowly disappears under a pile of pillows and clothing that she refuses to hand over. Axel arrives during the mayhem, his eyes widening as he tries to follow what's going on, Cade hissing to him under his breath.

Finally, we all collapse in Gabrielle's nest, watching her happily stack various shirts, hoodies and pillows around the room. She throws herself back, burying herself in them with a deep inhale.

"I feel better now," she says, her head popping up.

Bracing myself, I broach the subject that's been floating around my head as I've watched her.

"Kitten," I say carefully. "Do you think... you might be close to your heat?"

The room goes silent, everyone swiveling towards Gabrielle, whose ears have turned bright pink.

"It... might be possible," she says guardedly. "I don't know."

"I thought you needed to be Bonded to have a heat?" Hudson asks.

She turns to face him. "Bonded?"

She looks so uncertain that my chest aches, realization of exactly how little knowledge she has hitting us all. When I open my arms to her, she scrambles into them without hesitation, curling up on my lap like a cat.

Cade picks up the explanation.

"Have you ever heard of a mating bond?"

"Like a bitemark?"

Cade shakes his head. "A mating bond is something else. Bitemarks are what the Omega Compound used to keep omegas in line when they were sent to packs. The omega would be bitten, but it was one-sided. It was about control, nothing else."

Gabrielle is nodding. "I know. That's why I never wanted one."

Cade gives her an understanding smile. "We've learned a lot in the last few years, sweetheart. A true mating bond is something that grows naturally between a pack and an omega over time, if they're meant to be together."

Her mouth forms the words silently, taking it in. "So no bitemark?"

"There is, but it's the final step during heats. Natural heats, not forced ones. And it goes both ways – so you would wear our mark, but we would wear yours, too."

There's a flash of interest on her face. "So you think this is what's happening to me."

Cade nods. "You're showing some clear signs of the mating bond growing. Nesting, our clothes, wanting us close… it comes with the territory."

Her eyes slide to mine, a frown burrowing between those blue eyes.

"So… this. How I feel, how you feel – it's just biology?"

There's a resounding set of *absolutely not* and *hell no* coming from my pack, but I keep my eyes on our omega.

"Let me make this clear," I say firmly. "You are *it* for us, Gabrielle. We choose you. The mating bond is growing because of that, not despite it. If we weren't completely comfortable with each other, if something wasn't right, you wouldn't be feeling this way now."

She looks so vulnerable, it shreds my heart into pieces.

"I only ever wanted to choose," she whispers. "I've never had a choice before, Nate."

I cup her cheek, wanting nothing more than to close the distance between us.

"So choose us, kitten. *Choose us.*"

CHAPTER FORTY-TWO
GABRIELLE

My hands plunge into the hot water as I attack a pot crusted with some kind of sauce like it's my own personal nemesis. Bubbles fly everywhere, hitting me in the face and making me splutter.

I'm not focusing tonight. The conversation I had with the pack earlier keeps bouncing around my head, giving me thoughts and feelings that I'm really not sure about.

For five years, I've done everything possible to avoid getting a bitemark, to avoid being tied to an alpha forever.

But now... now there's the Reyne pack. Hudson, with his quiet care from the moment he found me. Axel with his protective nature and quiet sense of humor. Nate's joyful exuberance for *life* and making me feel that way too. And Cade, with his domineering personality that hides someone who likes to watch shooting stars and link our fingers together.

And now there's this mating bond, too.

I frown. I've never heard of it before.

Maybe I should go to the Omega Center. Find out more about who I am. I feel like I'm stumbling around in the dark, and I *hate* it.

I'm actually contemplating it when Veronica stomps up behind me.

"Gabby," she calls. "We'll need you out front tonight."

I swear my whole body shrivels up in horror as I swivel around. "Out... out the front?" I croak.

Veronica gives me a weird look. "That an issue? Hudson told me you had experience, and Daniela and Eve both called in sick, so we're short staffed."

Swallowing, I wipe sweaty hands on my apron. I don't want to let Hudson down when he's been so good to me. Plus, I don't want anyone to think I'm getting special treatment.

Forcing a smile, I nod. "Of course I'll do it."

Veronica sags in relief. "Thank fuck for that. Grab a uniform from the storeroom and head out."

After donning a close fitting black dress that skims my hips, falling loosely to my knees, and slipping into a pair of black pumps someone left behind, I pin my hair back and nervously make my way towards the main restaurant.

This is fine. I do have experience, even if it's more around serving sweaty beers and sloppy joes to even sweatier men.

Fine dining when you're as clumsy as I am could go pretty fucking wrong.

I try not to panic as Hudson briefs the front of house team, running through the table plan and key guests. My mind wanders, caught up in paranoid fantasies of dropping plates of food, breaking glasses and generally doing anything to embarrass the alpha who appears in front of me with a soft smile and a wink.

He whistles in a low tone, making a show of casting his eyes over my dress.

The heat in his eyes makes my stomach curl. "You," he says as he finishes his lazy perusal, "are a vision, Gabrielle."

My cheeks color as I tuck my hair back, fussing with the clip. "Thank you."

He slips a hand out to cup my cheek briefly, leaning in to look at me intently. "I mean it," he breathes. "You take my breath away, you know."

My own laugh is breathless, hiding the clench in my abdomen, the pulse of needy want that appears in response to the low timbre of his voice.

"Stop it," I murmur, biting my lip to hide my smile. "I won't be able to concentrate."

"I hope not. I'll be spending the whole evening thinking of you in that dress."

Now I'm grinning, the heat in my stomach growing to an inferno. "And what, exactly, will you be imagining?"

The teasing words slip out effortlessly, and Hudson's own smile grows in delight.

He takes a step closer, his arms caging me against the bar as he leans in to whisper in my ear.

"My hands slipping under that dress." His voice deepens, the faintest gravel in his tone making me lean back, my neck falling to the side as his lips barely trace my skin.

"You'd be so soft," he whispers. "Soft, and hot, and ready for me. Wouldn't you, sweetheart?"

My eyes widen as I stare at him.

"I'd trace that greedy little pussy of yours with my tongue. Make sure it's good and wet before I turn you over, spreading you open, nice and wide for me so I can see that pretty pink slit weep for my knot."

My slick appears with a gush, soaking my underwear so quickly that my knees wobble. Hudson's arm wraps around my waist as he pulls me in closer, his nostrils flaring as he picks up the change in my scent. I bite back a whine, my eyes falling shut as I feel his hard length press into me through the soft material of my dress.

"When we finish," he murmurs in my ear. "I'm taking

you to bed, Gabrielle. We'll see if you can be just as much of a *good girl* for me as you were for Cade."

My moan is swallowed as he captures my lips, his hands sliding up to cup my face as I fold into his body.

"There we go," he says huskily. "That's what I'll be imagining."

I blink at him dazedly when he steps back, the noise of the bar filtering back in and making me cast my eyes around in a panic.

"I… I should…,"

Hudson cocks his head to the side, a smirk on his lips. "Should what?"

Bastard, making me say it.

"You know what," I whisper-hiss. "I can't work like this!"

He laughs, his whole head thrown back before he steps in, dropping a kiss on my forehead.

"No touching," he warns as he steps back. "I want you needy when I take you tonight."

My legs wobble as I make my way to the staff bathroom, collapsing onto the lid of the toilet as my hands press to my flushed cheeks. My hands twitch as I bite my lip, the need Hudson stoked inside me pulling my hand down before I yank it back.

The anticipation might just kill me.

And if that doesn't, Hudson following through on his whispered words definitely will.

I shoulder my way through the kitchen entrance, carrying my plates over to my station and adding them to the teetering stacks piling up everywhere.

Mattias, another one of the servers, weaves around me,

adding his own. We both watch warily as it totters, then stabilizes.

He whistles. "Don't envy whoever's doing that later."

I bite my lip. Possibly me.

Eh, I'll worry about it later. We both head back out, and I smooth down my apron, checking for any stains as I move over to where Veronica is frowning over a folder.

She glances up, her frazzled eyes landing on me.

"You've done well tonight. I'm giving you the ten in the corner – big group, great tips. You alright with that?"

I nod. Despite my fears, working out front has been fun. I've had the odd side glance, but mainly people have been nothing but polite. And turns out the clientele here are far, far tidier than they ever were at the diner.

"Great. Matt will help you when it's time to serve. Off you go."

I take off, weaving my way in between tables in a way that's starting to feel more natural. I wonder briefly if Hudson would give me some more shifts out here. I enjoy my work, but it's kind of nice to be away from my little corner for a bit.

I spot the group Veronica was talking about, and plaster on my best customer service smile, pulling my notepad from my pocket and poising to take their order.

"Good evening, and welcome to *Il Piacere*. Have you decided what you might like to drink?"

The group chatters amongst themselves, and a woman glances up at me with a smile. She's beautiful, flaming red hair flowing down her back in loose curls and the prettiest amber eyes. I blink. An *omega*.

She tugs on the sleeve of the man next to her. "Rogue? What shall we order?"

The man turns around, pushing dark hair away from his face as vivid, forest green eyes land on mine. Recognition steals my breath away, my vision tightening to a single point.

I *know* those eyes.

I've had nightmares about those eyes.

The alpha – *Rogue* - gives me a cursory smile, glancing down at his companion with a much softer look. "Whatever you want. You choose."

Another alpha chimes in from across the table, his tone teasing. "Little omega, you know Rogue doesn't drink wine."

I know that *voice*.

She laughs, a husky, happy sound that sets my teeth on edge. Rogue just smiles, his arm curled protectively around the back of the omega's chair.

I'm frozen to the spot, my heart thundering inside my chest. My silence gets the omega's attention, and she grins.

"I'm so sorry! We're really bad at this. Could we have a few minutes?"

When I stay silent, her brow furrows, her eyes scanning me. Rogue picks up on the sudden atmosphere, turning his attention to me. I can't breathe. A combination of thick, cloying fear is choking up my throat. But right underneath that is pure, unfiltered anger.

"Are you alright?" the omega asks anxiously, but I ignore her.

Rogue frowns. "Do I know you?"

God. This man sentenced me to endure the hell of the Omega Compound, and he doesn't even *remember* me.

I wet my dry lips. "You… you lied to me."

Conversation around the table dies down, all eyes landing on me.

He frowns. "I'm sorry… have we met before?"

I turn my gaze to the blue-eyed alpha behind him. "And you. You lied to me too." My voice breaks, and I hate it.

Rogue's eyes widen as he glances behind him and back to me. He pushes his seat back, half rising as I take a step back, my pad dangling uselessly from my shaking fingers.

"Gabrielle?" he tests. "Are you… Gabrielle?"

Any trace of laughter disappears from the blue-eyed alphas face, and he rises too, his mouth opening as he looks me up and down.

Rogue's hand reaches out, and I flinch. The omega sets her hand on his arm. "Rogue."

He covers her hand with his, giving her a reassuring look.

It makes me want to vomit.

Does she know that he used to hand over omegas to the OC? Hand us over like cattle, to be bruised and starved and broken?

To be locked in the dark like *animals*?

He looks at me, pushing his hand back through his hair. "I… we've been looking for you for a long time. I wanted to make sure you were okay, but you disappeared after the OC closed down."

His words bounce around my head. He wanted to make sure I was *okay*?

My words are wooden. "Did you know, I was found a day after everyone else was released?"

Rogue's brows draw down. Next to him, the omega watches me, her eyes huge and sympathetic.

I don't want her pity.

He shakes his head slowly, his hand reaching out to rub at his chest.

"I was locked in a hole in the ground," I whisper. "They left me there. The guards left, and then the cavalry arrived, but nobody looked for me."

Nails scrabbling, whining, crying, screaming. Begging.
Nothing.
Nobody was coming.

And when I finally saw the sun again, hands lifting me out of the hole I'd spent days in, asking me questions, promising me things, I ran. Shaky on my feet, but I ran straight through the gates of the Omega Compound. And I didn't look back.

I'd learned my lesson about promises, and *safety*.

The omega gasps, and someone else gets to their feet.

Rogue's actions have defined my entire adult life. I begged him not to take us to the OC. I *begged* him.

And I was right.

Numbness steals the feeling from my hands, my heart, my entire body as I stand there and look him in the eye. "You… you promised me I would be *safe*."

Rogue looks as though he's been punched in the stomach. "Gabrielle… shit, I don't know what to say. I'm so—,"

I hold up a shaking hand. "I don't want your apology."

I never imagined that I'd see any of the alphas who took me from the traffickers and delivered me straight into the hands of the OC again. I've had nightmares about them, night after night of waking up, sweating and shaking, iron in my mouth as I choke back nausea.

And now they're here in front of me, I feel nothing at all.

Sudden heat breaks through the cold of my skin, Hudson's scent wrapping itself around me as he places his hand on my shoulder.

"Gabrielle?"

The sudden shame curls in my stomach. I've embarrassed him, his restaurant, in front of everyone. And for what?

Blinking back sudden tears, I turn away, pulling my shoulder from his touch and ducking past him. I weave through the tables blindly, tears starting to fall as I reach the main doors.

I need a minute. Just a minute, and then I'll go back and… my stomach clenches at the idea of apologizing to them. But I'll do it, if it smooths things over.

I'll explain to Hudson.

I just need a minute to pull myself together.

CHAPTER FORTY-THREE
CADE

My phone rings, the number for downstairs flashing across the screen.

"Yeah?" I ask, assuming it to be Hudson. But it's Veronica, her voice babbling down the phone in a tone I've never heard before.

Panic.

I make out shouting in the background, a crash.

Gabrielle's down there.

I'm flying down the hall, shouting for Axel and Nate as I throw myself down the stairs, hearing the commotion before I burst out of the stairwell door.

My eyes land straight on Hudson, his face darker than I've ever seen it as he lunges at someone. Others are holding him back, shouting things.

Jesus fucking *Christ*. What the hell is going on?

Axel and Nate arrive behind me, and Axel curses. "The fuck?"

We push our way past the full tables, everyone watching the drama unfolding avidly. Hudson is livid when I reach him, trying to reach the alpha in front of him.

There's no sign of Gabrielle anywhere. "Find her," I tell Axel.

Nate and I push ourselves between the two alphas. "Hudson. What's going on?"

Fucking hell, I've never seen him this angry. Hud is generally the most level-headed of us all.

"Ask him," he spits.

I turn, blinking when I realize who exactly Hudson is yelling at. "Rogue?"

Rogue Winter. Infamous for his father's role in destroying the Omega Creed for good. He looks blindsided, his hands up placatingly, but he doesn't say anything.

"Ask the fucker who delivered Gabrielle to the fucking Omega Compound."

My mind short-circuits. "You what?"

Rogue tries to explain, but my fist flies out before he gets a word in, and he rocks back.

Someone darts in front of me, and there are furious growls from all around us as the tension ratchets up by a good hundred degrees.

The omega darts between us as one of her alphas shouts, her face tight. "That's enough." She turns to Rogue. "You deserved that. You know you did."

He grunts, pushing at his nose. "Helluva shot."

Then she turns to me. "Rogue has spent the last five years trying to track Gabrielle down. To apologize, to try to put things right. He didn't *know*."

Hudson scoffs. "Bullshit. He knew enough."

"You're right. I did. But I didn't realize the extent of it." Rogue looks around, his eyes landing on the omega. "Not until we met Harper."

My heart hurts for Gabrielle. "She was *fifteen*."

Hudson snaps his teeth. "She's scared of the dark because of you, asshole."

Axel reappears, and I look for Gabrielle. He shakes his

head. "She's not here. She left."

Everyone stops. "She left?" Hudson repeated. "What do you mean, she left?"

Nate gives him a hard stare. "You tell us. You were here."

Hudson runs a hand over his face. "Shit. I wasn't thinking – where is she?"

Nate is already heading to the door. "I don't know, but I'm going to find her."

I stop Hudson from following. "Stay here, in case she comes back."

Rogue steps forward. "We can help."

His pack nods in agreement, but I shake my head. "Like hell you will."

The omega turns to me. "Don't be an idiot. They're professional trackers. If she's run off, they'll be able to find her."

I consider it for a second, my lips thinning. "Fine. But keep your distance if you see her."

We all move out, eyes and phones watching us go. Out in the street, we split up into groups, one of our pack and one of theirs. Rogue gets placed with me, and I fight back the instinct to snarl at him as we stalk down the street. My focus is on getting to Gabrielle as soon as fucking possible and bringing her home. I'd work with the devil himself if I had to.

We check every alleyway, every possible route that she might've taken if she came this way. There's no sign of her, no hint of her scent in the air. Frowning, I'm turning to Rogue, about to suggest we retrace our steps when we hear it.

Up ahead, tires squeal, the scent of burning rubber in the air. The air disappears from my lungs as a terrified scream rents through the air.

Gabrielle.

CHAPTER FORTY-FOUR
GABRIELLE

Storming along the street, I tuck my hands under my armpits for warmth, cursing myself for walking out of there without a jacket.

Hell, walking out of there at all. I should have stayed.

I really need to stop running away from things.

The fog of anger and upset starts to clear, helped along by the chill of the night air, and I take a deep breath. So I saw the alpha who took me from the traffickers and straight to the OC.

Maybe he didn't know. So many people didn't. Maybe he did. Does it matter?

More rational thoughts start to appear, until I'm chewing on my lip in agitation. I just left Hudson there to clean up my mess.

My throat thickens as I blink back tears. All I've brought this pack is trouble and issues to fix. Sniffing, I wipe my hand across my eyes to clear my vision.

The hair at the back of my neck stands up on end, and I slow my steps, my eyes flickering around me in the darkness. There's that damn feeling again. Except this time, without Nate by my side, in the dark of the evening, it feels more ominous. Closer.

My senses go on high alert as I walk past an alleyway, the shadows moving in a way that isn't normal. Glancing around, I look for possible help, but the street is deserted.

My mouth dries. *Stupid, stupid Gabrielle.*

I know what happens to lone omegas who don't pay attention.

Footsteps sound quietly behind me, and I run through my limited options.

But there's only one option. And it's what I do best.

I run.

Shouts ring out behind me. Footsteps pound along the sidewalk, drowned out by my shaking breaths. My feet slap against the stone as I put everything I have into running as fast as I possibly can.

I don't see the crater in the pavement until the heel of my stupid shoes catch in it, taking me down in a crash. They're on me before I can move, my terrified screech subdued by a stinking hand slapped over my mouth.

"You," someone snaps in my ear, "have been difficult to find, omega."

The familiarity of the voice makes my eyebrows crease, and I crane my head back to get a look at his face.

His weaselly, pointed face.

"What's a girl like you doing out here when you can be making money in there?"

Struggling, I try to push him off me, my bare feet scrabbling for purchase on the ground as I lose my shoes in my panic.

"I know some people who are very interested in meeting you," Elliot grunts. "Time to go."

"No!"

I suck in a breath to scream, but it flies out of me with a whoosh when his hand collides with my mouth.

"Mouthy bitch," he growls. "They'll soon train that out of you, don't you worry."

My vision spots, chest tightening until I'm wheezing in terror as a large van with blacked out windows reverses rapidly out of the alley in front of us. The doors slide open, revealing the dark space beyond.

If they get me in there, I'll be better off dead.

Twisting my head, I sink my teeth into the slimy bastard's hand. Elliot shouts, shoving me away, and I scramble to my feet, making a second run for it.

His feet pound after me, vile threats spilling out as he closes the distance between us. I try to push back my frantic sobs, pulling in the last of my breath.

And I scream with everything I have, until a hand twists into my hair, yanking me backwards so hard that my tailbone smacks into the concrete.

The beta drags me down the stones, agony radiating from my scalp as the pitch black emptiness of the van beckons.

Cade. Hudson. Axel. Nate.

They won't know what happened to me. They'll think I ran. That I *left* them.

My fingers wrap around the metal foot of a trash can, and I hold on for dear life as Elliot tries to yank me off. I can feel my hair coming away, his hand digging into my shoulder with long nails, digging so deeply into my skin I know it's cut through.

The low growl makes the beta pause.

A tiny piece of hope lights up my chest. Someone is here.

But the alpha who charges past me, his teeth bared in fury, is the last person I expected to see.

Rogue Winter whips out his hand, grabbing Elliot by the neck and slamming him to the floor. The tyres of the van squeal as they drive off, leaving him to it. Gasping, I curl myself tighter around the trash can, clinging on as voices reach me.

"Gabrielle!"

I jerk, my head snapping towards Cade. Then I'm untangling myself with a shuddering sob, trying to get to my feet as he reaches me, his hands cupping my face and running panicked hands down my arms, checking for injuries.

"Cade."

His arms wrap around me, lifting my torn up feet from the ground.

"I thought we lost you," he says frantically, his eyes still looking over me. "Sweetheart, your feet—,"

"I'm sorry," I gasp, needing to get it out. "I'm sorry I ran. Hudson – I made a scene in the restaurant and I couldn't..."

Cade presses his lips together, his blue eyes warmer than I've ever seen them. "None of us care about that," he says, tucking me in closer to him. "How many times do we have to tell you? All we care about is you. Everything else is just background noise, sweetheart."

Shuddering, I bury my nose into his chest. My muscles relax, the tension leaking out of them as I breathe him in.

"Gabrielle?"

I lift my head at the voice behind us. Rogue stands a respectful distance away, his eyes averted.

"Are you alright?" he asks roughly.

Swallowing, I nod. "I... I'm okay."

As I say it, my body starts to shake. My shoulder burns a little, and there's a pain in my ankle that tells me it's definitely twisted. My scalp burns from where he yanked my hair so hard, I'm fairly sure I might have a bald patch or three.

Cade pulls me impossibly closer, tucking himself around me protectively. "We need to get you to a doctor."

I shake my head, biting back the pain. "No doctors. I just want to go home, Cade. Please."

He searches my face skeptically, but he nods. "We'll take a look at you at home."

Summoning the last remaining shred of courage left in my stomach, I look to Rogue. "Thank you."

He dips his head. "You don't need to thank me for this."

"That's twice now."

"Let's not make it a habit." Rogue's mouth twitches, just the slightest bit. "I'll call the authorities, get this piece of crap taken care of. Will you let my pack know? Harper will be worried."

As Cade nods, I glance towards Elliot, who's starting to stir from the sucker punch Rogue gave him. My hands tighten around Cade's neck. "Put me down for a minute?"

Reluctantly, he lets me slide down his body, his hands gently gripping my hips as I catch my balance. Then I make my way over to Elliot, snatching up my heel on the way.

The scream he makes when I smash it into his dick is the most satisfying sound I've ever heard.

Rogue and Cade both look at me, slightly wide-eyed, when I make my way back to them. Cade catches me, pulling me into him as I nestle in.

"Now we can go home."

CHAPTER FORTY-FIVE
NATE

I wake up with a start, my chest thundering as I glance down at the sleeping omega beside me. Gabrielle stirs, a sleepy grumble furrowing her brow as she rolls over into Hudson, nudging into him as his arm wraps around her. Cade is on Hudson's other side, Axel's light breathing behind me telling me everyone is fast asleep.

I don't blame them. None of us got much sleep last night after Cade brought Gabrielle home, bruised and sprained and hurt. Axel nearly charged back out to get to the piece of shit that attacked her, but our omega wanted us all close.

So here we are, tucked up in her nest. Lying back, I try to calm the swirling emotions in my chest before they wake the rest of my pack up.

Fuck. If anything had happened to her, we wouldn't have known. Without a bitemark, we can't pick up on her emotions the way the rest of us can.

Axel stirs. "Nate," he mumbles, "I can hear you thinking."

I turn to him, relieved to have someone awake to spill my thoughts to. "We need to make this official, Ax. I want my bitemark on her. I want to wear hers. I don't want to panic like we did last night ever again."

Hazy green eyes start to focus as I talk, and he nods. "Agreed."

The barest bones of a plan start to form in my head, and I grin at Axel as he squints at me suspiciously.

"It's too early for scheming, Nathaniel," he mutters.

I'm about to spill the beans when a hand sneaks its way across my stomach, closely followed by a warm bundle nestling into my side. Shelving my plan for later, I give my full attention to the sleepy omega blinking tired blue eyes at me. Deep bruises sit underneath, highlighting her restless night, and I frown as I gently rub my thumb across her cheek.

"Kitten," I murmur. "How are you feeling?"

She buries her face into my side without responding, and I stroke my hand through her hair, waiting for her to gather her thoughts.

"I've felt better," she admits. I'm glad she's opening up to us. The Gabrielle of a few weeks ago would have told us she was fine and carried on.

I trace careful fingers over the dressings covering her shoulder and she covers my hand with hers.

"I'm sore. And I didn't sleep well. But I'm here, with you, so I'm happy, Nate."

I frown at her. "You don't need to hide things from us."

She shakes her head. "I'm not. Actually – there's something I want to do today. Will you come with me?"

"Always." The word flies out with no hesitation.

Wherever she goes, I'll follow.

As we stand outside the entrance, I glance down at Gabrielle where she's tucked securely under my arm. There's a nervous look on her pale face as she looks up at the sign above our heads, declaring our location.

The Omega Center.

I hold her more firmly against me as she chews on her lip. "We don't have to go in." My voice is gentle. "There'll be other days, kitten."

"No." Despite her nerves, our omega is determined as she looks up at me. "I want to do this today. I don't want to hide anymore, Nate."

Her bravery makes my throat tighten. "All right. I'll follow your lead."

It takes a few minutes, but she takes a careful, hesitant step towards the entrance, her hand reaching back for mine. I squeeze her hand as I follow her up the steps and she rings the bell, showing our faces to the security cameras outside.

There's a buzz, and I push open the door, letting Gabrielle slip past me before closing it behind me. I've been here before, when we first started thinking about an omega. We came to a few sessions held especially for alpha packs to help us learn more about group dynamics.

I nudge her towards the luxurious reception desk, offering a casual smile to the omega manning it. Gabrielle shrinks into my side, but she clears her throat.

"Hello. I was hoping to speak to someone about... um. Well, everything omega-related, really."

She stumbles over her words, but the omega smiles, her fingers tapping at a keyboard. "Of course. Take a seat, and someone will be right out. Can I get you a coffee?"

Gabrielle perks up immediately. Caffeine is absolutely the way to her heart.

We're only left waiting for a few minutes before a door swings open opposite it. The omega that appears isn't someone I expected to see. Gabrielle pauses at my side, clearly recognizing her face.

Ava Grey. The omega responsible for taking down the

Omega Creed and the closure of the Compound. I know the Center is run by her pack, but I didn't expect to see her here.

"Hi," she says to Gabrielle with an easy smile. "I'm Ava. I heard you'd like to have a chat?"

Gabrielle stutters, her eyes looking to me desperately. "Um. Yes. Please."

Ava's smile is understanding, her eyes softening. "First time?"

Gabrielle nods, her hair falling in front of her face.

"Come on. We'll find a quiet corner to curl up in." Pausing, she scans me. "Would you prefer to talk in private?"

I don't take offense when Gabrielle's eyes flicker to mine guiltily. Lifting her hand, I press a kiss into her palm.

"I'll be waiting," I promise. "Right here if you need me."

Ava gestures to the receptionist. "Megan will get you anything you need."

When Gabrielle tenses, I shake my head, making sure to move to the furthest seat away from the omega at the front desk as I sit, stretching my legs out. "I'm good, thank you."

Ava's face turns more focused, her eyes moving between us. "I see."

Gabrielle peeks over her shoulder as Ava leads her out, and I give her an encouraging smile.

I just hope she finds what she's looking for.

CHAPTER FORTY-SIX
GABRIELLE

I expected an office, but I'm surprised when Ava leads us into a bright, airy sitting room instead. Several deep couches frame a low wooden coffee table, and the room is filled with cushions, blankets and throws.

She waves a hand at my wide eyes. "This building is about omegas first. We do whatever we can to feel comfortable."

Sinking into a deep blue velvet couch, I pick up a cushion, hugging it to my chest. "This helps," I admit.

Ava settles herself down opposite me, curling up and tugging a blanket over her. "So," she begins. Her voice low, soothing, but my palms still start to sweat as she looks me over, her eyes lingering on the graze on my forehead. "Where would you like to begin?"

Pushing my hair back, I sit up straight, my fingers twisting in the pillow.

This is the issue. I have no idea where to begin.

When the silence stretches on, Ava purses her lips, a look of concentration on her face. "Do you mind if I ask how old you are?"

Well, that's an easy place to start. "Twenty."

She pauses. "You were in the OC, then?"

Vivid images parade across my mind. "I was." My fists clench. "I got out of there as soon as I could."

She frowns. "I was part of the group that went in to help settle the omegas, but I don't remember you. Have we met before?"

Darkness. Scrabbling, screaming, empty.

My nails dig into the soft material underneath me as I force out a shaking breath. "I was in the hole. They found me the day after everyone else was processed."

Ava pales, her hand flying up to cover her mouth as she looks at me, horror etched into her face as she searches for words.

"Gabrielle," she drops her face down. "I – I'm so sorry. I should have -there was so much happening—,"

I wave my hand, not wanting to delve into the details of my nightmares. "It's done. I got out."

Eventually.

Ava blinks. "Gabrielle," she says slowly, leaning forward. "Trauma like that doesn't just go away. It lingers, sticks to your soul like tar. Trust me, I know."

"I didn't realize this was a therapy session," I say weakly, avoiding her eyes.

"It's not. But we do have trained counselors that you can talk to, when you're ready. I think you may find it more useful than you realize."

Letting out a huge breath, I nod, staring down at my hands. I'm not ready for that. Not yet. But… maybe one day, I'll be able to talk about it properly.

"Now, then," Ava says crisply. "On to omega business."

She smiles at me, the corners of her mouth tipping up. "What would you like to know?"

I meet her eyes. "Everything."

When Ava and I exit her sitting-room-slash-office, Nate looks up from the magazine he's flipping through and pushes himself to his feet. He comes to me, his hands cupping my face and checking me over.

"Okay?" he asks roughly, and I nod, my fingers closing around his as I smile.

"It was good," I admit, and I'm not lying.

I feel much more informed about my own biology now than I did a few hours ago. Even though everything feels a little overwhelming.

Ava lays her hand on my arm. "Did you still want a tour?"

I nod, wordlessly turning to Nate, my eyes lifted pleadingly. He tucks a strand of hair behind my ear.

"I'll go and get some lunch. Are you hungry?"

On cue, my stomach growls, and he quirks his eyebrow at me. "Can't have you going hungry, kitten. I'll get us some sandwiches so you can eat whenever you're ready. Take your time."

Ava and I watch him leave and she turns to me, her eyes blinking mischievously. "That," she points out, "is the look of an alpha who is head over heels."

I try and hide my pleasure at her words, my stomach flipping over. "How do you know?"

"Gabrielle," she says patiently. "Not many alphas will sit in a waiting room for three hours and then volunteer for more."

"I- oh." I color. "So, that's a good sign that we might be... developing the mating bond?"

Ava's arm brushes against mine as we head to another part of the building. "Definitely."

I watch as she enters a security code, and she catches my wary look.

"Only omegas have access to this section," she explains. "Even my own pack isn't permitted here. We have dedicated spaces where alphas and omegas can meet and spend time together, but this section is sacred. All omegas have the code so they can come and go as they please."

I can't stop looking around as we move into a huge atrium, the ceiling high above us dangling with hundreds of bulbs in different lengths. More couches, large pillows, bean-bags – every kind of comfortable seating is scattered around, mixed in with shelves of books and long tables with coffee machines and snacks. A handful of omegas are curled up in corners, their eyes flicking to us and back to their books, completely relaxed.

"Wow," I mutter, and Ava laughs. "Not what you expected?"

My throat suddenly burns, and I shake my head tightly, my hand wrapping around the skin at the base of my throat. "Not exactly. I… I was so scared of this place. I thought it would just be more of the same, so when they tried to tell me, I didn't listen."

I could have been here the whole time. Warm, and safe, and settled. Cared for, the way these omegas look, well fed and happy.

Instead of starving, scraping my way through life, surviving on the bare minimum and living on the streets in between shitty little apartments and scummy landlords who didn't always understand the word 'no'.

Ava squeezes my hand. "I'm so sorry, Gabrielle," she says softly. "I don't know your story, but I hope you know that these doors are always open to you, whatever happens next. We never turn away an omega who needs us."

I nod, tucking away her words. I won't forget them.

I won't make the same mistake again.

We stroll down a hallway, and I glance to my right.

There's some sort of session happening, a group of omegas sitting around and talking animatedly.

"That's our Bonding class," Ava says, amusement in her voice. "It's rather popular."

"Do all omegas match with alphas when they come here?"

Ava's buoyant smile fades. "No. Some omegas... they don't want anything to do with the alpha population. They prefer to stay here. We have longer-term living facilities upstairs, and if and when they're ready, we support them to adjust to an independent life outside."

Someone pushes a door open in front of us, a younger omega bouncing through.

"Ava!" she cries, laughing. "I've lost them again."

I glance at Ava, who's biting her lip to hide her grin. "Oh, no," she says dramatically. "We'll have to call Luc to come and find them. Again."

There's a bright, happy giggle from behind the omega, and a little boy darts out, running to Ava and wrapping his arms around her leg. He's closely followed by a little girl with shocking white hair and purple eyes, her hand slipping into the omegas as she watches us warily.

I catch my breath.

I can't remember the last time I saw a child, let alone two. With betas no longer able to have children, the population relied on omegas to hand their children over into a foster system that no longer exists, thanks to the Creed being abolished.

"You," Ava scolds good-naturedly, bending down and popping his nose, "are supposed to be good for Molly. Do I need to call your fathers?"

"Noo!" The boy looks shamefaced. "I wanted to see you."

Ava lifts him up, balancing him on her hip as she turns to face me. "And so you have. Leo, this is Gabrielle. Gabrielle, this little munchkin is Leo, and the other munchkin over there is Emery."

They both wave at me shyly before Leo turns and presses a kiss to Ava's cheek.

"Love you, mama."

I think my ovaries just simultaneously exploded. These kids are *adorable*.

Briefly, I wonder what it would be like to have a child with my pack. A little pang of longing hits me, but I shove it down. Far, far down. Like down to the seventh circle of hell down.

Down, girl. I am in no way, shape or form ready to have any little Reyne babies running around.

As Leo runs over to the omega, her eyes lift up, catching on mine.

Recognition steals my breath away, her eyes widening. We both blurt out at the same time.

"Gabrielle?"

"Molly?"

My legs weaken as she takes a step forward, her face breaking into a smile. "It is you!"

I let out an oomph as she hits my middle, her arms wrapping around me. There's a sniffle, and she pulls back, wiping her eyes.

"Where'd you go, Gabby?" she asks me. Her eyes search my face. "I never – you never came. I looked for you."

The shame curdles my stomach. "I never meant to leave you, Moll. I'm sorry."

She smiles. "It doesn't matter. I'm just happy to see you again. Are you staying? Can we talk?"

I hesitate. "I have to get back soon, but… I can come back? I mean, if you… if you want?"

"Yes!" She laughs as Emery tugs on her hand, a determined look on her face. "Please do."

She bends down to listen to whatever Emery is whispering in her ear. They both look at me, Emery hiding behind her hair as Molly straightens with a grin. "Emery would also like you to come back, so she can braid your hair. It's settled – you have to come back now."

A small, genuine smile touches my lips as Emery sticks her thumb into her mouth.

"Well, then," I say to the little girl. "In that case, I promise to come back."

Her smile feels all the sweeter for winning it.

Ava's hand touches my back. "Shall we go back now?"

Taking a final look at Molly, I nod. "I… I'm a little over-whelmed."

"It's to be expected," Ava reminds me as we start making our way back. "Your heat is coming. This time is for nesting and spending with your pack. Enjoy it, Gabrielle. Remember that a heat does not equal a bitemark – and you don't have to take that step if you're not comfortable with it."

I choke back the nausea rising up my throat. Ava saying it out loud makes it all too real.

My heat is coming.

Which means… I have a choice to make.

Ava has made it clear that there's a place for me here, if I want it. An opportunity to learn more about myself, to focus on my own personal growth and decide what it is I truly want. And then there are the pack of alphas who have shown me so much love and support that the idea of leaving them physically tears at my chest.

But… what if we only feel this way because we were forced into a situation none of us saw coming? Given a little space, a little distance to clear our heads… would we still feel the same way?

Even the thought of pulling away from them makes the back of my throat ache. Nate picks up on my mood immediately, his eyes anxiously scanning me as he pulls me close and I bury my face in his chest, breathing him in.

How have they become so *essential* to me so quickly?

"Home?" he suggests, his hand stroking down my back. Even that one word chokes me up even more, how easily he offers it.

There are only two things I've ever wished for. Looked up at shooting stars and squeezed my eyes shut.

The first? Choices. To make my own way, to not be restricted by my designation or trapped.

The second? A home.

Now, it feels like I have to choose between them. And the unfairness of it all has me crawling into Nate's lap in the car on the way back, losing myself in his scent as I try to gather my thoughts and he holds me silently, giving me the space to think as he strokes my hair.

When we get back, I brush off Axel's concerned face, Hudson's offer of food and Cade's frown, and I bury myself in the soothing comfort of my nest, wrapping myself up in blankets and tucking myself in until I have a truly uncanny resemblance to a burrito.

I'm fighting a losing battle with the blankets and suffocation is becoming a real risk when it's tugged off my face. I take a great, gasping gulp of air, my face bright red.

"Little spoon."

Cringing, I let my head fall back with a thud as Axel leans over me. "Can we just pretend you didn't have to untangle me from my own nest for a second?"

I am a *terrible* omega. I'd probably fail the classes at the Omega Center.

Axel carefully maneuvers his large body into the small space left available, thanks to my overzealous blanket-wrapping. Propping his head on his hand, his green eyes bore into me, and I squirm. "Talk to me, Gabrielle."

I would, except I don't know how to put what I'm feeling into words. How can I explain this to him in a way that makes sense?

Huffing, I throw my hand over my eyes. "Just ignore me. I'm having a moment."

"What kind of moment?"

I move my arm up a crack so I can see his face. "One where it feels like my axis just shifted, and now I don't know what to do."

I feel the moment his body stills. Voice hesitant, he waits for a moment. "About us?"

Something in his voice squeezes my heart. It sounds a lot like hurt.

The back of my throat starts to burn again. The last thing I ever want to do is hurt this pack, but I seem to be making a real mess of things.

"Maybe," I whisper. "It feels like I'm at a crossroads, Ax. For the first time in my whole life, I have choices, and that feels too important to ignore. But at the same time, it feels like there's no choice at all."

A crease appears in his forehead as he frowns, trying to follow my admittedly very warped logic. "Explain to me?"

Thinking it over, I let the words spill out. "When I was a kid, I always had to follow my mom. We moved around from shitty trailers to motel rooms, to pokey little apartments. Sometimes we'd crash on sofas because she didn't have the money to make rent."

His hand pushes at the blankets until he digs mine out and wraps his fingers around it.

"I always wanted to be able to make my own choices. I never had any kind of choice, and I never had a home. They were the only two things I ever wanted."

I blink, and a tear slips down my face.

"At the Omega Center today... it felt like I made the wrong choice. I chose to run, and I lost the support I could have had to find my own way. If I had, I wouldn't have to rely on you. I'm so dependent on all of you, Ax, and I hate it. You give me everything, and I don't give anything back because I have nothing to give."

I'm crying openly now, and Axel pulls and yanks at the blanket until he can lift me into his lap, wrapping his arms around me and holding me as I sob brokenly into his shoulder.

"You think you don't give us anything?"

His hoarse voice breaks me out of my pity party. Shrugging, I try to turn away, but he holds my chin gently. "Answer me," he coaxes.

"Well... no," I say honestly, frowning. "You've given me everything. A job, a home, a nest. What exactly am I bringing to this table?"

"I always wanted a home too," he admits. I stare up at him curiously. "My mom... she drank a lot. My dad wasn't around. He had an apartment in the city and pretty much left us to sort ourselves out."

My heart clenches as I imagine a little boy with bright green eyes, sitting in a lonely house.

"I understand how it feels," he continues. "But I also understand that a home isn't made of bricks and mortar, little spoon. Home is a feeling. It's safety, it's the people you love, it's arguing over who gets the last of Hudson's pancakes and Cade grumbling over coffee. And for a long time, this apartment... it hasn't felt like a home at all. We've all been too wrapped up in our own worlds, barely functioning as a pack."

He rolls me over, leaning in. "You gave me a home, Gabrielle. Because my home is wherever you are."

He brushes his lips against mine just barely. My head stretches from the pillow as I move to follow him, a noise of complaint pulling from my throat when he presses a kiss to my cheek and pulls back.

"Take some time," he tells me. "Think it all over. Take

the time to decide what you want. And it doesn't have to be one or the other, little spoon."

On that note, he leaves me, wandering back out and leaving me breathlessly turning over his words.

Sneaky, silver-tongued alpha with his beautiful words and butterfly kisses.

CHAPTER FORTY-SEVEN
NATE

My knee jiggles as I sit a little too casually in the living room. Gabrielle is across from me, curled up on Hudson's lap as she sleeps. Neither of us are even pretending to watch the documentary we put on to fill the silence, both of us completely focused on the rise and fall of her chest.

Cade is down the hall pretending to work in his office, Axel taking a brief break from our mutual omega-watching to have a shower.

All of us are staying close to home, because Gabrielle's heat could kick in at any time. Her scent has deepened over the last few days, the sweetness maturing into something a little tarter. She hasn't been able to work, the scent pulses erratically spiking from her enough to keep her within the confines of the apartment.

She's sleeping more restlessly, seeking us all out through the night until we're tugged into her nest. We've slept together for the last three nights, all of us rotating to be close to her.

We're trying desperately to meet her needs whilst still giving her the space to make a choice.

On whether or not she stays.

My agitation jumps, and Hudson glowers at me as she stirs. "Nate."

"Sorry." My fingers tap restlessly on the arm of the chair. "Hud... if she doesn't stay—,"

"I don't want to think about that," he interrupts. His hand strokes some hair away from her face, his own more serious than I've ever seen it. "We won't lose her, Nate."

"But her heat—,"

We've talked about it as a group, all of us facing the fact that we're a pack of alphas with an omega who is definitely coming into heat. Cade insisted that we address it, so we could understand what she wanted from us.

She wants us there for her heat. But no biting. No marking.

Nothing permanent. Not yet.

I just hope we can keep the promise we've made.

None of us have been through a heat, Gabrielle included. The literature Ava sent over from the Center gave us some idea, but ultimately, every heat goes a little differently.

One thing is clear though. Our hormones will be the ones in charge.

Sighing, I stand up. I can't sit still any longer. "Want a beer?"

I've barely made it through the living room door when Hudson growls, and a shot of pure, melted butterscotch hits my nose. My back snaps ramrod straight as I spin, my feet tripping as I cross the room to Gabrielle. Her eyelashes flutter, eyes still closed as I feel the heat beneath her forehead.

The fever is unmistakable.

"This is it." Hudson swallows, his eyes meeting mine.

I stroke her hair back, my fingers shaking as her scent floods the room. "Kitten?"

It takes her a few seconds to rouse, sweat already starting to bead on her forehead as her core temperature ratchets up.

A door bangs in the distance, footsteps flying down the hall before Cade appears next to me.

"It's here?" His voice is hoarse, the sweet scent of her only growing the longer we stand around.

I nod. We planned for this, but now that it's actually here, I'm more than a little petrified that we're going to completely fuck it up.

Cade squeezes my shoulder. "Okay. We've got this. We planned for it."

He bends down, scooping Gabrielle into his arms as her eyes flicker open. There's very little blue to be seen, her pupils blown as she arches her back. A deep sugary burst of pure omega slick hits all of us, and my cock stiffens behind my sweatpants.

"Where's Axel?" Cade barks.

I move ahead as we decamp towards Gabrielle's room. Her nest should be all set up in the exact way she wants, seeing as she's been rearranging pillows and various items of clothing for days now, but it wouldn't hurt to check first. I want her to feel completely comfortable in her space, nothing to detract from her first heat experience.

I raise my hand to bang on Axel's door as we move past, but the door yanks open. He has a towel wrapped around his waist, his hair soaking wet as he stares around wildly.

"Fuuck." His nose lifts, his pupils darkening. Wordlessly, he tugs the door shut behind him, falling in line next to Hudson.

I didn't know what to expect. But the slow haze of her perfume grows into a knowing, pulsing need in my stomach – to comfort, to protect, to *take*. And it's far, far stronger than I expected it to be. I slam the lid down on my own wants, but I don't know how long I can hold out before I fall headfirst into a rut.

Gabrielle starts to struggle as Cade shoulders his way

through the doors, her legs drawing up as she doubles over in his arms.

"Hurts," she gasps. Cade places her down and she immediately curls up into a ball, visibly shaking. My knees hit the floor next to her. "Kitten. Tell us what you need."

She turns desperate eyes to mine as she shudders, a low, drawn out whine pulling from her throat that pulls on my own instincts. "It *hurts*, Nate."

"I know," I speak gently, mindful of the need to be very careful with her emotions. "What do you want, baby?"

"You." She groans, her hands rubbing at her stomach, tugging limply at the shirt she's pilfered from one of us. It takes me seconds to nudge her frustrated hands out of the way and flick the little row of buttons open, displaying her skin for us.

Hudson flicks on a set of lights in the corner, bathing her in a warm, golden glow. Her breasts gleam in the dim light, dusky pink nipples peaked and ready. She tosses her head, her hand sliding down into the dark curls between her legs.

"Don't make me beg," she moans, and I pull my head out of my ass.

"Just takin' in the view, kitten."

Her hand grabs mine as she yanks it down to her pussy, making it very clear that viewing-only time is over. My fingers spear through her curls, catching her clit between my fingers and rolling it as she bucks, her hips lifting from the mattress.

She's so wet that my fingers keep slipping, her slick coming faster as the heat fugue deepens. She cries out as I keep flicking, pinching her little nub until she's writhing in front of me, broken sobs falling from her lips.

"Knot, Nate. Please."

Nothing will help an omega in heat aside from knotting. The foreplay helps, but it's the endgame that matters here. I spread her legs, shoving my sweatpants down and kicking them away as I line up to her entrance.

"Kitten." When she groans again, my hands grab her chin, making her face me. Sweat beads along her hairline, her eyes gradually focusing.

"That's right, kitten. I want you to know exactly whose cock is inside you." I thrust, trusting my body to know what she needs, and I'm rewarded when Gabrielle screams out my name.

"Again." I pull out completely, making her sob before I surge back in, finding the perfect rhythm as our bodies slap together. I know the others are there, their eyes all too focused on us and the scent of pure arousal thick throughout the nest, but nobody interferes.

This is our first time, and I'm not sharing her with anybody. This moment is just for us.

I push into her as far as she'll take me, her legs stretched wide and my knot nudging her entrance. When she tries to push back on me, I pull out one more time, and her eyes fly open. "Get back here."

It takes a bare second to flip her over, my hand smacking against her ass hard enough to leave a mark behind before I sink back inside, her perfect cunt clothing me like a damn glove.

"Fucking perfect, kitten," I growl. "Made for me. Made for my fucking knot inside this tight little pussy."

She can't move, her shaking elbows holding her up and my hands holding her thighs in the air as I fuck into her so hard we move across the mattress. Her pants and cries are like fucking music to my ears, the perfect arch of her back a red card to a bull, drawing me on to move faster, harder as I brand her from the inside out.

My release hits me like a fucking freight train, Gabrielle soaking me with her slick as I flood her pussy with my own fluids, both of us shuddering. My knots slides inside with ease, and I ease her hips down to the floor, my hands running up her back as she pants, her cheek pressed to the mattress.

"Made for me," I murmur. "For us, kitten. Can you feel my knot inside you?"

She moans, pushing herself into me as I roll us to the side, my knot secure inside her. "More."

I kiss her damp hair. "Not going anywhere for a minute, sweetheart."

My hand strokes down her front, dipping between her breasts and down her stomach, tugging at her curls and playing with her clit. The high from her orgasm doesn't last, her movements becoming more frantic as I play with her body.

"I can't wait to see you take all of our knots." My voice is husky, and she shivers as I nip at her ear. Her throat is so damn close, all that perfect, smooth skin made to sink my teeth into.

I close my mouth over it, and she shudders. "Bite."

"Not this time, baby. Remember?" She mewls in frustration, and my knot loosens enough for me to reluctantly disentangle our bodies.

I kiss her throat one more time. "One day you'll be ours completely. And we'll wait as long as it takes."

CHAPTER FORTY-EIGHT
GABRIELLE

My head is a haze of pure, blistering need as Nate's knot slides from me, his teeth withdrawing from my neck.

No. Need their bite.

When I growl, a pitiful imitation of theirs, Axel appears in front of me.

"Steady, little spoon," he murmurs. "We've got you."

Heat squares up against my back, the fresh, minty scent of Hudson cutting through the thick tang of our bodies. He draws my hair back as he laves my neck with his tongue, dropping gentle, nipping kisses that make me stretch towards him with complaining noises.

"Not *enough*."

"Not this time," Cade interrupts us, his tone leaving no question about who is ultimately in charge. "No bitemarks, Gabrielle. We made you a promise, and we're keeping it."

I huff, but the heat starts to crest again, that craving in my abdomen that clenches painfully, needing their bodies, their knots. I push myself back against Hudson, butting my head into his shoulder as his hands lightly trace my side.

Axel moves in closer, until I can't breathe without my

skin touching his chest. He nuzzles into me, his lips tracing mine before surging in with a kiss that feels scalding, sending flickers of want down my spine. Between them both, they begin stroking, touching my body, two sets of hands turning me to putty.

When Axel shifts down, I'm unprepared for him lifting my leg, jamming it over his shoulder as he buries his face in my slit. I'm covered in juices, mine and Nate's, but Ax doesn't care as he cleans away every trace, thoroughly fucking me with his tongue until Hudson is holding me still, his hand still playing with my nipples.

"Jesus," Hudson groans in my ear. "So damn perfect, sweetheart."

Axel makes a noise of agreement that vibrates through my body, pulling another gush of slick that he licks up with gusto. When he reappears, his face shines as he presses his mouth to mine, giving me a taste that feels like a delicious mixture of the three of us.

"We're going to do this together," Hudson breathes. He pulls my hair back, wrapping his hand around it and keeping my neck stretched. "I want to see your face as we fill you up. Deep breath, baby."

Oh, *fuck*.

Axel moves first, hitching my leg over his hip as he nudges against me, slowly stretching me out. With my hair wrapped around Hudson's hand, all I can do is breathe in and out as he pushes in an inch at a time, my body welcoming him. Once he's fully seated inside me, he pauses, his eyes flicking over his shoulder.

Hudson kisses my shoulder. "Breathe."

But all the air leaves my lungs as I feel him pushing at my back entrance, the mess we've made more than enough for him to sink in slowly, stretching me with a slight burn as Axel leans over, spreading my cheeks for him.

"Fucking hell," Hudson murmurs. "Watching my cock

disappear inside you is heaven. Taking me so well, baby. Such a good omega." His words make me twitch, easing his way as he pushes past a ring of muscle and bottoms out inside me.

The sensation of both of them filling me so completely, our pelvises pressed together, is enough to recede the vicious ache between my legs, and I groan in relief.

"That's it," Axel praises. "So good, little spoon. Holding us both so well inside you."

He flexes, his movements slower than Nate's as he withdraws and pushes back again. I'm unprepared for Hudson to do the same, my cracked groan cutting off as his hand cups my throat, pinning my head against him as they both move in tandem.

My words stutter in the air, broken phrases pulled from me as their movements pull me closer to the edge.

"More – yes – please – *faster*—"

Axel suddenly pushes himself up against me, his knot nudging, big and hard and fucking pulsating as it pushes inside me. "Shhh," he coaxes, his eyes on mine as he swivels his hips experimentally. "You're gonna take both of these knots, baby. Both of us."

Dizziness hits as I feel Hudson pushing slowly against me. My whine is pure need as I push back with the little movement they've afforded me, the change just enough to open me up for his knot to push in fully. I'm full of them, knots and scents and fluid, so much so that I can't work out where I end and they begin.

Our bodies stay still as they let me adjust, their mouths moving over me as my release comes over me like a wave, growing and growing before releasing in a slow crash that wipes us all out. Axel bellows, his head thrown back as he fills me, and Hudson's head drops to my shoulder as he reaches his climax.

Our shared breathing is harsh and choppy, and they both

nuzzle against me, their soothing hands stroking at me and making my eyes flutter closed. I think I doze off, woken when they both pull away, and Hudson presses a cold bottle to my lips. I gulp down a tiny bit of water before I push it away, shaking my head as another cramp hits me.

Jesus. I think this might actually be how I die. This is going to last for days.

My eyes flick around me, panic rising when I don't see him. My last alpha.

"Cade?" Even I wince at the high pitched whine in my voice.

I gasp when a hand curls around my throat from behind, and he tugs my face back towards him. He's a shadow in the dim lighting, his beautiful face dark as he presses a long, lingering kiss to my lips. His fingers massage my throat, his grip tight enough to send a pulse of excitement through me as I lick my lips.

"You're so beautiful when you're knotted, baby," he murmurs. "I nearly came in my hand just watching you."

The mental image, Cade stroking his cock as his pack take me and fill me with their knots, draws a low groan from my throat. "Cade. Please."

"Please, what?" he asks. His voice is completely level as he continues his tortuous massage, the need growing stronger the longer he refuses to touch me. I wiggle, and he stops completely. "Cade!"

"Mmmm." He nudges me onto my back, his body following as he lowers himself over me. In the darkness, he towers over me, his eyes hooded as he slowly presses himself against me, his body pushing mine into the mattress as his forearms cage my head. He's careful to keep most of his weight off me, but I'm well and truly pinned beneath him as he carefully tugs up one hand at a time, pinning them above my head and making my breasts push up into his chest.

"Such pretty tits you have, Gabrielle." His voice drops to almost a whisper, his lips ghosting along my ear as his hard, heavy cock presses into my stomach. "Can I fuck them?"

The scent of my slick flowing, the sudden mess beneath me, gives him an answer, and he laughs darkly. My core is screaming for him, my pussy fluttering with the need to be filled, and I push my hips up impatiently, trying to spread my legs.

Cade leans in, pressing his lips against my throat. "Here," he murmurs. "Here's where I want my bite. Where everyone can see it, and know exactly what pack you belong to."

I'm desperate to move, desperate for him to move, enough that I shove my hips up with all my might, a broken sob slipping from my lips. "I need you inside me."

He smiles against my lips. "Good girl," he purrs. "I like it when you tell me what you want."

His knee pushes my legs apart, his strong hand sliding down to hold me open, my knee pressed against the mattress as he finally pushes into me. My eyes roll back in my head as he thrusts. "*Yes.*"

This. I need this.

He keeps up the same, slow and steady pace, gradually stoking me to an inferno before he pauses, just for a second but long enough for me to thrash against him.

"Give me your knot," I demand hotly. "Now, Cade."

He grins, a sudden, savage thing in the darkness, before his pace increases until he's brutally thrusting into me, every one hitting the very core of me, inching me closer to an explosive release. His face remains over mine, his eyes watching every expression, every flicker on my face.

"Eyes on me," he demands, when they flutter closed. "I want to see your eyes when you come around my cock, Gabrielle."

His words push me to the edge, that wave building to a crescendo that might destroy me.

My scream is loud as fuck, Cade's name on my lips when his knot finally pushes in, sealing my pussy around his cock to hold his cum inside. Cade's loss of control is a beautiful thing, his whole body shaking as he drops his face to my neck, his hands releasing mine to stroke down my arm.

"Perfect," he groans hoarsely. "So perfect for me, Gabrielle."

I shudder again as little aftershocks clench my pussy muscles around him, hot and thick and full inside me.

Four days of this? It's too much.

But it's not enough.

I don't think I can live without this feeling.

CHAPTER FORTY-NINE
HUDSON

My eyes feel like they're filled with cement as I stagger into our kitchen, blinking at the bright winter sunshine blasting through the windows opposite the doorway.

Four days.

We've been in full blown heat mode for four days. I'm pretty sure my nuts have shriveled to the size of raisins, but, *Jesus*.

Worth it.

A groan sounds behind me, Nate stalking in on wobbly legs and making a beeline for the faucet. He doesn't waste time with glasses, instead sticking his head straight under the cold stream and taking huge gulps.

My tongue sticks to the roof of my mouth as I watch, but I take an extra four seconds to grab a glass before I fill it up and down it in one.

Then I refill and down it a second time.

Once I feel moderately more hydrated, I turn to Nate. He's slumped in a bar stool at the counter, his hair sticking out everywhere as he buries his face in his arms.

There's a light snore, and I jab him in the armpit as I walk past to flick on the coffee machine.

He bolts upright, his head swinging around. "I'm ready! I- oh."

Fighting back my snicker, I lean back against the counter. Truthfully, I'm not in much better shape. Four days of non-stop sex has wrung us all well and truly dry.

But Gabrielle's heat has finally broken, her sleep finally restful after days of snatched dozes quickly interrupted by spikes of need.

"Hud," Nate mutters. "I'm a broken man."

I pour him a coffee and slide it over, watching as his eyes light up and he dives on it.

"Make one for kitten," he grunts. "She'll need it."

True. Gabby is even more exhausted than we are. Making up a selection and adding Gabrielle's pink cup to the tray, I carefully balance it as I carry it to the nest. The post-heat scents smack me in the face as I nudge the doors open, and Axel groans as he sits up.

"Coffee," he rasps. I hand out the goods, leaving Cade and Gabrielle's for a moment, both of them still passed out from the final, frantic few hours before the heat finally simmered down.

Sliding down the wall next to Axel, I swig from my coffee as Nate stumbles back in, taking up a position next to me. "Tell me you feel as wrung out as I do, or I'm going to wonder about my stamina."

Axel just grunts, and I dip my head in a lazy nod. Getting coffee is probably the extent of my capabilities at the moment. Although I'll need to prepare some food for when Gabrielle wakes up. She's barely eaten or drank anything, just a few sips of water here and there and a tiny bit of fruit Cade practically forced down her neck.

Cade stirs, and I hand him his coffee when he shuffles

over. If anything he looks worse than we do, having taken on the brunt of Gabrielle's needs in the last day when the rest of us were starting to flag. His dark hair sticks up everywhere, the suave lawyer nowhere to be seen as he glugs the coffee down.

He places the cup carefully on the wooden shelf before he flops back down, his breathing slowing as he falls back asleep. Axel's head slides onto my shoulder, huffing noises sounding in my ear. When I glance over, Nate is passed out too, his mouth wide open as his head rests against the wall.

My lips twitch. Post-heat exhaustion is no joke, but I can't help but feel amused at the sight of them all, brought to their knees by a tiny little omega.

A sleepy murmur floats over to me, and I put my cup aside, clambering past Cade to where Gabrielle is yawning. Her eyes slide to me and away, a blush stealing over her cheeks.

"Hey now," I chastise lightly. "No embarrassment here, sweetheart. How are you feeling?"

She stretches. "I feel… good. A little ache, but nothing I can't handle."

She crawls into my lap without asking, and I take it as a positive sign as she nestles into me. When she catches sight of Ax and Nate against the wall, she blinks.

"Think you wore them out," I tease lightly. "You want a coffee? It should still be warm."

She makes grabby hands as I pass it to her, letting out a contented sigh as she drinks it. I stroke her hair, both of us lost in our own thoughts.

Although I wonder if they're actually pretty similar.

"Hud?"

I kiss the top of her head. "Mm?"

"What do we do now?" she whispers. "Now my heat is over?"

I think it over. "You mean, about… us?"

A worried look steals over her face, her eyebrows

scrunching. "It's like... the whole world was locked out, and it was just us. But now everything is pushing to come back in."

My hand smooths over her hair. "There's plenty of time for that. Right this second, all you need to think about is recovering. Heats are exhausting, and you haven't had much rest. Do you want me to run you a bath?"

She nods, but she's still chewing on her lip, her own little tell that she's stressing. I let it go as I leave her for a few minutes, running the tub until the mirror is steamed up and it's full of bubbles. She tries to argue with me, but I scoop her up anyway, carrying her into the room and settling her gently in the tub. She reclines with a sigh, her eyes closing as I grab the cloth and start to wash her arms. She starts. "What are you doing?"

"Taking care of you." I motion her forward and run the cloth over her back, noting the faint marks around the base from our hands. We weren't gentle, giving her exactly what she needed, but it's left a mark on her.

Although not the mark I would have wanted.

Her hand rises up to cover her throat. "We didn't—"

I shake my head firmly. "We promised, sweetheart."

Her nod is a little forlorn, and there's a pulse of hope in my chest. Now that the heat is over, everything a little clearer, I pray that Gabrielle will choose to stay with us.

That our pack will be her choice.

After coaxing her forward so I can wash her hair, I bundle her up in the lilac bath robe Nate ordered, slipping the matching fluffy socks onto her feet. She points her toes, admiring the knitted pattern. "Oh, these are lovely."

"Blame Nate," I admit. "We're all fairly useless at that sort of thing, but he's definitely got the knack."

I don't mention the something else that's waiting for her, carefully packed and stored in various boxes along the back wall of Nate's room. He can handle that conversation.

She protests as I set her down on her bed and pull out a comb. "You don't need to comb my hair for me!"

"But I want to." I carefully section her hair, gently tugging at the strands to not hurt her scalp. "Let me look after you, Gabby. I need it just as much as you do."

I catch her frown in the dressing table mirror opposite the bed. "I didn't think of it like that."

I kiss a patch of exposed skin at the base of her neck, enjoying the light shiver of her shoulders. "In this situation, *need* and *want* are the same thing. Stop overthinking."

She flushes. "Am I that obvious?"

I pause, my fingers running through the ends of her hair. "I know that part of you is frightened that all of this is just biology. That it's not real. What can I do to show you that's not true?"

Her eyes are damp when I glance up, our gazes meeting in the mirror.

"I don't know," she whispers. "It's hard to break the habit of a lifetime, Hudson."

I continue working the comb through her hair, thinking hard. This feels like a precipice. If I say the wrong thing, I could push her away from us.

Tossing the comb down, I climb off the bed, circling around to face Gabrielle, and dropping down to one knee. Her lip wobbles when I take her hands. "Hudson—,"

"I love you." My voice is firm, no hesitancy whatsoever. "I *love* you, Gabrielle. You belong here, with us. And we belong with you. So if you decide to leave, to make your own way, I will wait for you. I will wait, and if that means that I'm sitting, gray-haired, in a rocking chair with an empty one beside me on the porch I'm going to build for us sixty years from now, then I will still wait. For as long as you're ready, even if that means forever. I. Will. Wait."

Leaning in, my thumb wipes away the tears from her

cheeks. "The only one I want sitting in that chair beside us is you. You understand me?"

She stares at me, her mouth open and her eyes wide.

"And if you need to take some time for yourself...," I force the words out, even though it feels like I'm smashing my chest wide open from the inside, "then you take all the time you need. We'll be here. All of us."

My eyes move to where Cade is watching us, his eyes dark as he lingers in the doorway of her nest. He nods, slowly, a tic in his jaw that tells me how happy he is at the thought of her leaving us.

But we'll do it. Even if it kills us to let her go.

CHAPTER FIFTY
GABRIELLE

L ittle hands stroke through my hair, incredibly gentle as they brush through it. "Pretty."

I smile, my heart clenching. "You think so?"

Emery Grey circles back around, her unique purple eyes narrowed as she carefully considers my hair. Her eyes move to my outfit, a cute little dark red knitted number with thick woolen tights and gorgeous buttery brown ankle boots, courtesy of Nate and his inability to stop buying me things. The latest being a whole new wardrobe that we're still battling over, but items still keep moving from his room into mine.

She nods seriously, and Molly laughs from where she's watching us play hairdresser. "That's a big compliment, coming from Em."

I can tell. Ava's little girl is so serious, the complete opposite of her little brother, Leo. He's quick to laugh, where Emery is quiet, but no less adorable for it.

In fact, something about her tugs on my heartstrings. I was more than happy to come back to the Center, to spend time playing innocent games to make her smile the way she did when I last saw her.

My eyes slide to Molly, and I'm mindful not to move

my head and dislodge Emery's careful pinning with butterfly clips. "Moll? Do you ever think about leaving here?"

She cocks her head. "Well, sure. One day."

"You want a pack of your own?" I ask. It's a little strange, having this conversation with her. Molly was only eleven when we met, the youngest omega in history, according to Ava and the records she was able to retrieve from the OC archives. But now she's seventeen, and she's clearly thriving here.

It's both a knife to my chest and the biggest relief of my life. I tried so hard to protect her at the Compound, and in the end, she didn't need my help at all.

She shrugs. "Maybe. But I'd like to work with omegas. Ones like me, I mean, who transition early. I've been talking to Ava and Max about setting up a specialist unit."

Max. One of Ava's pack, I met him earlier. He'd rushed in with a hasty apology for being late, his red hair still pinned with evidence of Emery's hairdressing skills as he handed her over to Molly. He works on the other, more public side of the building, acting as the head of medical services for the omegas here.

My brows lift. "I think you'd be fantastic at that." My words are genuine. Molly's optimism still shines through, even after all these years. The OC didn't manage to destroy that, after all.

She lifts her shoulders in a self-deprecating shrug. "It's a while off yet. I'm more interested in you, and your pack."

My eyes drop to the floor. "They're not my pack."

She scoffs. "Anyone with eyes can see that they're yours, Gabby. It doesn't take a bitemark on your neck to prove it."

I can feel the heat in my cheeks. "I haven't decided yet."

"You don't want them?"

My stomach revolts. "No! It's not that. It's more... I always said I didn't want a pack. I wanted to make my own way. I don't want my whole identity to revolve around being a possession. I want to be more than that."

Molly's voice is gentle. "You can't do both?"

I swallow. "I don't know how," I confess. "In my head, it was always so clear. I wanted my own home, that I'd paid for. I wanted a job, a secure one, with enough money for me to pay bills and have a little bit extra. That doesn't exactly gel with the pack life."

She frowns. "Gabby… that feels an awful lot like basic survival. And I get that. We went through a shi- a *bad* time, and it makes sense that those are things you would want. But it sounds like you're holding out for the basics, when you have so much more than that waiting for you."

Her words are a direct hit to my chest.

"Wow," I choke. "You should definitely press ahead with that unit. They could use someone like you."

Because her words have me re-examining every thought, every decision I've been debating for weeks now.

Her cheeks crease. "You think so?"

"I know so."

Emery pats the top of my head, and I turn my face, trying to pull my thoughts together. "Am I a princess now?" I ask, and she tilts her head to the side, considering my question before she responds with a single nod.

"I feel very honored," I tell her seriously. Molly gives me a thumbs up behind her back.

As I'm leaving, my thoughts in tangled disarray, I push open the doors to the main Reception area and freeze when I spot a familiar face. Rogue Winter is perched gingerly in one of the Reception chairs, his size large enough that he looks at real risk of toppling over.

He glances over and pauses. Taking a deep breath, I cross the open space to where the chairs are set up, and he stands as I approach him.

"Gabrielle." He sounds taken aback. "I – ah – I'm meeting Luc for lunch. Ava's mate."

I nod, chewing on my lip. "I've just been to see Molly," I offer, and he smiles. "She's doing so well."

"She is." I hesitate, taking him in. This man has been the boogeyman in my nightmares for too many years now.

And maybe I was focusing on the wrong person.

"I'm sorry that I called you a liar," I offer. He looks shocked, his hand moving down his face as he shakes his head.

"It's me that owes you an apology, Gabrielle. And I've been waiting to make it for the last five years. When we found you, I genuinely thought we were doing the right thing in taking you there. My father was the Director, and we thought… well. Truthfully, I never gave it much thought, but I *should* have. I met my mate a few days after we dropped you off, and I knew then that I'd made the wrong call."

He looks down. "My decision cost you something that I can't fix. I know that. I've learned enough about how the Creed truly worked that I know that's not something that can ever be atoned for."

"It's done now," I tell him gently. "It's a part of my life that I'll never forget. But we can't change it. All we can do is look forward."

"You sound a lot like Harper." There's a smile in his voice.

"Well, she sounds very sensible."

We both smile. The lightness in my chest is genuine, a weight lifting from me.

I meant what I said to Rogue. I can't keep looking back and using my shitty life experiences to stop me from living the life I want.

I don't have it all worked out. I don't know what I want to do with my life. But I do know that I want Cade, Hudson, Ax and Nate with me.

I want to sit with them on a porch one day and watch the sunset.

I just need to tell them. I've been drowning for so long, I couldn't even see the light when it was offered. But no more.

No more.

CHAPTER FIFTY-ONE
GABRIELLE

When I get back to Il Piacere, I'm intercepted by a frazzled looking Veronica. "Gabrielle!"

I shift on my feet. I haven't been able to work since before my heat, but my first shift is on the schedule for tomorrow. "Hey, Veronica. I know I haven't been around–,"

She waves me off. "I don't care about that. I know you're back in tomorrow. This is about Hudson."

My panic is immediate. "What's wrong? Is he okay?"

"Oh, he's fine. Except he's moping around my kitchen like someone kicked his puppy. Do us all a favor, and put the poor man out of his misery. Nathaniel too. In fact, him first. That way, he'll stop distracting all the waitresses."

I bite down a laugh. I don't think Nate will ever stop distracting the waitresses.

I can't really blame them.

"I'm working on it," I promise, and her eyes light up in glee.

"Excellent. I can't wait to have a functioning head chef again."

My amusement dies off, replaced by nerves as I get into the elevator, putting in the code for upstairs. My hands shake as I press the buttons and the door closes, running through the speech I prepared on my way here.

Come on. You can do this. They're not going to say no now.

But my nerves surge when I call out, my feet sounding loudly on the wooden floors as I walk through the apartment.

There's... nobody here.

My nervous excitement deflates like a popped balloon.

I wasn't expecting there to be nobody home. But I check every room, popping my head into Cade's office, the kitchen, their bedrooms... but I'm alone.

This is fine. I can hold it until they get back.

But my resolve shatters when I walk into my bedroom and see the black envelope on my bed. My name is scrawled across it in looped silver handwriting.

I collapse onto the bed in a heap, staring at it in horror.

Maybe they've given up on me. Maybe *they've* left.

No. Don't be stupid. They wouldn't leave their home.

My shaking fingers slide under the seal with trepidation. My shoulders hunch up as I pull out a note.

Meet me at Wrens.

Nate's name is swirled underneath, clearly his elaborate writing.

I flip it over, and something settles inside my chest.

Stop worrying, and hurry up.

Okay. So, they're not leaving me. But I'm intrigued enough to dig out the phone Cade handed me, filled with their numbers, that I hid in the bottom of my dressing table drawer in protest at them buying me such an expensive gift.

After a few minutes, I manage to work out where the messaging system is, and my fingers awkwardly jab out a message.

What are we doing?

Nate's reply comes a second later.

Get that beautiful ass over to the bakery, kitten.

I stifle a laugh. So he's clearly not going to give me any more information.

When I head back downstairs to call a cab, I stop short when I push the doors open. Cade is leaning against a long black car, his hair immaculate and dressed in a smart and sexy as hell dark blue suit. His eyes move to mine, an approving look in them.

"So you received our message?" he asks, opening the car door and gesturing me in.

"I… did." Climbing in, I smooth down the ends of my dress as he slides into the seat next to me. "This is all very mysterious, Cade. Do I need to be worried?"

I'm going for teasing, but the high-pitched tone at the end of my words gives me away. Cade picks up my hand and kisses my palm, folding my fingers over it.

"Nothing to worry about, Gabrielle. I swear it."

I chew my lip, but I let it go as we merge into the traffic. "So, you're taking me to the bakery?"

"I am."

"What are we doing there?"

"You don't like surprises, do you?" He grins, taking his face from devastating to boyishly adorable. "We won't keep you in suspense for much longer."

My feet tap out a nervous rhythm against the floor, and Cade squeezes my hand, holding it tightly against his leg as he drives. The contact settles me until he pulls into a space outside the bakery where Nate bought me my first cupcake.

"Go on." Cade nods towards the doors. "I'll see you later."

"Wait – you're not coming inside?" He shakes his head. "I have something to do. But you'll see me soon."

Well, that wasn't all mysterious at all. And also just a little bit sexy, the edge of a purr in his words.

I scramble out of the car, and Cade points to the bakery

door, his eyes watching me until I actually pull it open before he pulls off.

I turn my attention to the store in front of me, my fingers flexing around the door handle as I push back my nerves and yank it open.

Nate is stood in the middle of the deserted store, his feet shifting as he holds something in his hands. A little bell chimes above my head, and he swings his head up to meet my eyes, a smile spreading across his face.

My own smile grows, my anxiety melting away at seeing him. "What's going on?"

If there's a touch of suspicion in my tone, he can't exactly blame me. Nate has a habit of elaborate surprises. "If this is about the wardrobe — ,"

He coughs. "It's not."

Then he drops down to his knees.

My eyes widen as I step towards him, but he holds up a hand, his face pleading. "Wait, kitten. Let me say what I need to say."

My foot slowly moves back, my hands twisting around themselves. "Okay," I say quietly.

He takes a deep breath, his eyes not moving from mine.

"I didn't expect you. When you walked into Il Piacere that night. I was an ass, and I didn't see what was right in front of me. But I couldn't stop thinking about you, and now I know why."

I swallow. "Nate…,"

"I'm yours, kitten. And I know I can be too much. Maybe the wardrobe was overboard. But I'll work on that. All I know is that I want to watch you experience every beautiful thing life has to offer. I want to give you cupcakes and watch your eyes light up. I want to argue with you over gifts because you think it's too much and I think it will never be enough."

"Nothing on this earth is good enough for you,

certainly not me. But I want to spend my life with you, trying to be what you deserve. Because you deserve everything."

He looks down. "I guess I'm trying to say... please, don't leave us. We can work through everything else. But the only thing I can't cope with is being apart from you. And I understand that you need to find your own way. But I think we can do that together."

I'm crying now, my chest tight as he holds out a small box to me, rose gold with dark blue ribbon.

"It's not what you think," he says with a nervous smile.

Taking it, I undo the ribbon, expecting a cake inside. But there's a small, velvet blue box. When I open it, all the breath leaves my body. "Nate."

The small ring glitters in the light, silver with pretty stones set into the banding.

"I didn't buy it," he rushes out. "This was my mom's. She gave me that when we formed the pack, and she told me that one day, I would find a girl worth giving it to. And that's you, Gabrielle."

Carefully, I lift it free of the box, and Nate scrambles to his feet.

"If you...," he swallows. "If you choose us, will you wear it?"

I take a step closer, holding it out. "Will you put it on for me?"

It takes a second, but the smile that spreads across his face lights up the whole damn room. "You're staying?"

I laugh wetly, scrubbing my cheeks with the back of my hands. "I was coming home to tell you, but you beat me to it."

His fingers tremble as he slides the ring onto my index finger.

"It's a perfect fit," I whisper. He whoops, lifting me up and spinning me around as I clutch his neck. "Nate!"

"Sorry, sorry." He slides me down his body and I wrap my arms around him.

"I choose you, Nathaniel Reyne." I whisper the words against his heartbeat. "I don't need expensive gifts. I just need you."

His arms wrap around me tightly. "I can't promise that you won't have both."

I laugh, breathing him in. When we break apart, I admire the ring. "This was your mom's? It's beautiful."

"Yeah," he admits, running his hand through his hair. "They moved away a few years ago, and they run a farm a few hours away now, but we're still close. I want you to meet them."

"I'd like that."

Nate presses a kiss to my forehead. "Now that I've said my piece, there are a few others that would like to say something, too."

My eyes flash to the envelope he's holding in his hands, something leaping in my chest as I take it.

Where we first met – Axel

My mouth opens, then closes as I think it through. "The gym?"

Nate grins. "I'll take you."

Nate drops me outside the entrance to Axel's gym. "Just go on in," he assures me. "He's waiting for you."

His hand cups my neck, drawing me in for a long kiss that leaves me breathless. "I can't wait to spend every day with you, kitten."

My eyes close as he rests his forehead against mine. "Even when my hormones are going wild?"

He widens his eyes comically. "Oh, especially then.

You're far more amenable to gifts when your omega-ness is in charge."

He nudges me. "Go on. I'll wait until you're inside."

When I walk in, the room is dark, and I hesitate for a split second. Then a shadow moves, and the lights come on.

Not the main light. Hundreds, if not thousands of fairy lights are strung up over every wall, warm light bathing Axel where he stands in the middle, watching me.

He doesn't smile, shifting from side to side.

"I'm not good at this stuff, little spoon," he says abruptly. "Not compared to the others. But I'm going to give it my best shot."

My heart clenches, and I reach out my hand. He shakes his head, giving me a half smile. "Let me say this, first."

He shakes his hands out, his hair pulled back in its usual messy bun, kitted out in another sweatshirt I know I'll be stealing from him at some point.

"There is so much bad in the world," he says quietly. "So much bad, Gabrielle. And you've seen far more than your fair share of it. But there's so much good out there, too. And I never realized how much until I met you. Because you are what's good about my world."

"I told you before that you gave me a home, and I meant it. My home is wherever you are."

I shake my head, smiling. "And you say you're not good with words."

He still looks tense, and I walk up to him, placing my hands on his cheeks. "You feel like home to me too, you know."

I feel the moment the tension leaks out of him, his arms tentatively wrapping around me as he breathes me in, my head tucked under his chin. "You're staying."

It's not a question, but I nod my head anyway. "I've spent so much time looking for a home, Ax. So much that I didn't even realize when I'd found it."

Arms tighten around me. "Your home is with us. And our home is you. Everything else can work itself out."

I glance around at the lights. "It's so pretty in here."

The base of his neck is flushed when I look up. "Like I said, I'm not good at this stuff. But I thought you might like these."

"I do." In fact, I'm absolutely planning on stealing them for my nest.

Axel shifts, tugging out yet another envelope from his pocket. "This is for you."

My heart flips in my chest as I scan the words.

Our porch.

It's not signed, but I know it's Hudson, and I glance up at Axel curiously. He shrugs. "My lips are sealed, little spoon."

He drives me out of the city, the sprawling tower blocks and high-rise buildings giving way to rolling fields that decorate the landscape like a patchwork quilt in shades of green.

I have my nose pressed to the window for most of it. "I've never been to the countryside. I've never even been out of the city."

"You like it?" There's something in Axel's voice that makes me turn to look at him as I consider the question.

"I do." I glance back out the window. "It's so peaceful out here."

"Good." He turns off the main road, his truck moving slowly down a slightly rocky path before he pulls up to a field and parks alongside Hudson's car. He turns to scan my outfit before peeling off his sweatshirt and handing it to me. I take it with a grin.

Mine now.

When I look across the grass, a familiar figure is standing, arms crossed as he watches us.

Axel cups my cheek. "I love you."

The words hit me straight in the heart. "I love you, too."

He backs out slowly once I'm a safe distance from the

truck, and I wave before I walk over to where Hudson is standing, his smile soft.

"Hey, sweetheart."

I turn to look around us. The sun is shining, the winter air with enough bite to make me shiver. "This place is beautiful, Hudson."

His smile deepens. "You think so?"

I nod. "What are we doing here?"

He takes my hand, twining our fingers together as he begins to walk.

"This," he says, pausing and looking around, "right in this spot, is where our porch is gonna be."

My fingers clench around his, my shock drawing me to a standstill. "Our porch?"

"Yep," he says casually. "Right along here. Enough space for all of us to have our own chair, I think." He winks at me. "You in the middle, of course."

My legs are shaking as I follow his sweeping arm. "Here?"

"Mmmm," he says, shrugging. "I think we could all do with a fresh start, Gabrielle. And I can't think of a better one than this. I want you to have a home that you love. So how would you feel about building one here?"

He draws me closer to him, his eyes watching me seriously.

"You are our endgame," he says softly. "I told you that before. I want to sit on a porch with you when we're old and gray, watching the sunrise every morning. So I'm building our endgame, Gabrielle."

"The restaurant—,"

He nods. "It's not going anywhere, at least not for now, but they have these amazing inventions called cars, now."

I blush, shoving at his arm, and he laughs. "So... what do you think?"

I turn to look out, taking in the trees, the birds flitting

between them. I take a deep breath, sucking in the faint scent of the few wildflowers still growing at this time of year.

"I think this will be an amazing home," I say softly, squeezing his hand. "And I'm all in."

He scans my face closely, his chest barely moving as he holds his breath. "You are?"

I nod. "Looks like you're stuck with me."

His grin is a beautiful thing as he wraps his arm around my shoulders. "In that case, let's start planning now."

We spend a perfect hour wandering over every inch of the field, laughing and muttering as we share ideas, hopes, and plans for the future. I wouldn't change any of it, except to have everyone here.

"Hudson?" I ask, when we reach the parking lot. "Where's Cade?"

He winces. "I might have lost track of time a little. He's waiting for you." He opens his car door, leaning in and pulling out another envelope, waving it at me. "One more stop to go."

It's not signed, but it doesn't need to be.

Under the stars.

Nerves start to kick in again as Hudson drives us away from our future home. He leaves me to my own thoughts, whistling softly as he drives back towards the city, pulling up exactly where I expected him to.

The museum.

Hudson gets out, opening the door for me with a slightly goofy sweeping bow. "After you, madam."

I play along, even though my heart is pounding fit to burst. "Why, thank you, kind sir."

He pushes a strand of hair back off my face, giving me the gentlest kiss before he steps back. "We'll see you in a minute."

I retrace our steps from our previous visit, my boots

tapping out as I enter the empty, cavernous hall. It's completely empty, and I glance around.

I know where I'm going.

Every exhibit is lit up as I make my way through, from the thousands of lanterns to the aquarium. But my feet slow as I reach the double doors. I know Cade is behind there.

The planetarium is just as glorious as it was during my first visit, and I pause, taking in the night sky, so close that it feels like if I reach out, I could brush my finger against a planet.

"Gabrielle." Cade is watching me, his hands pushed deep into the pockets of his suit.

My heart feels like it's too big for my chest as I approach him. "I'm sorry I'm late."

He cocks his head. "Should I take that as a good sign?"

"Maybe." I chew on my lip. "I guess that depends on what you're going to say."

He saunters towards me, his eyes flickering with the light of the planets above our heads.

"I think you know what I'm going to say," he breathes. He stops, close enough to me that I have to crane my neck to look up at his face, our breaths mingling and his eyes hooded.

"I don't know. I've been surprised a few times today."

He smiles. "Did you like the field?"

My heart thumps erratically. "I did. I'd like to go back, with everyone this time."

"We can arrange that." His hands come up to cup my face. "I have realized that I'm not a particularly patient man when it comes to you, Gabrielle."

My eyes widen, my cheeks heating as he strokes them with his fingers. "You're not?"

I've always thought Cade had *infinite* patience. A little too much, even.

"Maybe in the bedroom," he acknowledges, his lips

twitching. "But not when it comes to you as part of our pack. I don't want to wait anymore, dancing around the subject. So I'm laying it out on the table."

I wipe my hands down my dress, trying to hide the shaking in my fingers.

"Gabrielle," he begins. "When I first saw you, running off down the street with my wallet—,"

I cringe at the reminder, and his finger tilts my chin up, his smile chiding.

"As I was saying," he continues, a thread of laughter in his voice, "I had no idea how important you would become to my pack."

His finger strokes along my lower lip. "Or to me."

"We'd become so stagnant," he breathes. "I didn't even realize how much, not until you came. You shine a light on all the dark and empty spaces in our lives, Gabrielle. Nate was slowly spiraling, Axel withdrawing more and more. Hudson was solely focused on the restaurant."

I wet my lips. "And you?"

"I was frozen. Doing the same thing, day after day. Watching my pack slowly splinter, everyone moving away from each other. And then I realized that what we needed was you."

He tugs my hand away from where it's picking at my tights, drawing it up and pressing a kiss to my fingers.

"We might have given you a place to stay, but you gave us a home. So I am asking you, on behalf of my pack and myself, to stay, Gabrielle. Don't leave us. We'll help you find your way, and we'll do it together."

He lets out an oomph as I fling myself at him, throwing my hands around his neck. "I already decided," I whisper in his ear, and he goes rigid. "I choose you, Cade. You, and Nate, and Axel, and Hudson. I want a forever with you."

I feel it, that moment when the tension leaks from his

muscles, when he softens in my arms, his hand cupping the back of my neck as he pulls me to him.

"That's what I'm offering," he says. "Forever."

I'm not sure forever will be enough, truthfully. Not to discover all the secret parts of them that I want to know. Not to do everything that I want to do.

But it feels like a pretty good start.

Epilogue
Three Years Later

Ava's name flashes across my screen, and I swipe it. "I'm leaving in ten, I swear."

We're working on the approach to a new unit at the Omega Center, one to complement Molly's support for younger omegas. I want to focus on older omegas. Ones that have slipped through the system, who linger on the edges of society and who are more at risk because of it.

Like the omegas in the dungeon.

But I'm late.

It's absolutely not my fault that I was held up by Cade and his meeting.

I was a little… tied up.

Rubbing away the ache in my wrists, I finally focus on the babbling in my ear.

"Turn on the TV! On the news…live broadcast…," Ava trails off, a conversation happening in the background. I can hear raised voices and what sounds like Luc ranting.

Frowning, I glance over to the screen, taking in the words scrolling across the bottom. Nate looks up from his newspaper, his eyes following mine before they widen.

"Cade!" My voice is shrill, my hands starting to shake.

Ava is just as panicked as I am, but her next words make me focus. "It's *Leah*!"

"Leah?" I ask dazedly.

Gentle hands push mine aside, Nate extracting the remote control and turning up the sound as Cade throws himself through the door. "What is it?" he asks, his eyes flying to my stomach.

"Not that," I reassure him. I might only be a few weeks gone, but Cade has been slightly overprotective since they first scented my pregnancy. "I'm fine. But, Cade, *look*."

My phone starts blowing up with messages. Hudson and Axel are both at work, but it's clear that word is spreading quickly. I leave them for now, listening intently to the man speaking on the news. Hundreds of cameras and microphones are pushed into his face, but everyone is completely silent as he talks.

Justice Imler, one of the five Supreme Justices tasked with overseeing the Justice system across the country, stares into the camera. He's a handsome alpha, his eyes a deep shade of green with thick dark wavy hair, but so cold.

He leans in, speaking directly into a microphone.

"We ask for privacy, to protect the health of our unborn child. That is our priority, and we will not be answering further questions at this time. We will of course provide relevant updates as needed to support any medical advances in this area. Thank you."

The camera cuts away to a clearly shell shocked news anchor. She shuffles paperwork on her desk.

"This is a recap," she says, her voice a little too high pitched. "Justice Emmett Imler has announced that he is expecting a child with an unknown partner." Her hand shakes as she looks up. "A beta partner. To confirm, this is the first beta pregnancy to be confirmed for more than twenty years. More information to follow as we receive it."

The bottom drops out of my stomach as I connect Ava's words.

"Leah," I repeat. "Leah is pregnant?"

Leah, Max's very lovely, very *beta* twin sister.

Ava hisses. "She didn't even tell us! Max just left to go and talk to her. And with *Justice Imler* of all people."

Even as Ava panics, something warm starts to fill my chest.

If a beta is pregnant... then it means that things are changing. Really, truly changing.

It means that we might not spend the next twenty years or more constantly looking over our shoulder, worried about pro-Creed groups targeting our children.

It means that we might actually, finally be free.

THE END

Omega Fallen playlist (in order)

Find it on Spotify

She Will Be Loved – Maroon 5
Put a Light On Me – Sam Ryder
The Man Who Can't Be Moved – The Script
Collide (Acoustic) – Howie Day
Please Don't Say You Love Me – Gabrielle Aplin
Please Keep Loving Me – James TW
Can I Jump? – Freya Ridings
I Won't Give Up – Jason Mraz
Grow Old With Me – Molly Hocking
Praying – Kesha
Who You Are – Jessie J
Shake It Out – Florence + The Machine
Here – Tom Grennan
I'm Gonna Be (500 Miles) – Boyce Avenue
Holy My Girl – George Ezra
Celestial – Ed Sheeran
You Are The Reason – Calum Scott & Ilse DeLange
Brighter Days – Emili Sande

A NOTE FROM EVELYN

I know, I know.

I said this would be the end. And it is.

For now.

When I was writing Omega Lost, Leah was one character who I felt deserved more. She's a beta who gave up her whole life to support her twin brother and her pack, and I feel quite strongly that one day, I'll be revisiting the world of the Omega War and telling her story.

For now though, this is goodbye, and it's bittersweet. These are characters who have lived inside my head for a pretty long time, and to send them out into the world is much harder than I thought it would be.

There are many other characters jostling around inside my brain (it's a pretty chaotic place), and I'm really looking forward to sharing them with you.

Next up is Sienna and her pack in *Denied* and *Devoted*, the Bonding Trials duology, which is coming really soon.

I hope you'll stick around, and if you'd like to keep up with the latest news and updates on my releases, come and hang out in my Facebook group, The Evelyn Flood Collective.

Evie x

Keep reading for a sneak peek at Denied, coming soon from Evelyn Flood…

"It's here! *Sienna!*"

My best friend looks up at me sharply. The nail polish she's been using to paint my toes a bright silver dangles precariously from her fingers, threatening to tip over my cream rug.

"Jessalyn!" I make a grab for it, but she pulls away, waving me off with wide eyes.

"You don't think…," she breathes. "The Hub?"

Excitement unfurls in my belly as my mother bursts in through my bedroom door, waving a gold, official-looking envelope in her hands. Jessalyn squeals, abandoning my half-painted toenails to dance around the room.

"*Sienna Michaels*! Didn't you hear me calling you?"

Helena Michaels is a beautiful woman. My father likes to say that she's the most beautiful omega in Navarre, and it's hard to disagree, even if he is blinded by his Soul Bond. But despite her infamous beauty, my mother's voice can hit levels only heard by dogs when she's pissed… like now.

She plants her hands on her hips, glancing between me and Jessalyn with a frown. "It's rude to ignore your own mother, Sienna."

"Sorry, mama." Jumping up, I plant a kiss on her cheek in apology, seizing the opportunity to snag the golden envelope. Turning it over, my chest tightens at the sight of the familiar Omega Hub emblem etched into the thick card, the 'O' split open by a curved line on either side at the bottom.

"Holy shit," I wheeze. Jessalyn crows as my mother lights up all over again.

"Language, Sienna! If Ollena heard you, that invite would disappear faster than I could snap my fingers." My mother sniffs indignantly.

"Sorry," I mutter again, still turning the envelope over in my fingers. Nerves start to twist in my stomach.

I've been waiting for this envelope for *years*. Well, it feels like years, although I only reached my majority three months ago. Omegas aren't eligible for the Bonding Trials until they turn eighteen.

Right on cue, my mother sniffles, daintily whipping out a handkerchief from her elegant blue dress and dabbing at her cheeks. "I'm sorry," she hiccups, when Jess and I turn to her. "You're just growing up too quickly, Sienna."

Not quickly enough.

"You still have Elise, Mama," I say, and she nods, although her face crumples a little as she comes to sit next to me on the bed. Her arm wraps around my shoulders, a familiar support, and I lean into her embrace.

"You will be perfect," she whispers to me. "I know it, sweetheart. I'm so proud of you."

My throat closes up as I blink back unexpected tears.

Everything is going to change now.

The Bonding Trials are the culmination of everything we omegas work towards. All of us are sent to the Omega Hub for tutoring as soon as we reach thirteen. We're taught every possible skill that an omega might need in her arsenal to please her future pack. When we've been assessed as suitable, we're matched to packs through the Trials.

I speak four languages, know every possible form of etiquette there is, can identify every type of fork in existence from a good ten meters away. My painting is passable, and my music speaks for itself. Plus, my nesting skills are on *point*.

I'm ready for this.

Even if the idea of standing up in front of dozens of the most important people in Navarre to pledge myself to a group of unknown alphas is making me break out in hives.

Taking a deep breath, I slide my finger under the envelope, lifting the flap and pulling out a letter written on thick, cream paper. Jessalyn settles on my other side, my mother and best friend both peering over my shoulder as I scan the flowery script.

"Read it aloud," Mama urges, and I clear my throat.

Dear Sienna,

Congratulations! I am delighted to offer you the opportunity to participate in the Bonding Trials.

You have been matched with the Cohen pack.

In order to be accepted as a pack omega, you must progress through the four stages of the Bonding Trials and win the formal approval of your alpha pack.

1. *Scent marking*
2. *Nesting*
3. *Heats*
4. *Mating ceremony*

If an omega does not meet the standards expected, they may be returned to the Omega Hub. Should this occur, you will be offered another opportunity to participate in the trials at a later date.

In exceptional circumstances, a pack may decide to Deny an omega.

This means that you will no longer be permitted to come into contact with alpha packs. You will be stripped of your omega status and must leave the City to live amongst the beta population.

Please be reassured that no omega has been Denied in the history of the Omega Hub.

We're delighted to welcome you to the Bonding Trials and wish you the best of luck with your mating process.

Kind regards,

Ollena Hayward
Head of the Omega Hub

My voice trails off, and we all sit for a moment. My head feels a little dizzy.

"It's happening," Jessalyn whispers. "Sienna! And it's the Cohen pack!"

Both my mama and I turn to her. My head feels too slow to keep up with her excitement.

"The Cohen pack?" I push out through the lump in my throat.

Jessalyn squeals. "I *said* you needed to keep up more! The Cohen pack are *the* pack. Jax Cohen is this seriously hot singer, and Tristan Cohen is going to be the next Council leader!"

She hugs me. "I'm so happy for you, bitch face," she mumbles into my shoulder. Her voice shakes a little as I hug her back. "I'm not going anywhere," I reassure her.

"You're going to be the mate of the next Council leader," Mama repeats numbly. "Oh, Sienna."

I chew on my lip, but don't bother pointing out that I'm likely to be absolutely terrible at being a Council leader's mate. I'm not exactly the best at managing social situations.

"What if they're your Soul Bonded?" Mama gasps, her hands to her chest. My heart jumps a little, but reality soon steps in.

"I doubt it," I remind her gently. "Once in a lifetime, remember? You and Dad were lucky to find each other."

Soul Bonded. That incredibly rare moment of connection, of meeting the eyes of an alpha – or *alphas* – and just… knowing. That you're meant to be theirs. The way my parents describe it, the heavens open up and the angels sing. But we have to take their word for it, since my parents have been the only Soul Bonded pairing to appear in Navarre in more than a hundred years.

There's not much point in waiting around for something none of us are guaranteed.

Clearing my throat, I turn back to Jess. "So, tell me about my future mates," I tease her. "Who else is in the Cohen pack?"

Jessalyn shakes her wild bronze curls away from her shoulders, holding up her fingers in the air. "We covered Jax and Tristan. Then you have Logan. He's an amazing artist. His paintings and sculptures are incredible – he has a gallery in the Artist's Quarter. Then there's Gray Cohen. He's an architect. He designed the Opera House when he was fourteen!"

A bottomless pit of inadequacy opens up in my chest.

She flops back dramatically on the bed. "You lucky bitch," she breathes. "They're all super hot, Si."

My mother yelps as I tug her back and we all sprawl out on the bed. "Looks aren't everything, Jessalyn," she says primly.

I turn my head to her. "They don't hurt, though, right?"

"Well… no." My staid mother actually giggles. "Certainly not."

I can't help but join in her laughter, a heaviness lifting from my shoulders as the worry I've been carrying around for weeks evaporates.

The Cohen Pack.

Sienna Cohen.

I'm on the verge of pulling out a notepad to practise my future signature when my little sister bursts through my bedroom door.

"Sienna!" Elise gasps. Her blonde hair dances around her face in ringlets. "Is it true?"

I sit up, opening my arms, and she dives into them as I drop my head to breathe in her soft, flowery scent. "I don't want you to leave," she mumbles. Stroking her hair, I lift up her face to look into her blue eyes, the exact mirror of my own.

"I'll still be around, 'Lise. And it means you get to have my room."

She shakes her head stubbornly. "Don't care."

"Now, Elise," Mama scolds. "Be happy for your sister. It'll be your turn soon enough, miss."

Elise retches dramatically into my stomach. "Blech. No, thank you."

A grin tugs at the edges of my lips. All we have to get through is the Bonding Trials, and they're only a formality, a stupid process set up by the Council when Navarre first separated from the mainland more than a hundred years ago. I've been preparing for *years*.

What could possibly go wrong?

Denied is available for pre-order now!

Stalk me!

Facebook: https://www.facebook.com/groups/evelynflood/
Goodreads: https://www.goodreads.com/evelynflood
Bookbub: https://www.bookbub.com/profile/evelyn-flood
TikTok: https://www.tiktok.com/@evelynfloodauthor
Instagram: https://www.instagram.com/evelynfloodauthor/

Printed in Great Britain
by Amazon